ANTISENSE

ANTISENSE

R.P. Marshall

ISBN-13: 978-1493615421

ABOUT THE AUTHOR

Richard Marshall trained in medicine at University College, London, specialising in respiratory and critical care. Motivated to find new treatments, he quickly moved into research, obtained a PhD in medical sciences at UCL and has published widely in scientific journals. He now leads a research team trying to find new drugs for severe lung, kidney and liver disease.

Writing has always been an essential part of Richard's working and creative life, his skills were originally honed writing medical texts and journal papers. *Antisense* is his first novel, combining literary fiction with the pace of a thriller, drawing on his experience as both a Doctor of Science and of Medicine.

He lives in Hertfordshire with his wife and his *Les Paul* guitar.

To Rachel with thanks for her support and insight.

. . .

Thanks also to Dexter and Harry for seeing potential in the book, and for introducing me to my agent, Lisa Eveleigh. Without her faith and perseverance no one would be reading this.

Words are trains for moving past what really has no name.

Paddy MacAloon

PART ONE

CHAPTER ONE

Someone broke a window the day we buried my father.

The low murmur of conversation in the front room stopped for only a second. And when that second had passed the mourners were still standing exactly where they had been before, except now their heads were bowed towards the scattered glass about the furniture and floor. There had been no time to flinch.

The projectile, I recognised instantly. It was a stone from the small rockery at the entrance to my parent's driveway. As a young boy, I must have come close to throwing that stone a hundred times and I felt a curious bond with the unknown assailant who had managed to succeed where I had failed. Good for you, I thought.

The first sound after the breaking of glass was the clink of china, of teacup reunited with saucer. A large man lurched from the shadows and began to work his way through the startled gathering, heading for the front door with his eyes fixed firmly on the driveway outside. Like everyone around me, all I could do was stand and watch as his awkward figure moved across the sharp light of the leaded window, silhouetted against its giant screen, and then wait in suspended disbelief for his breathless return – a hand pressed to his chest – and for the rueful shaking of his head that confirmed his short sprint down the gravel had achieved little more than a damp shirt and a small twinge of angina.

The mourners became animated again. Released from the tension of whispers, the mood of the house rebounded to a buoyant clamour. Everyone had something to say and something to do. Some of the women began picking glass from the carpet, watched by men who said 'careful love' with a sympathetic buckling of their brows, while others worked collectively on a fresh supply of tea. I remained by the fireplace, holding onto the mantelpiece where for over an hour I had managed to avoid justifying my existence to a group of people with whom I shared little beyond a small portion of genetic material (and for most, not even that).

Amidst this hum of activity, my mother's solemn figure appeared from the kitchen holding a bottle of Chivas Regal at the end of an outstretched arm like the head of John the Baptist. The women exchanged knowing looks, while the men urgently tipped back their cups. I forced a smile, lifting my cheeks until a warm moisture enveloped my eyes that might have been joy or sadness, or it might have been nothing at all. A state of relative stupefaction soon returned, though, because, with the aid of a little local knowledge, I had discovered the Chivas almost an hour before.

My mother kept herself busy with the administration of beverages. Holding the bottle precariously by its neck, with her mid-riff flexed to pour, she served a row of fat men folding slowly into the padded jaws of a large chintz sofa. She must have sensed my gaze because she turned to me with a thin smile, and, for a moment, I was able to reach beyond the depths of my unease and feel a little compassion for the woman I still held responsible for making most of my childhood a misery.

The man who had taken it upon himself to chase down the driveway turned out to be my Uncle George, my father's brother. I hadn't recognised him. The few memories I had of him were of a thin man with thick *Harry Palmer* glasses who wore grey suits and green ties you could cut yourself with. He was a shy man, I recalled, but used that shyness to his advantage like a nervous salesman you can trust. Since his return from beyond the window, he'd been standing alone at the opposite corner of the room to me. I'd caught him glancing in my direction a number of times, and in doing so I had exposed a particular weakness of mine all too readily. No matter how much I might want to be left alone, I can't find it in myself to ignore people. I can't look through them when they pass me in a corridor. I always manage a wink or a smile or a widening of the eyes, which means that, in the end, the lonely people at functions come to me. And with my subliminal invitations sent, it wasn't long before Uncle George's figure came wading through a sea of dark suits towards me with all the subdued excitement of a kindred spirit.

He still had the skinny shoulders and the flat chest I could vaguely recall from childhood, but in the interim had acquired an almost globular middle. His suit barely fitted the definition, more a sheet of loosely draped cloth. There was more hair on his face than on his head, and his beard – full of autumn colours – had the appearance of an abandoned nest. His eyes, though, were harder to appreciate, hidden behind greasy lenses in wire frames and by a pocket-handkerchief he used intermittently to dab sweat from his forehead. Around him, everyone was talking and smiling. The somber atmosphere had been broken as easily as the window.

I turned to find it again. Two of the glass diamonds had been shattered into coarse granules of light, but no attempt had been made to seal the holes. We might even have welcomed the chilled air, considering it appropriate for the occasion. It made our skin and our mouths hard. It made us suffer a little, and lent a medicinal quality to the scotch.

Uncle George introduced himself as 'Uncle George' - pretty quaint considering I was forty-six. And there was obviously a little too much facetiousness in the smile and the weakened grip I returned because I could see the skin above his beard redden briefly. He was as painfully shy as I had remembered, and I wondered if the beard had been acquired to conceal the fact.

We made a few half-hearted efforts to talk to each other, but neither of us were born conversationalists – I through boredom, he through timidity. Inevitably, though, we came around to the subject of the window. From what my uncle had overheard, the predominant theory in circulation (though never uttered within my mother's earshot) was that Heddersley was a small hamlet – even by Kent standards – and opportunities for excitement limited. (I was already familiar with this concept, having been trapped there myself for the best part of a quarter century). The blame for the stone throwing had therefore been laid squarely upon the shoulders of the Drewson brothers from the Castlebridge Estate. They had been spotted driving a dishevelled Ford Fiesta at high speed through Aylesham late at night on more than one occasion. And their parents were as bad. Always the last to leave the Friar's Arms at closing time, the overgrown patch of grass in front of their house forever strewn with the innards of cars and motorcycles destined never to comprise whole vehicles again. The father had longer hair than the mother, the mother had more tattoos than the father, and the grandmother had a fouler mouth than both of them.

Quick to confirm he had seen nothing outside, my uncle was in agreement with the rest of the crowd. 'Just a yobbish prank,' he said. 'We shouldn't let it spoil the day.'

I suppose I knew what he meant.

'You still working at the university?' he asked me. 'Neuro-something wasn't it?'

'Neurobiology, yes.'

'Pretty amazing stuff that.'

'My other half would be quick to convince you otherwise.'

'I didn't know you were married!'

'Marcescent, more like.'

'Sorry?'

'It's a botanical term.'

'I see,' he said, nodding slowly.

With the conversation effectively smothered, I grew anxious to leave. I have never been able to bear the end of those events with their embarrassed goodbyes and false amity, like the end of a disco when the lights come on. Worst still, was the chance I might be left alone with my mother.

My excuses were quick to arrive. 'Work beckons,' I explained, and was amused by how readily and how courteously Uncle George offered to give me a lift. The nervous salesman again, always willing to please.

At the front door, with a weak apology still stumbling from my mouth, I bent forward to kiss my mother on the cheek. We held each other for a moment too long before she withdrew her hands from around my shoulders and clasped them in front of her again. In her quivering smile I sensed the hope that perhaps all this would somehow bring us closer together, but I think we both knew that not even my father's death could take us back.

As I turned to leave, my mother, suddenly seized by some new imperative, told me to wait and then disappeared off into the shadows. The distant opening and closing of drawers and wardrobes followed before her flustered re-emergence, trembling faintly.

'Some old stuff of your father's,' she said and handed me a small brown shoebox without distinction.

'Thank you.' I replied, flummoxed.

I buried the box under my arm and stepped out into the light. It was a sharp day in late November, more autumn than winter, with the garden still awash with chlorophyll thanks to the shrewd placement of evergreens and a generous September rainfall that had flooded the banks of every major waterway that year. I stood shivering while Uncle George pushed a pile of redtops, road maps and empty sandwich cartons from the passenger seat onto the floor of his *Volvo* estate. Once enough room had been cleared, I edged into my seat and stared out through the already-frosted windscreen. The air freshener suspended next to me smelt very much the way the fruit it was mimicking would have done if it too had been left dangling from a rear view mirror for a similar length of time. The whole interior was mildewed and musty. I noticed the back seat had been garnished with long white hairs and realised with disgust that my suit was likely to have acquired a similar coating.

George soon abandoned any attempt to circumnavigate his waist with the seatbelt and sent it ricocheting back into its holster with a high-pitched whine. I tested a smile, which I'm certain would have drawn a further blush from him if it hadn't been for the cold.

'Rufus,' he said, cryptically.

My head nodded without knowing what it was agreeing with. I was too busy struggling with his accent. Half *Archer*, half Barrow Boy, it made me immediately self-conscious of my own upper class twang. (Though, luckily, mine is an accent acquired more by association than by breeding and therefore easily moderated to avoid contempt.)

'The dog,' said my uncle, throwing his head back towards the hirsute upholstery. 'Big bugger. Just like his owner,' he added, tapping his stomach with pregnant pride and tittering nervously to himself with the same recurring distress as the *Volvo* now spluttering to life beneath us.

I'm not sure whether I began a new smile at this final inanity or simply extended the previous one; they were all beginning to merge. Either way, I was grinning like a fool as the engine ignited and the car began to crunch across the drive, distancing us from the house, and with my spirits lifting in direct proportion.

Throughout its length the driveway was shielded from the front garden by towering Leylandii and dense hedging. Indeed, the whole house was shrouded in a similar growth that rendered the plot a small oasis amidst the silvered furrows and singular trees of the surrounding farmland. It had been my parent's home for almost thirty-five years, and as we drove out into the laneway, a shiver of recollection brushed my neck. There were memories in every fallen fencing pole and abandoned farm vehicle.

As an only child I'd had to work hard to occupy myself in such rural isolation. I spotted birds and cars, and the planes leaving

Gatwick with their atomic regularity. I collected mushrooms and leaves and broken bird's eggs. I read every Enid Blyton and C.S. Lewis and acted them out – with chairs for cars and blankets for houses – in lengthy rituals that extended long into the summer twilight. And, of course, I studied. My father made sure of that.

Like many men, my father wanted to be someone else. For him it was mathematics, the practice of medicine never enough, and the two of us spent many an awkward evening together poring over the hidden languages of algebra and calculus. Frequently, I would pause, and often for uncomfortably long periods of time, apparently deep in calculation when really it was my father I was trying to figure out. A chance for me to study him more closely, that youthful sweep of hair he retained well into his sixties, the beaked nose, the chaotic wrinkles that ran like exposed wires across his moled skin. At first, I thought his fascination with numbers was about the challenge, stretching himself intellectually when all those hours he had to spend dealing with petty ailments at the surgery must have been terribly dull at times. Then I realised how lonely he was, and I grew to despise my mother for not recognizing the despair even I could see buried behind those dark green eyes. For not even trying to save him. Always hiding in the kitchen, tiptoeing around, inching cupboard doors open, teasing ingredients from packets, and all the time listening for the restless sounds of discontentment that would signal my father's withdrawal. Avoiding him. Avoiding us, it seemed.

At the end of the long lane that led from my parent's cottage to the Canterbury road, the short row of council houses that was Drovers Lane emerged. At first just another shade of the sky's grey palette, their outline gradually hardened into an ugly conglomeration of slate and stone, disrupting the horizon like a vulgar fraction.

The car swerved suddenly towards a ditch, only righting itself after a sharp tug on the wheel from George. Still clinging to a strap above my head, I could see the folds of his face were gathered in moist concentration, and yet despite the possibility of ice, the road ahead was empty and dry and seemed to offer little resistance to our progress.

In the silence that followed, I became aware of a dull ache in my ankles. Up until then, the debris on the floor had forced me to keep my feet in precisely the same position, placed in the only sliver of space that would accommodate them. But now, mindful of my uncle's renewed attentiveness at the wheel, I felt able to edge the papers and packets out of the way until there was just enough room for me to twist round on the seat and bend my knees to one side, as if riding side-saddle. The change in posture brought an immense relief to my legs. Unfortunately, it also attracted the attentions of my uncle.

'Don't worry about any of that, Daniel. Make yourself comfortable.'

I shifted in my seat, but this time only to acknowledge the permission he had just given me and to disguise the fact I had already made myself comfortable without it. Nevertheless, the trigger of conversation had been pulled.

'Sorry I haven't managed to see more of you over the years,' he said. 'Last time I saw you, you were only....' He seemed to pause self-consciously at the thought of an impending cliché. '...Been what, thirty years?'

'It must have been,' I said.

We made another sharp turn into a road barely wide enough for the estate. Wayward strands of thicket and bramble clawed the sides of the car.

'He was a good man, though, your father,' said George, his eyes firmly fixed on the road ahead, as if it was easier for him to imagine he was talking only to the tarmac and not to some long-forgotten nephew. 'But if you don't mind me saying, I reckon you didn't get on with him too smartly?'

'Nothing I'd go rushing to my analyst about.'

Despite the flippancy of the remark, I knew I had underestimated George and, as a consequence, I had let my game go. To be a champion you always have to play at your best, no matter the apparent frailty of your opponent. It was one of the many reasons I had never made Professor. I was too ready to accommodate the weakness of others. I had about as much killer instinct as I had a talent for maths – no more likely to understand *Krapp's Last Tape* than I was Fermat's last theorem. I don't believe my father really expected me to get all of the answers right, but there was no mistaking the disappointment in the click of his tongue and the slow whistle of air from his nostrils as he struggled to follow my clumsy derivations. A distance began to form between us, subtle at first, and strange that it should have evolved from such proximity and in spite of all my efforts to provide the company my mother seemed incapable of. But there it was, like a gas-excited, expanding to choke the life from us.

Could Uncle George have known any of this, I wondered? I grew more wary of him, and respectful too, if not for his insight then at least for the apparently innocent nature of his questioning. I sat upright in my seat and kicked away the rubbish beneath my feet, determined to be more on my guard. But from what? From the ramblings of an old man or from the images my own mind had chosen to conjure up along the way?

Outside a gloom began to seep across the fields and hedgerows, the road ahead an endless tunnel we were being sucked into along with a few confused bugs glimmering in the headlights. Yet George continued to hurtle us through the serpiginous laneways at an alarming speed, making no obvious allowance for the fact he could only see a few yards in front of him. And at another near right angle in the road we were thrown to one side of the car, a flood of drinks-cans and papers surging across every surface towards my uncle, threatening to bury him at the wheel. Spinning on a seemingly endless arc, the g-force had him pinned to the door and me bent so far over to one side I was almost in his lap.

We came out of it with a jolt, tyres skidding and bodies flung upright. George's grasp of the wheel may have tightened a notch but, otherwise, no recognition, apology or explanation for our near-demise was forthcoming, and that shyness of his began to seem nothing more than sheer impudence.

'Are you a betting man?' he said breathlessly.

I wondered if he was going to quote odds on us finishing the journey alive, my heart still pounding from the shock

'No, I find gambling rather puerile,' I snapped.

'I'm sure you're right,' he nodded repentantly. 'I'm sure you're right. I've lost a fortune in my time. And won a few, mind. Your father never gambled. Good with numbers though. Could have used him at the racetrack. Course, it's all much more complicated now. Nobody has a two-way bet any more. It's all Trebles and Yankees. I could never get the hang of it myself. You get the same excitement from a simple First Past The Post, if you ask me. But it's like everything else these days, nobody's happy with what they've got. We already have everything, so we have to start inventing new things to want, just for the sake of it. A thousand shades and variations. A hundred kinds of everything. It's almost impossible for the likes of me to make a decision. Takes me all morning to buy a loaf of bread.'

'Paralysed by choice,' I heard myself mutter, my thoughts distracted by his sudden show of fluency. It was hard to imagine this man being related to my father, and even harder to predict what would come out of his mouth next.

He sighed and shook his head slowly from side to side. 'It's a shame when people don't communicate properly, isn't it? Never leads to any good.'

I wondered if he was he commenting on my silence during our drive together rather than on the innate silence of families. 'I have buried my father today,' I reminded him.

George's face slowly startled. 'Oh goodness, no, I didn't mean you, Daniel. I was talking about me and the fact I haven't seen you or your parents all these years.'

It didn't seem a shame to me at all that our contact had been so severely limited.

We entered Aylesham in silence and in darkness, though thankfully in synchrony with the South Eastern Rail Network because I could see a stubby locomotive grinding its way into the station ahead. I thanked George for the lift (he barely looked in my direction) and made my way across a small, desolate car park. Where it not for the train now pulsing impatiently at the platform, I could easily have believed that the Ticket Office was no longer in use, save as a shelter for dead leaves. Already shut up for the night (although it was only early evening) it gave me a legitimate excuse to board without paying my fare. The train, too, was empty and I was easily able to commandeer a first class compartment.

Settling back against the headrest's chequered tapestry, I moved my hand across a sweaty window just in time to see the *Volvo*'s headlights sweep out onto the road. As the car receded from view, I couldn't help feeling George had been trying to get at something, to tease some mote of information from me, and that the brief but irritating prattle I had just endured had been his own peculiarly nervous way of working up to it. I was also certain he had been lying about what he'd seen outside my parent's house that afternoon.

CHAPTER TWO

Leaving the underground station I had to walk briskly to keep warm. Then at the end of my road a wave of anger purged my skin as if I had moved against the current of a fast flowing river and suddenly I was perspiring in spite of the cold. I might have convinced myself this state of agitation was about being back at my parent's house, but really it was about coming home.

A sheet of blonde light broke through the frosted glass of the front door, which made finding my key an easier task than it would have been had I had to rely solely on the dim flicker of a Chiswick street light. I could have knocked, but knocking would have meant facing Jane straight away, whereas now I had a chance to gauge the mood of the house and, perhaps, give my simmering anxiety an opportunity to settle.

At the end of the hallway, my eye caught the familiar sight of an empty wine bottle perched on the kitchen table. Next to me, behind the closed door of the sitting room, Jane's presence loomed like a pressure threatening to warp and crack the wood, and for a moment, I foolishly considered pretending I wasn't there and heading straight up to bed. Then I remembered the loud clunk with which I had let the front door slam.

'Hello,' I called out in a neutral tone, knowing it was never good to betray my mood so early on.

'Hi darling.' Jane's voice was unexpectedly soft and conciliatory.

I pulled my coat over a hook and let my forehead fall against the wall. My lungs emptied. My body drained instantly of energy, the day at last coming to its conclusion.

Her disembodied voice reached me again. 'How was it?'

I continued to grip my coat tightly as if it was the only thing to stop me from falling to the floor. Did the lights in the hallway dim for a moment? I couldn't be sure. I let go of the coat, but my mind caught hold of something, a fraction of an image, some prehistoric rumbling. A tension in my mother's face staring back at us from the kitchen, a coarse light reflected in the yellowing glass of my father's spectacles, the tarry beams of the cottage hovering overhead.

Another sound from the living room: wine glass and coffee table in sudden contact. I turned to find Jane lolling in the doorway, her face hidden in the shadow cast by a wave of auburn hair.

'I said, how was it?'

'You don't really want to know, do you?' I replied.

'I was more than happy to come with you.'

'Well, thanks, but you being there would only have dragged things out even longer. At least on my own I managed a quick getaway.'

'I thought you were a bit bloody early. You can barely have touched your cucumber sandwiches.'

'Mine aren't the posh lot remember? I just went to a good school.'

'Alright, bread and dripping then!' she said and smiled.

I nodded towards the kitchen. 'I see you've been enjoying yourself.'

Her face darkened. 'For Christ's sake, Daniel!' she sneered in that upper class tone alcohol seemed oddly prone to encourage in her.

'I was just making a joke,' I said, trying to force an unnatural lightness into the words and failing.

'And I was just sitting here quite happily sipping a glass of Beaujolais until you turned up to piss me off.'

'You never sip.'

'No. Just like you never joke. Is this the way it's going to be every time? We seem to have our roles reversed here. Isn't it me who's supposed to be telling you to slow down a bit? You're hardly dragging me back from the pub every night, are you, for God's sake!'

It was difficult to follow her logic (if indeed there was any), my head still full of unwelcome thoughts: my mother's distant tears, the cool innards of the cottage, images less easy to bury, it seemed, than my father's enfeebled corpse.

Jane continued to rail in front of me. I had to decide if this was an argument to be won or an argument to be withdrawn from self-righteously. I was wrong about not having the killer instinct. I had it with Jane. I could make up for all my weaknesses with her, attacking without fear of reprisal.

Before we were a couple, Jane had lived with an actor. He had all the bleached denim and carefully manufactured stubble befitting a typecast rogue. A flowing mane of jet-black hair framed the near-diabolical good looks with which he managed to charm women and directors alike with conceited indifference. Jane, too, had been quite the gorgeous thing in her youth, and so between them there had certainly been enough on the surface to attract, but, as it turned out, not nearly enough beneath to interest. And when the veneer of our vanity wears thin it reveals the differences that ultimately bury us all.

Jane was besotted, all too easily drawn by his rather superficial lures, and willing to do anything to please him. It was inevitable that when his drinking became a serious occupation, all Jane could do in response was drink to mirror his drinking. 'In loving mimicry' I used to call it.

I found them in an underground station, a place that would normally have offered little hope of meaningful contact but on that occasion presented me with a rare opportunity. I'd been watching them along the platform. Jane sitting quietly with those plaintive dark eyes, him standing above her, a rucksack swinging from his shoulder to the rhythm of wild ideas. At first, I couldn't tell if he was arguing or pleading with her. Then I noticed the empty bottle in her hand and the screwed up paper in his, and the lines of black tears on her face, and I felt an instant of love for her that I realise now was almost certainly pity.

The paper in his hand was a rejection letter. These are pieces of paper I know well. They arrive regularly to tell me of articles unpublished and grants un-funded. They are always 'regretful'. This particular piece of paper concerned another mediocre audition for Hamlet rather than another mediocre attempt on my part to crack the riddle of the human mind, but it amounted to the same thing.

The actor became more agitated, his gestures increasingly wild, until his contempt of all things artistic was clearly audible to a platform now swollen with delayed passengers. A few of the men around me lowered their broadsheets like gunslingers twitching at their belts, but The actor remained rapt in self-pity, oblivious to the attention he now commanded, even though it might have been one of the larger audiences he had played to.

There was a new violence to his movement. He gripped the edges of Jane's raincoat and lifted her into the air, and yet she remained oddly indifferent, all too familiar with his tantrums, it seemed, waiting for the storm to pass. The same could not be said for the rest of us. A shadow fell across the platform beside me. The largest man amongst us was on the move with the certainty of purpose only a body-builder can possess. I suspect I was not the only one who breathed a quiet sigh of relief as we drew in behind his massive shoulders, suitably emboldened and enfranchised.

It was a bloodless coup: an old-fashioned shove to the shoulder that only highlighted the rather juvenile nature of the whole incident. The actor – all too lightly built – crumbled instantly to the prodding of that giant hand, and although Jane tried, briefly, to defend him, she failed to convince anyone, least of all the actor who made a snarling retreat towards the exit.

The mob disbanded to the weak splatter of applause and was quickly absorbed again by newspapers and diffidence, whereas I lingered with Jane a while, and found that, for once, I knew exactly what to say. I had my own lures then – of empathy, at least – and yet I can only imagine how desperate or how drunk she must have been to accept the meagre comforts I had on offer. We made a strange pair: neuroscientist and thespian stray, she twenty-two and me thirty-five, oddly bound by curiosity and fear. In the beginning, Jane maintained her close relationship with the bottle – getting over him perhaps, or getting into me – but I decided to ignore it, almost to the point of losing her. My nerve and my patience held until, finally (and with no particular intervention on my part beyond my continuing disinterest) her drinking slowed to a more even pace that smoothed and tenderised more than it lacerated. Still, she managed to consume enough to remain largely hidden from me. Partner was the right word. Our togetherness was functional. It was ballroom dancing.

Jane had cocked her A-levels up first time round, so she had one thing to thank her ex for when he'd persuaded her to temp her way through night school and obtain the necessary grades to enter The Maria Swanson School of Music and Drama. At one point she did appear to possess a modicum of talent. In her early twenties, I saw her in an above-average production of *Cat on a Hot Tin Roof*, in which she played a 'Maggie' well beyond her years, conveying a bitterness that should have served as quite a warning. But as time drew on, her performances became more erratic (though in some ways more life-like) and the roles more scarce. Small parts occasionally came along to jerk her back into life again, granting me small glimpses of this woman I hardly knew, but those short off-West End runs didn't even cover the *Sunday Times Wine Club* bill. If they had offered us 'wine-miles' I believe we might have circled the globe.

The difference in our age seemed to suit us almost as much as our similarity in temperament. A thirteen year gap, but there was no clash of the generations, aided by the fact neither of us had enough friends to form a circle. We had dinner with Adam and Claire every couple of weeks, and now and then a girlfriend from Jane's old school would come to stay in mysteriously coordinated visits that coincided with one of my impending grant deadlines. While I was trying to sell myself and my derivative science to charities for incurable diseases, they toured the bars of West London in search of the perfect Pinot. But even these intrusions were not enough to make our relationship feel unusual in anyway, and we stumbled towards that state of inurement so typical of a relationship in mid-phase.

A few years after we'd moved in together, perhaps my one chance of escape from the drudgery of British academia came in the form of an e-mail from an ex-PhD student of mine offering me a job. The little sod was heading the Department of Neuroscience in Auckland (in my experience, the success of one's juniors often fails to flatter.) It was a good position though: a Chair, a low-rate mortgage, as much fresh air as I could contaminate. But for Jane it was a problem, and in the two weeks of deliberation that followed in what seemed like a very cramped Victorian terrace, we let it all fly. An environmental protection order could only have been a Judge's signature away. Needless to say, I passed on the offer, and though I would likely never have taken the Job, this 'lost opportunity', much like Jane's drinking, became another stick with which I could beat her from time to time.

The firelight from the living room cast a soft halo about Jane's knotted face, and I realised I had dragged her into my life without considering whether I might have anything meaningful to offer. I took a deep breath and pulled her towards me. She stiffened at first then gave way at my insistence. It had always been like that with us, even on the night we had first met and had found ourselves walking out into the cool London air above-ground, absorbed by each other's stories and by every sign and streetlight that dared punctuate the night sky, that intangible force between us so frighteningly feeble if we had stopped long enough to think about it.

Jane fell away from me and we paused to inspect each other like sculptors. I pushed the hair back from her face, revealing sultry eyebrows above soft brown eyes and an elegant nose that might have been altered but Jane swore had not. Alcohol had already donated a dry, coarse texture to her skin like fine sandpaper, which had only encouraged the formation of lines and creases. I wanted to love her but knew I did not think enough of her to do so; and Jane's recognition of that fact seemed all too visible to me now.

I nodded to the bottle on the kitchen table. 'I don't suppose there's a glass left for me?'

'I'll open another one,' she said and stared into my eyes as if trying to reassure me of something.

During the night, I awoke into blackness with an aching in my spine that made it almost impossible for me to move, forcing me to turn slowly on to my side like a stubborn screw in the hope that the pieces of my dream might settle. But by then I was awake and I was thinking about the stone.

The verdant outline of my parent's cottage stood out so clearly against the stark surrounding landscape. The nearest cover was Drovers Lane, almost half of a mile away, and anyone fleeing the house would easily have been spotted against the open ground. I supposed for a moment that whoever had thrown the stone might have made their get-away by car, yet nothing had been audible from inside the house and, again, George would surely have seen something?

It was a stupid lie, and it could only have been grief or boredom that had prevented the rest of us from believing otherwise at the time. Still, I could persuade myself that I might have done the same if I had been Uncle George. Returning to the cottage with tales of marauding youths would have been a nerve-shattering experience for him, I'm sure, exposed to the inquisitive attentions of so many. Summoning the courage to go out there in the first place was quite possibly a subconscious reaction on his part given the nervous disposition I'd just witnessed, and the truth of what he had seen would also have been highly distressing for everyone else. And so, as the night wore on into morning, I began to convince myself of my uncle's restraint, and, to the sound of milk floats and magpies, I silently commended him for it.

CHAPTER THREE

Humour in science is rare. I have no notion of whether Dr Edwin Southern is a funny man or not, but for me his name has come to epitomise such weakness of wit as we possess.

Much of my working life has been spent trying to understand what goes on inside the human brain. This is strictly in the neurobiological sense, not only because my own grey matter apparently lacks the capacity to asccommodate both science and humanity, but also because mice don't talk back (although in time it will almost certainly become possible). Thus, aided and abetted by my merry band of itinerant pre and post-doctoral fellows, and under the infrequent guidance of Professor Charles Baxter in the Department of Neurology and Neuro-Psychiatry, I have toiled long and hard to match the behaviour of, said, mute and humourless rodents with changes in the activity of certain genes and proteins in a shadowy region of the brain called the Amygdala. It's Greek for almonds, which gives you some indication of how much we know about it.

Over the years, my team and I have studiously tracked the translation of DNA to corresponding protein via its faithful intermediary: ribodeoxynucleic acid, or RNA. A laborious, thankless, and frankly shitty task – mouse shit, if I am to be precise – which for unknown reasons (that if we could fathom we might truly unlock the secrets of the human mind) we pursued with an almost insane delight.

And what of Dr Southern? Well, in the course of trying to piece together the inner workings of our cells and tissues, we have learnt to extract and analyse specific fragments of DNA in a process developed by one Frank Southern, and which bears his name: The Southern Blot. By this process, DNA is made to travel through a sheet of clear gel using an electric current to form discrete, dark bands we can measure and quantify. Taking his lead, others soon developed techniques that visualised RNA and protein in a similar manner, and by the droll logic of our peers these techniques came to be known as the 'northern' and 'western' blot respectively. Apparently, we ran out of things to blot before we could head east.

And on that particular Monday morning, it was the outline of Brian Lindgren I could see standing at the dark end of the seminar room, throwing another slide of a northern blot onto the wall with his thumbprint and smiling smugly to himself. Except there was nothing funny about it at all.

Holding the weekly departmental meeting at 9 a.m. on a Monday was a strikingly unoriginal ploy of mine, intended to encourage the slower-moving members of my flock to work more promptly at the start of the week. In reality, the timing served only to tire them so profoundly that it took the rest of the week for them to recover. By nine-thirty, most had managed to stagger in from the four corners of the public transport network, ready to witness the toil of one poor individual whose turn it was to update us on their research.

Enter Brian.

Brian is a hybrid. He is a coalescence of cultures, and yet he has none. They cancel each other out. He is fine and fair and clean: that's the Lindgren. He is overweight and stubborn: that's the Brian. He has inherited the worst from each of his parents. He has neither the neatness nor the precision of a Swede, only the humourlessness and the monotonousness. He is neither the strong-willed, yet introspective, Brit either, but rather the wet and superficial type. A truly awful combination that not even the most profound of scientific endeavours could have compensated for, let alone the nonsense he was trying to convince us of that damp and sombre morning.

The temperature in the room, I remember, was appropriately bland. They call it climate control, but the machines they nail to our walls neutralise climate, lending the air the same featureless quality as the décor. Beyond the window a winter made impotent by global warming was trying its best to scare us with soft winds and a thin form of rain that had barely managed to moisten us during the short lunge from Underground to institute, but which now gave the room the faint smell of damp jean. Dutifully cooled and redistributed by the air conditioning, the smell only compounded our suffering. I was particularly depressed to consider that amongst a team of fifteen scientists with over forty degrees to their names, none of us had thought to question the need for air conditioning in the middle of November.

I wasn't sure if I'd had too much coffee or too little. Occasionally, I looked up to catch something Brian was saying, but I could only stand a word or two before drifting back into torpor. I knew I would eventually have to ask a question, if only to prove to myself that I was still alive. But it wouldn't be a problem. I had a well-prepared stock: my icebreakers and my confidence breakers, questions to place people and questions to put people in their place. But with Baxter in the room I had to keep my silence, for the time being at least.

Baxter wasn't always at the Monday meetings. There were usually too many committees for him to sit on – those quasi-corporate gatherings of the university elite with all the brutality yet none of the productivity of their industrial counterparts. Charles fitted in perfectly, of course, with his double-breasted suits, his gaudy silk ties and a permanent frown of dissatisfaction; failure was a bark, success a grunt, these the distinctive calls of the egos that inhabit the upper boughs of the academic tree. It was unlikely Charles had seen the inside of a test tube since...well, since we had stopped using test tubes. Yet, ever faithful to the obtuse timing of one's superiors, it was typical that he should have been there on that particular morning.

Brian's morning.

Intermittently, Baxter made a rasping noise that I initially mistook for snoring but soon came to fear was more likely a sound of contempt. He had his questions too, of course, a raft of snipes and put-downs log-jamming his throat. The only hope for Brian was that Baxter might have a 'ten o'clock' and would have to leave before the end of the presentation. But I knew Brian didn't have enough data to last even that long, and so rather than expose him to my own particular form of ridicule (which only risked making us all look bad) I nodded silently towards Gavin.

Gavin belongs to a specific sub-species of mature student with a dress sense ten years his junior: jeans without hips, trainers without laces, a good complexion and a bad haircut. He had been a distinctly immature student when he'd first started in the lab, but now he was trying to break some sort of record for the time taken to write up a PhD. The fact I hadn't harassed him too much because he was reasonably good fun to have around may not have exactly helped to spur him on. It did, however, mean that we had come to understand each other pretty well. He nodded knowingly at my gesture and slowly lifted his hand.

'Brian?'

Brian's laser pointer died. He turned to Gavin with unguarded irritation.

'Yep?'

'Sorry Baz, could we go back a few slides? I wasn't sure about the first graph you showed. I thought the serotonin levels fell after exposure?'

There was a soft groan from the rest of the audience.

'They went up,' said Brian, indignantly. 'They showed a clear rise.'

'Didn't they fall at one of the time points?'

'At four hours, but it wasn't statistically significant.'

'Really?' Gavin raised his eyebrows and scratched a non-existent itch through a sorry looking T-shirt. 'I was pretty sure they went down at more than one time point. Have you repeated the experiment?'

'Of course! I've pooled the data from three experiments into that graph.'

Gavin got his way despite the prevarications. Brian tracked back through the slides and we reviewed the data. We managed to keep the debate going for a full ten minutes before Baxter finally left the room and I shouted at Brian to get on with it and stop wasting everybody's time.

She seemed to be there in front of me the instant the lights went on. Everyone in the room was rising to leave, and there was Gavin introducing me to Erin. With the distraction of the funeral, I'd forgotten she was due to start that day. Slimmer and taller than me (though neither presents much of a challenge), she wore trousers that appeared too well pressed for someone her age and a neat but nondescript V-neck above which the fine ends of her light brown hair teased the pale and sparsely freckled skin of her chest. There was an immediate calm about her, an understated air that captivated as it disarmed. And when I knew her better, I understood why. It was because her face said so much about her. It gave her away at once. And it said she could never be angry or bitter because it simply wasn't in her nature. Honesty and warmth were there, imprinted about the small of her mouth and the slow curve of her cheek.

'Erin,' she said in a polite Scottish accent, her voice as soft as spring water.

My handshake was purposefully brief. 'Of course,' I said. 'I remember you from the interviews.'

I clearly hadn't remembered her at all. How could I have? The image of her would have seared itself onto my memory. I assumed I must have been hung over or ill that day, and thanked God someone on the interview panel had been paying attention.

'Oh, right.' She looked confused. 'I'm not sure I performed that well. I didn't think I'd have a hope of getting it.'

'No! You were marvellous. Quite a star-turn, if I remember.'

Which I did not.

Gavin and Mark hovered next to us, trying to get a closer look at the girl who could make their boss say things like 'marvellous' and 'star-turn'.

Girl. She was twenty-two; twenty-one had she not taken a year out to survey the frozen lakes and impoverished citizens of Russia after her Bachelor's Degree in Pharmacology. There wasn't even the extra year of a Masters to fill the vast chasm of age that fell between us.

'Are you OK?' said Gavin.

Everyone was staring at me, no doubt imagining they had just witnessed some mournful aftershock from the funeral. Nothing could have been further from my mind. I forced Erin back into focus. She looked older than her years – or certainly carried herself beyond them. Gentle, yes, but there was a confidence there too, feminine but firm, and, I surmised, already quite skilled in dealing with men, whom she neither encouraged nor repelled.

'I suppose we should discuss your project.' I said, rousing myself.

From the seminar room, the three of us walked together along the bright corridors of the institute discussing the new *Metro* paper and the woes of London travel until we reached a small kitchen serving the fourth floor.

Gavin leant towards my ear. 'You didn't interview her,' he whispered. 'It was Baxter.'

I nodded and frowned and indicated to Gavin that he was to leave.

I made coffee for Erin (as if it was something I routinely did for all the members of my group) and then took her back to my office. I noted a flicker of surprise as we entered. The décor was a devoutly institutional mix of nylon and MDF. My desk was strewn with forgotten articles and unread manuscripts. A blind dangled like a man half-hanged in front of a grimy window no one had been able to open for years. Cacti desiccated slowly in a corner. I think she was more than a little impressed. I expect she had the same naïve notion of The Intellectual I had had at her age: that truly creative individuals lead chaotic lives. She didn't see that mayhem as the slothfulness it really was.

Erin settled into a chair and crossed her legs, looking immediately comfortable. Whereas I, fretfully conscious of her gaze, fumbled with papers but could only make modest headway towards locating the surface of my desk.

'Coffee?' I said, looking up.

Erin raised her cup into the air and smiled.

I felt pubescent.

'What did you make of this morning?' I said.

'It was good. Great.'

She was being polite.

'You managed to keep up OK?'

'Sort of.' She took a slow, delicate sip from her cup. 'Brian's trying to show that an increase in Secretory Neurotrophic Factor is linked with the development of aggressive behaviour.'

'Trying is indeed the word. We've been working on the role of SNF as a positive regulator of aggressive posturing for a few years. We cloned the gene in…'

'…In 1995, I read the article in *Nature*.'

'And, as you'll discover, five years in science is a bloody long time. Christ, you must have only just finished your O'levels?'

'GCSEs,' she corrected.

'Well, one *Nature* article can only sustain a department for so long.'

'So when do you start work on the knockouts?'

She knew all the right questions to ask. Knockout mice were genetically engineered to remove a specific gene from the pool – in our case, the gene for SNF. By comparing their behaviour to wild-type mice that still had the gene intact, we could get a handle on the function of SNF. The experiment would be vital to the continuation of my research. If SNF was important in modifying the aggression response, the knockout mice would remain calm. I wasn't admitting it to Erin just yet, but I had been dragging my feet getting around to them. The experiment was too important to rush into unprepared. Brian's latest exploits in the lab should have been an important step along the way, only there was something quite unusual about the data he had just shown us. Luckily most of the lab hadn't twigged yet, which would give me some much needed time to figure out what the hell I was going to do about it. I'd already earmarked Erin to assist him on the project. I hoped she'd be able to help overcome the shortcomings in his data and then be the first to have a crack at the knockouts.

'There are a few preliminaries I need you to help me with first,' I said.

'Like trying to figure out Brian's data?'

I smiled. 'Go on.'

Erin hesitated, I suspected more in the interests of diplomacy than ignorance.

'Say what's on your mind,' I told her. 'You have to get used to being critical. It doesn't do anyone any good to worry about sensibilities. If we ignore potential flaws in our data now, you can be damn sure a reviewer will pick them up in our manuscripts later on, and then we'll be lucky to get them into the Malawian Journal of Un-publishable Results.'

Erin uncrossed her legs and bent forward to place her cup on the desk. Her outer composure belied an inner conflict I knew would leave her no choice but to cross the boundaries of tact.

She took a deep breath. 'There were a few things. Taken at face value, Brian's data suggests there's no change in SNF expression after running the aggression protocol.'

'According to Brian we're wasting our time.'

'But I wasn't convinced.'

'Neither was I. The sense controls didn't look any different from the antisense, which immediately casts doubt on what's really happening. I can only assume it's a problem with the probes.'

'I think you've lost me.'

I pulled the paper tray from the printer, pinched a sheet of A4, and began to outline Brian's experiment. The hypothesis was, in essence, straightforward enough. In the wild-type mice we had asked the question: did SNF increase in the brain as they became more aggressive? If the answer was yes, it suggested SNF might be responsible for the behaviour and therefore something you could make a drug to block – a chemical ASBO, if you will. We quantified the production of SNF in the brain by measuring its RNA. Pieces of RNA are rather like magnets – opposites attract – so we designed an artificial RNA with the exact mirror sequence (the so-called 'antisense' probe), and then by adding one to the other and running them out on a northern blot, we could visualise where they had bound together as a discrete black band. And just to be sure what we were seeing wasn't due to artefact or chance we also used a 'sense' probe on another lane of the blot that had the same sequence as SNF, to which nothing should bind. It was old technology (by then everyone was switching polymerase chain reaction), but it worked.

As these words poured forth, retrieved from the countless lectures I had flogged unappreciative students with in terms-past, I became mesmerised by the smallest of movements in Erin's face, the muscular codes of her mental labour. She was quite beautiful when she was deep in thought.

'But can you be sure those particular antisense probes are specific for SNF?' she was asking me.

Clearly, she'd forgotten much during her Russian sojourn. Plus, undergrads aren't given anywhere near enough time in the lab to help all the theory they're forced to cram in stick. So I had to remind her that with the complete mouse genome now sequenced, we could readily predict the RNA for any individual gene. Sometimes you had to try a few different probes to get the best binding, but by in large they were fairly easy to design, and by making them of sufficient length we could be sure to within a few billion decimal places that they would be highly specific.

'I've obviously forgotten more than I thought,' she said.

'Am I going too fast?'

'No I'm OK. But you're quantifying the RNA by northern...?'

'Yes, a little behind the times, I know, but it's worked so well for us in the past. I just can't explain how Brian managed to get the same degree of binding with the sense probe as he did with the antisense. We've no idea if the increase in SNF he was crowing about back there is real or not. It could all be non-specific, though it's difficult to imagine how.'

Another thought seemed to take her away from me.

'Listen,' I said. 'I know it's only day one, but I'd like you to take over the knockout project, when we get there.'

'Really? I thought I was going to do the cell stuff?'

'I need some fresh thinking on the mice. I'll put Brian onto the cells.'

As if on cue, a weak knock rattled the door behind me. Erin's mouth opened but I silenced it with a raised finger.

'Come in Brian,' I said and smiled at her.

Brian edged into the room, parting the door just wide enough for him to squeeze through, though this was still a considerable distance given his size. There was something odd about his appearance: dark, puffy rims beneath his eyes, his face distorted like an artist's impression of himself.

'New contacts, Brian?' I ventured.

Brian mumbled something to the affirmative.

'You've met Erin.' I gestured abstractly in her direction. 'We've just been discussing your data.'

'There's still work to be done,' said Brian, feeling his way down onto the seat behind him, 'but the northerns were pretty impressive.'

'Well you certainly managed to get everything to bind, as far as I can tell. Who designed the probes?'

'I did,' Brian said firmly, 'but you approved them.'

It was true; there was little Brian did that was not verified by me.

'Actually,' Erin looked at us both. 'I was going you to ask about that.'

Brian leapt forward. 'I had all the right controls.'

Erin raised her eyes. 'Yes, I could see that. But what kind of probes were you using?'

The irritation in her voice pleased me. It meant she had read the balance of power correctly, comfortable to let her annoyance show.

'They were from *Genotractics*,' grumbled Brian.

'That's odd,' said Erin, 'If I remember, they're usually pretty good?'

'It's just a technical issue. The sense probe's probably binding randomly to something. We just need to tweak the sequence.'

I rose for effect. 'Well, if we can't make this work with the wild-type mice, there's no way we can go on to the knockouts. The very least we'll have to do before we start using them for behavioural experiments is to be sure they're the genuine article. And I was relying on your bloody northerns for that.'

'Can't you just assume they're knockouts?' said Erin.

Streaks of drizzle appeared on the window. The blind juddered down a notch for no obvious reason.

'We can't assume anything,' I said. 'We've had all kinds of cell-lines and mouse strains in the past that didn't turn out to be what we thought they were. And the reviewers will want to see proof. If all this pans out, it's going to be controversial, so the data needs to be squeaky clean.' I looked at Brian. 'Which is why I think Erin should run with the mouse work from now on.'

Brian's face tremored, point ten on the Richter scale. 'I can sort this out,' he stammered. 'And Erin hasn't done this sort of work before. It wouldn't be fair on her.'

'I appreciate your concern, Brian, but I'm more than happy she'll be OK. She certainly couldn't do much worse.'

'Actually, I did quite a lot of *in vivo* work during my Bachelors,' said Erin, joining in.

I liked her more and more.

'No offence Erin,' said Brian, 'but there's a big difference between being nursemaided through a two month degree project and taking over a complex behavioural experiment. There's no way you'd be able to do it on your own.'

'She won't have to do it on her own.' I said. 'I'll be helping her.'

Brian's mouth visibly gaped. 'You don't have the time.'

'It'll be a change from marking exam papers.'

Brian didn't have the nerve to take it any further in front of Erin; there was some element of subtlety to him at least. He would wait for his chance to win me round in a series of chance conversations in corridors and lifts, perhaps, or by e-mail – the true voice of the introvert.

Another knock at the door, this time more an announcement than a request for permission, and Charles Baxter was in the room before any of us had a chance to react. Clad in a grey suit with cream stripe he looked more Captain of Industry than science, but then he was a consultant to most of the major pharmaceutical companies. I noticed his half-head of lightly greying hair had been flattened by moisture, but that the rest of him was distinctly dry. Together with the ruby smear on his cheeks, I guessed a particularly energetic game of squash had recently been completed. I certainly didn't think his secretary was up to it.

Brian stood to offer his seat but was waved away like an annoying smell.

' I wanted to talk about this morning,' said Baxter, eschewing the niceties.

'We've just been discussing the data,' I replied, with a withering glance at Brian who was busy trying to meld with his chair. 'I'm sure we can turn it around.'

'Turn it around?' A forced laugh from Baxter. 'I have a great feeling about this, Daniel. It could be the next *Nature* paper. It'll certainly keep the Provost off our backs! And me off yours!'

Success didn't last long in the eyes of people like Baxter. His comment was a less than veiled reference to my 'disappointingly low productivity, of late', the phrase he'd used at my recent yearly appraisal. Predictably, though, and in-keeping with his hopelessly weak grasp on molecular biology he seemed delighted with Brian's results, and I could only sit there, muted by disbelief, as he gave him a big thumbs-up, while Brian crumpled a little further into the chair, only this time under the sheer weight of Baxter's approval.

It was the bland leading the bland.

CHAPTER FOUR

On as many evenings as I could stand them (or they me), I dragged my underlings to a subterranean wine bar near the institute. We were close enough to the City to have numerous such barrel-ridden watering holes within our reach, and by six-thirty they were usually close to capacity, although many of the evening customers (I had noticed during the occasional daytime session of my own) were simply those washed over from the lunchtime sitting. Unless it was one of his karate nights, Gavin tagged along, Brian almost never came and, of course, that evening there was Erin. She couldn't possibly have turned down my offer on her first day. That particular confidence would take a little longer to surface.

To my surprise, though true to her Celtic heritage, Erin shunned the Chardonnays and Chenin-blancs and plumbed for a pint of Best instead. Drinks ordered, I moved away from her and Gavin to let them establish a conversational base-camp. It was rare for me to find the impetus for being sociable in a single drink. I had to give myself time to ease into the evening, to muster the courage or interest or whatever it was I seemed to need to engage. I tried to look lost in higher thought, evincing a strong show of disinterest in the conversation they were struggling to hold above the piped-pop. But my mind was concerned only with thoughts of Erin, and what she might think of me, and how I had performed earlier in my office. Firm but fun, I hoped. Commanding, but relaxed with it. Whatever I felt towards her, I already knew it amounted to more than routine desire.

By the second round, I was able to face them again, but my newfound enthusiasm for conversation was met by an awkward silence. What had Gavin told her about me, I wondered? Of what had she been warned?

'How's the thesis going Gav?' I asked with all the innocence of a lion cub in the gazelle enclosure.

It was Erin who answered. 'Gavin was just saying he's almost finished writing up, actually.'

Clearly Gavin had put his time with Erin to good use by rallying her support against a possible attack from me. Shrewd, if transparent. Then again, Gavin had been with me for over five years and if he hadn't learnt to take care of himself in that time there would be no hope for him. As for Erin, it might have been wiser for her to have stayed out of lab politics, at least until she was more sure of the game. But there was loyalty in the gesture, at least. And balls.

'He's been saying that for two years.' I said. 'His funding runs out in three months and we've already had to extend his PhD once to get him this far.'

Gavin took a nervous slug of his pint. 'I've been working on papers too,' he whined. 'And not just my papers either.'

'You've got to be able to do both if you want to survive. A few less weekends with your girlfriend in Brighton.'

Gavin turned to Erin. 'Can you believe this? I've been working my tits off for him.'

'If only Brian could do the same!' I laughed.

Erin gave an uncertain smile, hoping, I'm sure, that this banter was all part of some clever team building strategy on my part and not the public humiliation it appeared to be.

'You need to set a good example for Erin, here,' I said to Gavin. 'We wouldn't want her to end up wasting her time with a boyfriend when she should be working in the lab, do we?'

'Absolutely not!' said Erin, going along with it. 'Horrible things, boyfriends. Waste of time.'

'He's just trying to wind you up,' said Gavin.

I winked at Erin. 'Cheeky bugger. I've still got your thesis to read, remember?'

'How could I forget?' He said, and let his glass fall clumsily to the bar. 'I'm off for a piss.'

Erin and I gazed in silence at the pinstriped drinkers. My glass emptied quickly, but although Erin had ordered a pint like a Scotsman, she was drinking at a Scotswoman's pace. I made a hand signal to a pretty young woman behind the bar. Over the course of the evening I'd been tracking the curves beneath her satin pencil skirt and starched white blouse with a studied indifference, as if to confirm just how unusual my attraction to Erin was, the fascination I felt towards her so easily distinguishable from the usual middle-aged infatuations. The effect she was having on me was difficult to comprehend. The opportunity to learn something new about oneself tends to diminish with age, particularly as one grows accustomed to one's shortcomings (if not oblivious to them), but she seemed to make so many things possible.

Erin placed her elbows onto the bar next to me, clasping an empty glass with interlocking fingers. A rim of froth exposed a series of fine hairs above her upper lip like a fingerprint revealed by powder.

'Same again?' I offered.

'Yes please. Thanks.'

'Good girl. I can see you're going to go far.'

'And, at this rate, I can see it's going to be a pretty tough three years.'

'Absolutely!' I bellowed. 'I hope your liver's suitably prepared?'

'I'm Scottish remember?'

'It's in the genes then!'

'Well, I'm an orphan, so I'm not entirely sure about that, but I reckon I can still handle myself.'

A clichéd image of Erin is in my mind at that moment: a pig-tailed girl in a duffel-coat, gloves on strings, kicking a pile of autumn leaves, the endless wait for prospective parents. I imagined her to be too gentle for an orphan. She should have been more obviously hardened and embittered by the experience. There was certainly an edge to her, though; witness her treatment of Brian, her confidence with me, and the ease with which she had blended with us all so quickly. There was no easy solution to her equation.

'I'd better keep my eye on you or you'll be dishing out the Glasgow kisses next!' I quipped.

She smiled uncertainly. 'You're safe enough. And I won't try and 'chin' you either, in case you're worried.'

I was sure her telling me she was an orphan had been a mistake, and now she was cursing herself behind the smiles for letting it slip, for trying to keep up with the Boss's drinking.

'Are you really from Glasgow?' I asked her.

'No I am not!' she said with mock offence. 'Edinburgh, it's a totally different planet. You're talking to a Hibs supporter.'

'Protestant or Catholic?'

She looked bemused for a moment. 'You mean Hibs? Oh, they don't seem to bother much. Probably whoever's buying the next round.'

The barmaid arrived with our drinks and tossed my change into a puddle. I didn't mind. I would rather have fished for pennies than have seen that place with the lights on. Gavin lolled back from the toilets. He'd been gone for quite a while and I wondered if he was the type to 'snort' or 'drop' something, though he would have been hard pushed to afford a decent habit on his miserable salary. I'd tried coke myself once, but it had only made me feel foolish. That was in the early days with Jane, when she still had her connections to the more peripheral elements of the drama scene, and when I still had my concerns regarding the age gap. I felt a short spasm of longing for those wilder elements of our fledgling relationship, for that infusion of promise.

'Erin was just telling me she's a wee orphan from the Gorbals,' I said to Gavin.

'Really?'

'No, not really, no' said Erin. 'Well, an orphan, yes, but not from Glasgow.'

'Oh. Sorry.'

'Don't be,' she said, quietly lowering her head, 'it's no big deal. I'm used to it.'

Gavin turned a little paler than usual.

Erin arched backwards and slapped him on the chest. 'Will you look at your face. I'm taking the piss!'

'Sorry,' said Gavin.

'And stop saying sorry! Come on, I'll buy you one.'

Erin leant forward into the downlighting along the bar and I noticed the brown of her iris soften and lift from her eyes like watercolour. We said nothing more about it. She and Gavin left together a round later having discovered, by chance, that they both lived on the outer reaches of the Piccadilly line. Unusually for me, I felt awkward drinking alone and disappeared up the stairwell shortly after them, leaving the roars of ex-rugby players echoing behind.

The air at street-level felt surprisingly mild, at first, but the donated warmth of the bar soon abandoned me to the cold. I shivered and watched my dark figure in a shop window as it turned the buttons on my overcoat, the night and the glass playing tricks with the angles of my face in cubist's style. I ran a hand through my short, greying curls, but to no avail. Glancing down to the junction with Jacob Street, I could see Gavin and Erin laughing together by the traffic lights, arms entwined. Red fell to green and they moved off in the direction of the tube. I lifted my collar and followed.

The overflow from what must have been early Christmas parties crowded the streets, women in short skirts tottering across the pavements led by men in low-slung ties. Erin and Gavin set a brisk pace, forcing me to dive between a snaking chorus line of tuneless workmates. In the station, the ticket hall was similarly congested, but here the crowds aided rather than hindered my movement through the barriers and down the escalators to the tunnels below.

Oddly, the northbound platform was almost deserted, so I took cover in the archway of an exit, leaning my shoulder against an advertisement for photocopiers in which a woman was trying to photocopy her arse. In the distance, the students' arms had uncoiled and now Gavin was hopping from one foot to another at a courteous distance from Erin, his skinny hands lost in a bomber jacket. He flashed a broad but essentially desperate smile from which I deduced he had all but abandoned his attempts to pursue her. She was too mature for him, too clever. He must have known he was out of his depth.

A train tilted in along the platform. Following the students' lead I made a well-timed leap from my surveillance post and found a seat in a compartment next to theirs where I continued to spy on them through the connecting doors. The windows had been pulled down and a heavy, ferrous air bruised its way along the carriages as the train gathered speed.

By Finsbury Park they seemed to have nothing more to say to each other, the conversation exhausted. An Albanian-looking woman in a headscarf shuffled towards them with a ragged mouth and a hand outstretched as if testing for rain. She wore *Nike* trainers and carried a child that looked old enough to join a militia. Erin dropped coins into her expectant palm and Gavin followed suit. Erin was a fool, but Gavin was an amateur. The gesture didn't do him any favours at all; Erin would want a man who could think for himself. Then, as if to heed my advice, he leapt to his feet at the next station and only just managed to slip out through the fast-closing doors into the commuter slurry.

I stayed with Erin until we both left the train at Wood Green. From the endless kebab houses and minicab sirens on The Broadway we turned into streets lined with tessellating houses and pavements newly christened with frost. I kept a full block's distance between us on the straight and then sprinted to catch up as she rounded each corner, drawing frantic gulps of air while at the same time trying to limit the noise of my breathing. At one such juncture, as I paused to recover, hands on thighs, an Asian couple in traditional dress emerged from a house across the road carrying plates of what looked like ornate pastries and began loading them into the back of a large white van. The woman stopped and pointed me out to the man. From the curious expression on their faces, and the fact they weren't immediately running for cover, I supposed they were more concerned for my safety than for their own. Before I was strictly ready to, I stood upright and waved a reassuring hand. Ahead, Erin was about to turn the next corner when the sound of the van's engine caught her attention. She looked back in my direction, and suddenly I was grateful to be panting in the shadow of an oak tree, because she recognised someone in the van and waved as it went past, by which time I had summoned sufficient reserves to continue.

The house was a double-fronted Victorian detached over four floors. Through the naked branches of a hedge bordering the roadside I watched Erin ascend a narrow array of stairs to the upper ground floor. As her key hit the latch, the door opened and the large silhouette of a man stepped out to take her firmly in his arms. His eyes looked out over her shoulder towards the place I was hiding. I froze, trying to convince myself that he couldn't possibly have seen me. But if he couldn't see me, then I could have walked away, and yet I did not, mindful, perhaps, that the perception of movement is heightened in low light. Their embrace broken, they walked inside and closed the door. Not a word had been spoken – the silence only lovers can bear.

I stayed put for a while longer, trying to catch glimpses of them through the windows, but once the curtains had been drawn there wasn't much point. It was an intriguing end to the evening, heart quickening in its own way, though my excitement was small defence against the increasingly bitter cold. I checked my watch. It was neither late nor early, an awkward hour to be returning home, and I decided to stop off for another drink en route to ensure my breath, at least, would bear witness to my alibi. A few wrong turns delivered me to a random pub with an uninspired name. The inside was like somebody's front room. Wrinkled men drank quietly above floral pile, while women in matching earrings huddled together in mother-daughter pairs. I like that kind of place. Beyond the first few seconds, nobody cares about you. They leave you alone. A distinct lack of competition. There is no one to feel inferior to.

I ordered a boilermaker and let the beer and whisky clash swords in my throat. Then I ordered few more. Erin's boyfriend could have been her brother, of course, or her step brother (or whatever it was called when you were an orphan) brought all the way from Edinburgh to watch out for his 'wee' sister. Or he might just as easily have been a good friend, despite the distinct warmth of their embrace, although that seemed less likely. The students around campus certainly appeared to be far more intimate these days than anything I had ever experienced, but it was an asexual chemistry they displayed, a text-message universe without desire I couldn't buy for a moment. Neither could I relate any such sterile relationship to the scene I had just witnessed on Erin's doorstep.

I turned my head and caught a group of women by the door pull their eyes away from me. So much for being ignored. One of them laughed in a way that made me want to check my flies. I finished my drink and sloped off to the toilets. They were a classic: cold and dank with cigarette burns on the condom machine, papier-mâché on the floor, and urinals blocked with the shrunken rings of toilet cleaner. Lowering onto a cold seat, I pushed my foot against the door of a cubicle in lieu of a functioning lock. My spine came to rest awkwardly against a pipe on the wall that emptied a high level cistern. With the bar's babble no longer able to find me, only the draw and release of my own breath remained to breech the silence, and, foolishly perhaps, I allowed my eyes to close to the rhythm of it.

I was standing in the largest of the fields bordering our house. It was summer and the corn was taller than I was. And it was early morning, the sky bleeding colour, the air heavy with pollen. I was on my way to catch the school bus that collected the scattered children from the farms. I must have been twelve, maybe thirteen. I had a black steel-rimmed briefcase with a combination lock. Inside there were green and mauve exercise books with margins drawn in red biro. My mother had made me sandwiches neater than my English teacher's handwriting.

A tearing of corn to my side. An irregular, clumsy movement. Someone running through the field towards me. Heads of corn falling. I hold my breath. A light wind gathers, brushing feathery buds across my face. The field sizzles and dies away again. The handle of my briefcase has dug deep into my palm. I release my grip and watch the colour flow back into my skin.

'Are you alright in there?'

Someone was rattling the cubicle door. I roused in considerable pain. My head had fallen sideways against the tiling and my back had become rigid and unwieldy.

'I'm fine,' I stammered. 'I'm OK.'

I staggered out into the pools of piss on the floor. Standing over the basin, I pushed a handful of cold water onto my face and with it a numbing pain that burrowed deep into my skull.

At home, Jane was making the noise of saucepans and drawers in the kitchen. I stood in the hallway drowning in tiredness, the strains of the weekend and my North London pursuits closing in on me, gaining footholds amidst the soft ground of my inebriation. I felt suddenly liquid, floating in the soft glow of the hall light and the warm odours of the Kitchen, glad to be back in this otherworld with its thin gloss of familiarity, and to send my lingering thoughts of Erin and Heddersley baying out on to the streets.

Another clang of steel reverberated down the hallway.

'I'm in the Kitchen,' Jane shouted.

'Yes, I gathered that,' I cried jauntily, trying to shake myself and perhaps, at the same time, to emphasise how unremarkable my appearance was at such a late hour.

The overcooked dinner promptly served, we ate dry bolognaise by the light of a candle flame through parchment, me drunkenly chasing spaghetti across my plate with excessive moans of delight. I imagine Jane enjoyed the respite. I was harmless like this. She had nothing more to do than simply be there.

'Good day?' she asked.

'OK.'

'You're a bit late.'

'We had a few drinks after work.'

A short laugh. 'And I gathered *that*. Any news?'

'Not really.'

For a while there was only the sound of me trying, fruitlessly, to wind pasta.

'You haven't said much about the funeral.'

'There isn't much to say.'

'Is your Mum OK?'

I lifted my shoulders. 'How would I know?'

'Well, did she seem OK?'

'She always seems OK. She's resilient. It's something she picked up in the war: a 'get the hell on with it and stop whining' attitude our generation apparently lost in favour of a point of view on life.'

'And are we doing any better?'

'At least we're alive,' I snorted.

'That's a matter of opinion.'

I put down my fork. 'I could really do without the argument tonight,' I said, even though this was the phrase most guaranteed to start one.

Jane let the remainder of a cheap Chablis tumble into her waiting glass. 'Oddly enough, Daniel, I was just trying to be nice. I actually wanted to know if your mother was coping, that's all. '

'Don't worry about my mother, she's always managed to take care of herself.'

'Well I still think you're unbelievably hard on her. She can't have been all that bad?'

My stomach refused entry to a lump of food left hovering in my gullet. I took a mouthful of wine and choked rather pathetically. The mention of my mother was a sure way for Jane to get under my skin, but I wasn't sure if that was what had made me feel so ill at ease. I brought my glass down to the table in a slow, deliberate arc, trying to concentrate, trying to dredge some self-control from the muddy depths of my weak character.

'She's never given a damn about anyone else,' I said.

Jane took another gulp of wine. 'I'm just trying to have a normal conversation, Daniel. Like normal people do!'

I sighed heavily. 'Alright. There was a room full of people I hardly knew. I slipped some whiskey into my tea and tried as best I could to avoid the small talk.'

'Which you hate.'

'Which I hate. My mother was rushing around serving drinks, even though she never touches a bloody drop herself. We hardly said a word to each other. She buried herself a long time ago and, personally, I've given up trying to dig her out.'

Jane looked at me with what I sensed to be a form of understanding, that feminine insight which makes children of men.

'Was it at least a nice service?' she said.

I had to smile. Women always find something to say, something to fill the silence rather than become preoccupied with it. And there was Jane, framed by candlelight, hazily redolent of something. Of love, perhaps?

'I can't honestly say the day had any redeeming qualities. Except when some yob threw a stone through the window.'

'A stone?'

'Uncle George ran after them but couldn't see anyone, or at least he said he couldn't. I think he was just trying to avoid upsetting my mother.'

'Your 'Uncle George' being...?'

'My father's brother. I haven't seen him since I was a kid. He looks like a tramp. I think he lives in his Volvo.'

'Christ, your family!'

'Everyone seemed pretty certain it was a couple of tearaways from the local sink estate.'

'I expect you were grateful for the intrigue. Must have livened things up a bit. Talking of which, I almost forgot, your solicitor rang.'

'I don't have a solicitor.'

'Your *mother's* solicitor then.'

I let out a desperate laugh. 'It's a bit late for her to divorce him now!'

'He wants you to go and see him on Friday.'

'Just me?'

Jane looked exasperated. 'With your mother.'

'Marvellous,' I said flatly, and thought of the last time that word had passed my lips.

'You could show some compassion, Daniel. She has lost her husband.'

It was easy enough for Jane to find some small excuse for kindness towards my family, that particular strain of sympathy only detachment allows. Though she must have known better than to expect the same from me, and I rose from the table, the gathering storm in my eyes saying all I had left to say on the matter.

CHAPTER FIVE

Kent was a blur of green at my periphery. It was rare for me to drive and I had to concentrate hard to avoid swerving into the onslaught of traffic on the A2, which was annoyingly dense for a Wednesday afternoon. I had no car of my own; this was Jane's *Renault Megane*. It had the strong odour of plastic and a glove compartment brimming with spent face-wipes and boiled sweet wrappers. It was my second trip to the home country in as many weeks, but this time I had decided to drive myself to avoid any possible dependence on lifts from forgotten relatives or, even worse, from surprise offspring, the types that lurk behind veils in Agatha Christie novels poised to inherit the estate.

I didn't imagine there would be much to cover. My father had been a General Practitioner all his working life, in the days before private practice became a serious source of income. Even when the potential punters did start to migrate from The City to their listed buildings and profitless farms, my father was too old to be in any real demand. His pension was above average, but that only meant enough to live on.

I used to blame his patients as much as the National Health Service for sending him home each night with only the energy to brood silently behind newspapers or torture me with mathematics. I'm not sure when I first came to recognise this detachment in my father, but for a time I even blamed myself for it. If I had been better at maths; if I had been quieter at dinner… I used to think he wanted me to be more of an intellectual companion for him, the way my mother never was, and I longed to be older faster so that I could understand more of the books in the study and the politics and the other unfathomable topics that preoccupied the news headlines and the late-night documentaries he seemed so interested in. But I could not escape my childhood. I could not wrench myself free of its gravity quick enough to save him.

We had lived in the same house for as long as I could remember. My mother had a job in a bank before I came along, but soon gave it up for that rural and, frankly, servile existence. And there should have been more children. I knew of the miscarriages before my birth and the emergency hysterectomy that hastily followed my arrival. It was another childhood burden I carried: that maybe I was only part of the family my parents wanted, that I, alone, was not enough to defrost my mother nor reanimate my father. But there were other reasons, unknown and unspoken, I could only vaguely sense, like old scars the cause of which you can't remember.

I had arranged to meet my mother inside the solicitors' office, and I was late. I had shunned the 'Park and Ride' scheme offered by the city perimeter and had driven unabashedly into the one-way madness of Canterbury Town where the streets are paved with lines of gold. I finally abandoned the *Megane* behind a shopping precinct and made the rest of the way on foot.

The offices were situated at one end of a passageway wedged between a chemist and a shoe repairers on Watling Street, which led out onto a brick courtyard and then to a narrow flight of wooden stairs winding up to the first floor. It was a secluded location that rendered the town a distant drone like a passing train.

I half expected the plump secretary who greeted me to be using quill and ink, so dim and grey were the surroundings. In a darkened corner my mother sat beaming earnestly as if she'd been saving up to greet me. A thin sheen of makeup lent further pallor to an already pale complexion. She wore a navy tunic dress, a grey woollen overcoat, and dark shoes with a modest heel. In her hands glove fingers drooped like wilting stems.

With barely a word spoken, I took my place on the seat next to her. Living with my father, we had at least grown accustomed to each other's company, if not at all comfortable with it. We were more than used to being trapped alone together with only the sound of clocks ticking and pages turning, which meant we were able to endure those slow minutes, perched on the edge of a worn leather couch in the smoky light of *Forsythe & Silverman*. That didn't mean I wasn't irritated at having to be there. Considering we were at the start of new millennium, it seemed a little old fashioned to have to attend the reading of a will when one could just as easily have had a 'faxing' or an 'emailing'. And what revelations awaited us? How many skeletons where poised to fall from the locked cupboards of my father's life, I wondered?

Suddenly, and by virtue of some unknown prompt, the secretary lifted her head and gave us permission to go in. The office door swung open and a small balding man brushed past us with a briefcase bulging under one arm. In his wake was left the lean figure of Mr Edward Silverman. A younger man than I'd imagined, he had a sleek face but with a rounded jaw to spite the sharpness of his nose, and a wave of blonde hair swept back from a high forehead. His boldly striped shirtsleeves were rolled to the elbow, freed from their cuff links in a studied manner that said he was a man that meant business, a man who wasn't afraid to get his hands dirty. Although it was with a particularly manicured hand that he offered to guide my mother through the doorway, smiling back at me over her head with a mischievous sparkle in his eyes. And as the door closed firmly behind us it became clear that the quietness in the waiting room had come courtesy of that most discrete of monoliths.

Tea was offered and refused as we shuffled chairs around a desk before my mother and I took our places. It was Silverman who spoke first.

'It's wonderful to see you Margaret, Daniel.' He smiled at my mother and nodded at me. 'This is actually a pleasure for me, if you can understand that. I mean, to be dealing with friends and not just someone trying to grab money from someone else. It's nice to feel I'm doing some good for a change.'

I wanted to ask him why he was so certain we weren't the sort to grab money from other people. Then I thought perhaps this was his subtle way of telling us that there was no money to grab.

Closer inspection confirmed his youthful exterior, yet he continued to conduct himself in a distinctly elderly manner. He had the deliberate, neutral tone of an undertaker. He was also one of the smarmiest men I had ever encountered, and it crossed my mind that he might easily have managed to wangle his way into my father's will. No need for any veiled relations.

'People are so greedy these days,' he continued to sermonise.

'The blame culture,' I said.

Silverman raised his palms plaintively. 'Exactly. It's always somebody else's fault.'

I remember thinking this was rich coming from a lawyer.

'You're very kind, Edward,' said my mother, her comment apparently suffering from some sort of time-delay.

I shared a patronising glance with Silverman before his face took on a more grave expression. 'It was cancer, wasn't it?' he said. 'Terrible business.'

But not terrible for business, I thought.

My father's life had receded slowly from us with an acute transformation of chronic lymphoblastic leukaemia, succumbing to the dwindling blood counts, and to the infections and bleeding they encouraged. I'd stayed well clear of his admissions and infusions, telling myself that my father wouldn't have wanted any fuss. I certainly had no desire to cause any. Better for him to keep his dignity, and me mine.

'You have the will?' I said, peering at the papers on his desk, trying to move things along.

My mother looked sternly at me. Lawyers and Doctors were still venerated by her generation. They were not to be questioned, let alone told what to do.

'Yes, indeed I do.' said Silverman and proceeded to rearrange no more than three sheets of headed notepaper. The reading would be as brief as expected.

'It's all very straightforward,' he began. 'The estate passes directly to you, Margaret, and Edward's life insurance policy, of course.' A pause for further examination. 'Now, the share portfolio he wanted to be put in trust for any future grandchildren, or for you Margaret in the event of Daniel turning fifty without children.'

'Jesus,' I blurted.

'I see,' said my mother. 'Is there anything else?'

Silverman gathered himself with a further inflation of his chest and the slow donning of some antique-looking spectacles, although why his eyesight suddenly needed correction wasn't clear at all.

'There is one further matter,' he said, holding us briefly in his gaze. 'The other *Lloyds* account.'

I sat upright in my chair with unconcealed curiosity. 'What other account?'

'A separate deposit account your father opened thirty-odd years ago,' said Silverman, removing his glasses again. 'It's left to you, Daniel.'

I looked at my mother expectantly but her eyes stayed pinned on the solicitor. Was there to be a touch of the Agatha- Christies to the proceedings after all?

'This is the current balance,' he said and handed me a thick square notepaper from the branch in Aylesham. It was an unfamiliar type of statement, almost entirely bereft of numbers, which I was forced to read in its entirety before I could find a balance buried deep within the turgid prose. Even then, I had to re-read the sentence several times to take it in, all my arithmetical inadequacy returning to me in an instant.

'A hundred and twenty thousand pounds?' I exclaimed.

Edward Silverman leant back on his chair and nodded slowly. 'It's a pretty good interest rate.'

...

Mid-morning tea in the *British Home Stores'* Restaurant. My mother and I, and twenty other mothers eating Danish pastry. I had bided my time. I had said nothing. I had accepted the account details, shaken Edward Silverman's hand and had escorted my mother from the premises with only the most routine of pleasantries. The secretary had smiled at us like we were lottery winners, worrying me for a moment that there might have been a Press Corp for us to face (was there a 'no publicity' box I should have ticked?). But outside the small car park 'For Patrons Only' had been empty and the passageway to the High Street filled only with the stench of stale urine. I bit into a baked currant the consistency of a bullet. My mother was saying what a nice day it had been for the funeral and what a shame it was about those Drewson boys and the broken window. I pretended my mouth was full and nodded, trying to let the ramifications of what had just happened sink in, trying to put this revelation into some sort of context, and to at least prepare for – if not actually give it at the time – the consideration it demanded. It was an increasing problem for science too: the absence of any time just to think. Experimental data are only as good as the analyses applied to them. And now, above all else, I needed to understand why my father had kept that money a secret for so long? The man who had never been on a foreign holiday; the man who could make a pair of shoes last five years and a quadratic equation last even longer.

Suddenly my mother said 'Your father loved you very much, Daniel.'

'Is that what the money's about?' I retorted.

'In a way, yes, it is.'

'Where did it come from?'

'He always wanted us to be secure if anything happened to him. I wasn't much of a breadwinner, that's for sure.'

If my mother was expecting me to defend her in the same way she seemed to be defending my father, she was mistaken.

'But why in a bank?' I asked. 'If that's how much there was after thirty years of compound interest, think what he would have made if he'd invested it properly.'

'You heard Silverman about the interest rate and, besides, your father didn't care much about money. He didn't like the idea of getting rich at other people's expense.'

'Then perhaps he should have given it away.'

My mother sighed. 'Well, he didn't, did he, Daniel? He left it to you. Try to stop being so suspicious!'

'It's my job to be inquisitive.'

Those crass words silenced us for a moment

'Why don't you have it?' I said.

My mother looked confused. 'I'm fine. More than fine,' she said. 'The life insurance will take care of me, and judging by the way you and Jane are going I'll have those shares to look forward to when you turn fifty.' She smiled, the jibe almost a term of endearment between us.

'Well, I won't touch it anyway, just in case.'

'Don't you understand? I don't want it.' Her tiny hand slapped the table, toppling our teacups over in their saucers. 'Why don't you pay off your mortgage? Or get out of London and buy that place in the Loire? Do something useful with it. It's been lying there all this time, rotting away.' She was as close to tears as I had seen her that day, and yet, still, she managed to refuse them their release.

My offer of a lift home was refused; lunch with a friend, my mother said. I left promising her that Jane and I would visit soon, and she nodded and smiled. Over the years we had learnt to absorb each other's lies all too easily.

CHAPTER SIX

It was a day that refused to start. The sky a grey cauldron of soup above the city, the windows smeared with rain, my umbrella limp and wounded by the office door, my coffee stripped of its warmth, and my nerves jangling like wind chimes. Things could have gone either way. I might have been on the verge of a great epiphany or a great sleep. The moment before the starter's gun. The moment before you turn over an exam paper. The last thought before you drown.

I'd spent a restless night ruminating over the *Lloyds* account, which didn't help matters, wondering where the hell all that cash had come from, and knowing, no matter how tempting it might be, that I couldn't talk to anyone about it – least of all Jane – for fear of looking a complete fool if any of the secrets my father had been hiding came to light. So I went to the office early, hoping for sanctuary but finding, instead, new horrors.

On my desk lay an innocuous square of transparent film, a jumble of journals and manuscripts visible beneath its smoky outline. I could only presume Erin had left the northern blot for me the previous evening. I dropped my briefcase onto the floor and thumped the power button on my computer. For as long as I could I deleted unwanted files, sent terse replies to the pointless mail that seemed prone to clog my inbox each morning, and tried my best to ignore the blot on the desk. But it continued to distract me, apparently all too eager to reveal its secrets. And when I could stand the anticipation no longer, I swivelled towards the window and held the film up against the brash winter sun.

My eyes flitted erratically from one area of the blot to another, and yet my mind seemed incapable of making any useful interpretation of the information they gathered. I tried to re-focus with greater intensity but the more I stared at the lanes of RNA that streaked the film the less sense I could make of them. Outlines began to form within their blackened smears like faces in a cloud. They tested me as well as any *Rorschach*.

It didn't matter. My subconscious had already seen all it needed to see in that first glance towards the sky, its conclusions instantly drawn by the reflexes of my profession. They were the same results. The same results Brian had presented to us only two weeks earlier.

I was less than thrilled. To compound my disappointment, I realised Erin's new data would also absolve Brian from any charges of incompetence. The results were not just similar to his; they were identical. I even rooted out Brian's original northerns to make sure Erin hadn't given me a copy by mistake. But no such luck. I had put my faith in Erin. I had asked her to repeat the northerns using the RNA from Brian's aggression experiment, and she had paid me back with unfaltering honesty. There was nothing to blame her for. She had executed the experimental protocol faultlessly, I was sure. Neither could she have fabricated the results so perfectly to match Brian's. And why should she have? She still had the naïve luxury of being able to seek out the truth, no matter the consequences, whereas I had Baxter, The Provost, and my industrial sponsor, Quintex, lining up to put the boot in.

I inspected the film a final time, staring deep into its grainy shadows, trying to make the darker spots lighter and the lighter spots darker but they would not yield. The sense and the anti-sense probes had bound to the RNA with equal avidity. The bands could not have been more similar. Hope alone could not have altered their density.

The scientific validity, or otherwise, of Erin's data was irrelevant. Whether the product of poorly designed probes or just bad luck, they were now a reality compounded by replication. They would have to be confronted, dealt with. In the past, when faced with such results, I might simply have filed them and moved on – another hypothesis disproved another hypothesis forming – but the grant deadlines, the impact factors and the struggle for tenure had long since superseded the science. I could no longer afford such purity of thought. With the SNF receptor cloned, we should have been well on our way to revealing its function. Our next big result was long overdue. I would have to squeeze what little advantage I could from those smudges, spin them in whichever direction they needed to be spun.

Through the half-raised, half-fallen blind the sun that had been so revealing just moments before was now obscured by a sheet of low cloud like a tide coming in over the sky. In front of me, a screensaver kicked in, showering the monitor with brightly coloured bubbles in some awful metaphor for inspiration. A phone rang and was ignored. I knew exactly who it was. I was late for Baxter.

The lift in the institute was out of order and I had to climb four punishing flights of stairs with a mild discomfort in my ribcage to get to Baxter's office, where his PA smiled and directed me to a sofa. It wasn't until I sat down that I realised I was the only one in the room. Was Baxter seeing us one at a time, I wondered, or were the other department heads even later than I was? Perhaps they were holding a pre-meeting of their own, trying to get their "ducks in a row"? To my relief, they began to appear in ones and twos until there was standing room only, and we waited together as our appointment time slipped into the distant past. It seemed Baxter had his own pathetic methods for trying to toughen us up.

Mentally I went around the room trying to weigh up our chances. Yokota and Mendes from Neuropharmacology sat confidently in one corner. They had three papers between them in the

Journal of Clinical Investigation (impact factor: fifteen) and were very much the opening batsmen. Tensmith and Hatfield sat close by, each with one paper in the Journal of Biological Chemistry (impact factor: seven point five – respectable, but hardly stellar). Anthony Beswick was the last to arrive, looking a little annoyed to find us all still cooped up like battery hens. He had had a less than successful year: only two papers and not one in a journal above impact factor four. The one female head amongst us, and the only American, Sally Levitz, was as badly dressed as ever in a voluminous dirt-brown suit. Sharp as an axe, and hypomanic with it, she was perpetually engaged in low volume, high intensity conversations with anyone who would stay still enough for long enough. Meanwhile, Jack Williams from Neuropsychiatry and I swapped notes on London house prices before our conversation, like all the others in the room, ran dry. The rest of our wait we spent in silent solidarity, our scatter plots and our reprints reluctantly primed to please our Master.

Every department in every university went through the same process every five years – The Research Assessment Exercise. It was a government audit, which like all its attempts to quantify any human activity that requires more than the ticking of a box, only encourages our public institutions to manipulate their figures and focus their efforts on achieving the highest quantity of the lowest quality activity required to meet the targets. And we were no different. How many publications had we achieved? In which journals? How many graduates? How much funding had we raised? Not how creative we had been, nor how daring our science. And not how rounded our students were either, or how prepared they were to go out into the world and have any credible shot at making a living.

Our department had a '5' point rating at the time (one point short of the highest possible '5-star'), but from my calculations, that particular run of good fortune was about to end. I certainly didn't expect there would be any eleventh hour *Nature* papers to add, nor faxes from the Nobel Committee. We were ready to drop, and it was written on the lines of every brow in the room.

Baxter's door opened and we were beckoned in, shuffling silently, to take our places around the conference table like a line of stooped lemmings. In any performance-related environment, one is usually required to achieve a certain proficiency in the art of hype; and the great and the good of the Neurosciences Department were no exception. We all had our doctorates in bullshit. Not that we had entirely under-performed that year. There had been a few high points, a few surprise fellowships, an occasional high impact paper, but nothing spectacular, nothing that could detract too significantly from the otherwise mediocre departmental statistics.

There were some mitigating circumstances, however. One couldn't forget that we were, to a large extent, at the whim of biology. As I knew only too well, experiments had a habit of throwing up unexpected data, and with them came new hypotheses ready to cover the old like fresh layers of coral. But a new hypothesis doesn't guarantee success; it's just new. In other words, you have to work with the hand Nature deals you in the lab, just as you do in life. You have to go where the data tells you to go. And so no one could possibly have expected any of us to be leaders in our respective fields all of the time.

Of course, I didn't expect someone like Baxter to appreciate these subtleties, and so I was initially perplexed by how gracious and beneficent he appeared as we gave our edgy, flittering presentations and spirited apologias, before I realised his predicament was really no different from our own. He also had his Masters on the Provost's Committee to answer to, which made it very much in his interests to shine a kindly light on our achievements.

Our optimism dared to swell. It was a tough funding environment for everyone, we agreed, perhaps the toughest ever. The journals were getting more picky about what they published, the reviewers more pedantic and more paranoid (they were our competitors after all). Everyone was finding it difficult to compete with the American powerhouses in California and New England. The whole scientific community in the UK was feeling the pinch, courtesy of an ever-dwindling public purse and charities stung by a series of stock market-tumbles. Relatively speaking, we had actually performed better than most. At least we had funding. At least we had a few citations on *Medline*. Not up for a 5 this time round, but at least a 4, maybe even a 4-star (suddenly we were grateful for the incorporation of a star into the rating system). Our average journal impact factor was a very credible 6.1, we'd raised 5.2 million in funding, and as we went around the table, a tentative enthusiasm crept into our language. We said, 'great data' or 'interesting approach' or 'he's an excellent post-doc' and we parted like old friends at a college reunion with new collaborations blossoming and new sources of income ready to tap. More seals than scientists, it seemed to me.

. . .

A gingerly knock at my door, and then Erin peering in at me through the narrowest of cracks. She seemed to be fizzing with excitement, relishing the intrigue and the gossip Baxter's meeting had undoubtedly generated throughout the institute. She could afford to feel exhilarated rather than beleaguered by it all, of course. She had yet to write grants and papers of her own – documents like children we struggle painfully to produce only to see them perish in obscurity far short of their prime. There were, as yet, no such dependents to sap her enthusiasm, so why shouldn't she have enjoyed our feeble manoeuvrings for as long as she could?

'Well,' she said, drawing the word out like old chewing gum under a school desk, 'how did it go?'

'Not too bad,' I replied. 'Come in for goodness sake, I can hardly see you out there.'

She stepped into the room in pale chinos and a green silk blouse. Her hair had been tied back into an ornate lattice like a puzzle waiting to be unravelled by the tug of a vital strand. She walked over to the window, looking gorgeous and making it difficult for me to concentrate on the complex of feelings – the syndrome, I suppose – that I experienced upon seeing her again.

'Did you show them the repeat northern data?' she asked tentatively.

'I did.'

'And it went OK?'

'It did.'

'Really?'

I laughed. 'They do understand these things, you know. I showed them the results. I told them we still had plenty of adjustments to make to the protocol. They've all been where we are. They know what a bugger those probes can be.'

'I guess. Do you fancy a drink?'

It was barely midday but my desire to be with her was far greater than any desire I had to remain sober at such an early hour. Lunchtime drinking generally made me soporific and useless for anything bar the misfiling of old papers, but I convinced myself I had earned a slug of something and said, 'yes'.

This time we stayed above ground and found a place by the river in mid-transition from public house to wine bar. Food was being served, but *coq au vin* and *boeuf bourguignon* had taken their place alongside the cheeseburgers and the ploughman's' on the menu. There was a jukebox, but no slot machine, and the music was quiet enough to allow conversation. The prices matched the waterside location, even though the windows were small and low set and denied us any serious view of the Thames. We ordered at the bar and waited for the waitress to bring us our thick sandwiches. Now and then an icy draft blew in from the unseen riverbank as customers came and went, though mostly they came.

'Don't get me wrong,' I was telling her, 'the meeting with Baxter was still pretty tough.'

'But I can take tough, remember?'

'Ah yes, Little Orphan Annie, I forgot.' I smiled quickly to imply flippancy, hoping I hadn't overstepped the mark. 'I'd like to you to run a new experiment with the Wild-Types.'

'Sounds good.'

'The same aggression protocol Brian ran, but start all over again. And I'll supervise you directly, this time. I don't want Brian cocking it up. We'll use some new probes for the northerns, and see if we can't have a bit of better luck with a new batch of mice.'

'Just as long as he doesn't get too pissed off with me; I still have to work with him.'

Why the sudden deference, I wondered, to someone she had been happy to vilify only a week before?

'Don't worry. I'll keep him out of your way. He won't have any reason to poke his nose in.'

'It's a relief about the meeting,' she said. 'I thought Baxter was going to go ballistic. Are northerns always this much of a pain, or is it just me?'

'It's not the most straightforward technique to begin with, but that's usually because enzyme contamination from your skin degrades the RNA. But that wasn't the problem, you had plenty of the stuff.'

'So I'm just unlucky then?'

'Honestly? I'm not sure. It's a bit of an old chestnut, but you do learn something from every experiment, successful or not. Great discoveries and serendipity and all that.'

Erin raised her pint. 'Here's to chance then!'

Our glasses joined briefly.

'There was something else,' I said. 'In the meeting today, I can't be certain, but I think Mendes is working on the same animals.'

'The knockouts?'

'I think so. Not here, a collaboration in the States.'

'But that's absurd. Why wouldn't he collaborate with us?'

'Because he wants control. Nobody wants to rely on anyone else for data, or have any more authors on a paper than is absolutely necessary. He's a big enough noise. He'll have struck a deal with another group in exchange for lead authorship. He knows he'd have to share it with us if he used our mice.'

'What do you think he's doing with them?'

'I'd guess something on neuronal regeneration, but if he publishes first, it'll take the wind out of our sails and make it a hell of lot harder for us to get our papers out.'

'But there's some amazing stuff coming out of Mendes' lab, why would he bother working in the same areas as us?'

'From what I saw in Baxter's office today, that's all about to dry up. His latest data's not looking good at all, and Mendes needs publications like everyone else. If they use our knockout mice, he knows I'll want to be senior author on the paper. And at his level that's what counts. No point being stuck in the middle of the author list with all the technicians. It doesn't get you points for the Research Assessment Exercise.'

Erin looked confused. At the time, I must have thought that a good dose of subterfuge would help motivate her, galvanise her loyalty to the project, but she might just as easily have concluded that senior academics were all as despicable as each other. I decided to lighten the mood a notch.

'Anything planned for the weekend?'

'No, nothing really. I think I'll work on the slides of those northern blots for the lab meeting.'

I hesitated. 'Listen, I wouldn't bother showing those for now.'

'No?'

'It'll only get everyone twitched. And there'll be a round of idiotic questions I can't be bothered to answer just yet.'

'And Brian will have a gloat, no doubt.'

'Already you know him so well! And you haven't seen him in full gloat yet. It's not pretty.' I put a hand on her shoulder. 'Go out and see London, for goodness sake. Pretend you're a student. There must be someone who can show you around?'

She seemed confused by me bringing us back to the topic of how she should spend her weekend. 'I'm sure I can dig someone up,' she said.

'Anyone in particular?' I said, trying to probe more obviously now in an attempt to hide my true curiosity.

'Well I wouldn't bloody well tell you, would I? You'd probably have him assassinated!'

'I can assure you those rumours about post-docs' better halves going missing are entirely without foundation.'

'You mean they are foundations by now.'

'Please! Credit me with a little more finesse. I've always preferred acid to concrete, far more discrete.'

'Sulphuric or hydrochloric?'

'A little of both, I find, works a treat.'

'You should publish your methods.'

'Crippen Quaterly, 1990,' I mused, 'a landmark publication.'

We laughed briefly but I made sure to stop before Erin so I could watch her for a moment, imagining that she was laughing not here, but alone with me in my office or in the high-ceilinged rooms of her house, her boyfriend peering impotently at us through the wizened branches outside not knowing what it was we had found so funny.

I lifted my glass. 'To the knockouts,' I said.

The heads around us turned.

We grinned like schoolgirls.

CHAPTER SEVEN

Every other Thursday I returned to being a student again. I'd known Adam since our first day at university together, and by virtue of our mutual oddity a life-long friendship had been forged. In our early thirties, he'd seen me through a testicular cancer scare and I'd seen him through a bout of 'clinical' depression (as if there were importantly different ways to feel suicidal), and although we were never certain which of us had had a worse time of it, we were at least agreed upon the therapeutic significance of the Thursday evening sessions that phase of our lives had spawned.

On Thursdays the watered-down lager in the Student's Union Bar was watered-down further still – and the price halved accordingly. Sadly it was enough to keep us coming back for more, our bi-weekly ritual only further encouraged by our failure to realise that the young women in the bar looked at us not because they possessed any sordid form of physical attraction towards us, but because they believed we might have some influence over their exam grades.

Adam was typically late and I thought nothing of finishing the first two pints on my own listening to the retrospective offerings of a nearby jukebox. He might not have expected me to turn up, of course, given recent events, but I'd been determined to go along, regardless of, or perhaps even in spite of, my father's demise. Besides, it was hardly a chore, with the evening fast living up to all my expectations of weak beer and random adolescence.

When at last he did appear, Adam looked different. I have always been wary of the acting profession, not just because of Jane's worrying ability to find work, but because it appears to be based solely upon the portrayal of human emotion through gesture and speech. This is a concept at odds with all my experience, which is that people go to enormous lengths to hide what they really feel, and one only discovers anything of worth about them in brief flashes of tragedy like the opening of wormholes in deep space. Drama, for me, is strictly the art of concealment, and a technique in which Adam is unwittingly proficient. An economist in every sense of the word, I cannot imagine the intensity of boredom that the combination of his inert features and Keynesian theory must generate during lectures.

But that Thursday, as I spied him at the entrance to the bar, I had to brace myself because his face was so obviously and so uncharacteristically wrought with emotion. It looked as though every sinew in his cheeks, jaws and brow was trying to contract simultaneously, each one antagonising the movement of another in a kind of muscular stalemate, such that when he reached me I wasn't sure if he would be able to speak at all.

He managed, 'Hi,' and dropped down onto a seat.

Although the lager I'd purchased for Adam nearly an hour before was no longer troubled by gas, I pushed the glass towards him. Well accustomed to the rhythm of each other's drinking we finished our pints on almost the same swallow without a word being said. I left for reinforcements but still kept an eye on him. He had that look – something with a broken glass, perhaps?

Nothing happened. I jostled my way back through the crowd, beer slopping over my fingers, to find his angular profile still frozen against the youthful blur. His cheeks were more hollow than usual, and his were eyes cupped with darkness. It seemed almost indecent for me to see him like this, and I hesitated to sit down again. It wasn't what those evenings were meant to be about. It was the emotional void I looked forward to, not this smouldering despair.

'New PhD student in the lab. Erin. Seems pretty smart,' I said in a half-shout, setting what was left of our drinks down onto the table. 'Attractive too. Scottish, though, but I guess you can't have everything.'

Adam remained silent.

'Is everything OK?' I ventured. 'Is Clare OK?'

Adam and Clare had surprised us all by remaining blissfully married for eight years. Not that Adam was the type to stray; it's just that there was so little outward expression of any bond between them. Clare is no great beauty either. Indeed, on the basis of their relationship I had formed the theory that a couple's attractiveness is inversely proportional to the sustainability of their marriage. Ugly people tend to stick together.

'It's my mother.' said Adam from nowhere, reminding me of his high-pitched voice and the modifications London had made to his Lancashire burr.

'Your mother?' I said, as if I was surprised he had one.

Adam went back to gazing at the wall.

'Is she ill?'

Nothing.

'Adam, you're going to have to tell me what's going on. Is she dead?' (Insensitive phrasing, perhaps, but apt to generate a response.)

'Dying.'

'Shit. What is it, cancer?'

'Worse.'

My mind was instantly grappling with the most bizarre of afflictions.

'Huntington's.' He spat the words.

Huntington's chorea is a disease of the nervous system: onset in adulthood, abnormal writhing movements of the limbs and torso, a dementia of biblical proportions, and then death within ten to fifteen years. There was no treatment, of course. I knew people who worked on gene therapy in the States.

'Sorry,' I said, digging for empathy. 'But presumably it could be years before it starts to affect her?'

'She's already had it for twelve. She's almost a vegetable.'

My throat closed. Huntington's was genetic. Being a dominantly inherited condition meant Adam had a fifty percent chance of acquiring the disease himself. The problem was you didn't know it was in your family until it was too late for you to wish you had never been born. And that was the life sentence: not knowing whether you were next in line. There were tests, but with no cure who would want them?

'You could be tested?' I offered, despite my inner conclusion.

His face distorted suddenly. 'Would you want to be?'

'Why didn't you tell us? Maybe Jane and I could have helped.' I was trying not to sound too pissed off with him. 'It would have been good to know, at least.'

'Well I'm sorry if I've let you down Daniel, I really am.'

'I'm just frustrated for you, that's all.'

'Frustrated?' Adam was shouting now. Even above the heavy rock let loose by the sound system, people were beginning to notice us, no doubt half-expecting and half-hoping for a fight.

'We should talk about this somewhere else,' I said and lifted him from his seat by the sleeve of his leather jacket. He offered only the resistance of gravity.

Together we forced our way through groups of laughing faces and plastic glasses to find the exit at the back of the building. We stumbled down a metal stairway outside, Adam growing heavier in my hand. A small crowd of students gathered on the stairwell looked at us like we were two old farts who couldn't hold half a lager-shandy between them. The air was humid from the exhaust of an air conditioning unit and the pavement was greasy from a light rain, and as we left the final step, I slipped and almost brought Adam to the ground with me.

More laughter behind us. 'Fucking hammered,' I heard one of them say. Half of me wanted to go back and punch a sneer or two from their mouths, but I still had Adam attached to my fist, and I still had a passing financial interest in my position at the university. By the time we reached the main road Adam was lolling across my shoulder like a corpse.

'You can't let it get to you,' I was muttering into his ear. It was a strange time for counselling.

I adjusted my stance, trying to accommodate his weight with a less painful group of muscles. 'How long have you known about this? You must have thought it through enough times?'

Adam could give me nothing intelligible. He toppled sideways onto the bonnet of a car that buckled and then regained its aerodynamic line as I quickly pulled him away from the bruised metal. I allowed him to fall again, gently this time, against the window of the driver's door, and heard the air escape from his chest in a soft groan as he slid down onto the pavement. His hair was matted to his face, and suddenly everything felt damp and uncomfortable. For a while I just stared at him lying there, feeling sorry for him (and a little for myself, no doubt) until, finally, assured of his stability, I stepped out into the traffic, arm aloft.

...

Jane was used to the ritual. I couldn't blame her for the well-rehearsed look of disgust she gave us as we fell into the hallway, a taximeter ticking gleefully at the roadside. I leant against the wall with my arm around Adam's waist, the pair of us like wounded soldiers returned to the trenches, while Jane paid off the driver. I wondered how long it would take her to realise it was Adam I was struggling with and not the booze.

My first assumption was that it was some strange property of grief that had exaggerated the effect of the two pints Adam and I had shared in the Union, because he was now so emphatically drunk. But the stale whisky I could smell on his breath said he had been drinking hard long before he'd come to meet me that evening. Had he been trying to summon or drown the courage to tell me about his mother, I wondered? It was absurd to imagine I was someone in whom people could easily confide, but I didn't expect friends I had known for twenty-seven years to have to get shit-faced either.

I raised my eyebrows at Jane and allowed Adam to fold onto the carpet.

'His mother's dying,' I said, dolefully.

The anger drained from Jane's face.

'Huntington's chorea,' I added, knowing full well she wouldn't know what it was. 'It's genetic. Drives you round in a wheelchair before it drives you round the bend. The problem is you don't know you've got it until one of your parents has already been diagnosed.'

'I've heard of it,' said Jane, still staring at Adam. 'There's no real treatment for it, is there?'

I glanced downwards. 'What do you think?'

Jane's eyes moistened. 'Daniel, could you stop baiting me for a minute and just tell me what happened?' She bent down for a closer look. 'Is he alright? How much has he had? You seem OK.'

'He must have been pissed before he came to the Union. He's so quiet it's hard to tell sometimes. He only had a couple with me.'

Adam gave a resonant snort.

'He can sleep here,' said Jane.

'Someone should phone Clare,' I said.

We put a still-clothed Adam to bed in a series of comical manoeuvres, and then Jane left me to make the call to Clare, which I wasn't best pleased about. Adam's state didn't appear to come as much of a surprise. According to Clare, he'd been hitting the Irish since two that afternoon, and she seemed oddly nonplussed by the whole thing. I wanted to ask her about the tests for Huntington's but didn't have the nerve. There was something vaguely impenetrable about the woman that always managed to scare men like me off. Nothing tangible, just an instinct.

Adam's predicament was the sort of issue two adults should have been able to sit down and talk freely and openly about. Jane and I might even have learnt something about each other in the process. Instead, I quickly opened a bottle, intent on drowning such impulses, and made for the sanctuary of late-night television. After sorting Adam out, Jane came to join me in the living room. She sat on the edge of an armchair, cradling a wine glass, her eyes brimming with fresh tears. The depth of a woman's sensitivity never fails to amaze me.

'Would you want to know if your mother had it?' Her voice was tremulous.

Slumped in the corner of the sofa, I still managed a fairly emphatic shrug of my shoulders.

'Poor Adam,' she said. 'It's awful. It's a life sentence. Knowing you might have to face this awful illness, I mean, Christ!' She took another slug of wine.

I sighed. 'At the risk of sounding trite, we all have to die of something. The only difference in Adam's case is that, usually, we don't know what we're going to die of.'

'But that's all the difference in the world isn't it? With this Huntingdon's...'

'Hunting*ton's*,' I corrected.

'...You have a chance of knowing. A chance to change your life, to do something about it.'

'We can change our lives anytime we want to, with or without a terminal illness. It's just that most people choose not to bother.'

'Yes, I know,' she said. 'The rest of us are all running around in circles wasting our bloody time while you're pushing forward the boundaries of human knowledge, blah blah.'

Jane was close to falling into one of my conversational traps: an attack on my profession. Scientists were intellectual masturbators, the argument would go, generating meaningless paperwork solely for the furtherment of their own careers and wasting hard-earned taxpayer's money in the process. I would play the altruism card in return. That to work in science was to work for the greater good, for the advancement of mankind and, in my case, for the benefit of its health. The financial rewards were undeniably poor and fame was, at best, limited to a brisk round of applause in a foreign auditorium. Plus there could be little argument against the principle that I was generating knowledge. Whereas acting, I could always contend, was a profession borne of frivolous exhibitionism.

My face hardened. 'I don't think we want to go there just now, do you?'

'You're just pissed off that Adam didn't tell you about his mother,' she said, audibly slurring now.

I killed the television. 'You must be joking?'

'I mean, do you think you're really any kind of a friend to him?'

'What on earth are you talking about?'

'He told me before.'

'Told you what?'

'About his mother.'

'When?'

'I'm not sure, a few weeks ago.'

'OK, Jane, I'll go along with it. So why would he tell you?'

She slid down onto the seat of the armchair. 'Because he'd rather tell anyone else, Daniel. Because nobody can fucking talk to you. Because you never fucking listen!'

'Is it a wonder?'

'You don't see it, do you?' she said. 'How like your father you are?'

'You hardly knew my father.'

'That's just my point, Daniel. No one did.'

Later, reaching out into the darkness of the spare room for sleep, Jane's argument made a fresh impact on me. Why had Adam told her about his mother and not me? I had always thought of Adam as my good deed; that I was doing my relatively unattractive and uninteresting companion a favour by remaining friends with him when – beyond a few brief and begrudging smiles in corridors – I generally ignored everyone else. I had convinced myself that I was his only friend, the person to whom he would have revealed his innermost secrets. But Adam had seen through me. He hadn't taken me seriously at all. He had another life kept hidden from me. And what I couldn't quite come to terms with at the time was that I might have needed Adam more than he needed me. That it was me who didn't have anyone to turn to, and that I could never have confided in Jane the way Adam had been able to, three sheets to the wind or not.

...

The thought that there was a burglar in the house quickly passed, the noises far too blundering. But whatever it was moving out there at such an ungodly hour, it had me sitting breathlessly upright staring out into cold, blank air.

A slit of white light appeared under the bedroom door. Then another noise: glass bottles rattling on ceramic. It was Adam engaged in a series of pain-staking attempts to find painkillers in the bathroom. The once phosphorescent hands on my old alarm clock said 5.00 am. The Hangover Hour.

In the kitchen I boiled the kettle and Adam sat quietly. I poured the tea and Adam sat quietly. I thumbed the leaves of an old *Evening Standard* and Adam sat quietly. I wanted to take his pulse in case he'd died prematurely during the night and it was an apparition sitting there in front of me, hands wringing and head bowed. I pitied Clare for having to face the sight of him each morning, ashen-faced, congealed hair, his nails soiled and chewed. Despite my annoyance at being kept in the dark about his illness, a part of me was relieved to have survived the twelve years of his agony in honest ignorance.

'Why did you tell Jane about your mother?' I asked him.

Adam's stare broke. His face drew up from the table. 'My mother didn't want anyone outside the family to know.'

'When people tell you they don't want anyone to know, it usually means the exact opposite.'

He looked coldly at me. 'The least I could do was respect her wishes.'

'It still doesn't explain Jane.'

'Jane was just...there.'

'There when?'

'A Thursday. We'd come back from The Union. You went to bed. I was waiting for a taxi and I just blurted it out. I don't really know why.' He paused. 'I'm sorry, by the way.'

'Sorry for what? I might have been able to help you, that's all. It's no skin off my nose.'

'I meant about your father. I expect my problems are the last thing you need.'

'I wouldn't worry about that. I probably knew your mother better than I knew either of my parents.'

'Was it difficult?' he said with a genuine tone of interest, as if insights into the pain of his future might be gained from the pain of my past. Though I was certain my family's parallel lines would be of little relevance to the tight matrix of his own.

'Fairly ghastly,' I said, 'but not in the way you'd imagine.'

'And Jane?' Adam lifted his eyes just short of catching mine. 'I mean, is everything OK between you two?'

'Jesus, Adam, you've got your own problems. Stop worrying about me.'

He was oddly persistent. 'Not good then?'

'No.' I smiled thinly. 'Not good.'

'Sorry.'

'Don't be.'

I took a breath. 'So, are you going to have the test?'

I immediately felt cruel for having brought up the Huntington's again so bluntly. I could see it all coming back to him. And for the first time since our rendezvous in the Student Bar he looked directly at me. Bringing his hand up to eye-level, he first waited until I had convinced him of my fullest attention before spreading his fingers slowly apart. The half-light and my fatigue made clarity of vision a privilege rather than a right, and I had to blink hard to find my focus, uncertain, at first, if Adam's hand was shaking as much as it appeared to be. But it was definitely shaking. Like a drunk without a drink.

CHAPTER EIGHT

Christmas came late for us that year. Christmas, The Holiday, surfaced at the same time it always did; it was just the lab party that was late, delayed until the Eve of Eves. None of us, it seemed, had anywhere more important to be.

The routine in the lab would have been all too predictable. Work would have stopped by four, the laptops placed into hibernation, the water baths cooled, the isotopes returned to fizz and click in their leaded tombs. A youthful anticipation would have filled the air, a sense of impending frivolity over which I would have had little control, and so, as always, I made certain to avoid such moments. I made sure I was out 'doing some last minute Christmas shopping', and I made sure everyone knew about it.

In truth, I was with Erin in the animal house.

She had already shown me the baseline behavioural data, but I wanted to see it for myself. It was difficult for me not to look as though I didn't believe her – but I didn't. She wasn't lying, she was just new to this type of work and had obviously made some beginner's mistake. Perhaps I was partly to blame. Perhaps I had exerted too much pressure on her – enough to perform, I had hoped, but not enough to fail.

Back in the lab, the northerns from Brian's original experiment had continued to defy us. He and Erin had tried seven new probe pairs from three different companies on the RNA from his experiment, but each time the sense probes had bound as keenly as the anti-sense. And it didn't make any sense. Despite my best intentions to see the data through to its natural conclusion, I ended up stuffing the blots into the back of a filing cabinet and praying for a fire to engulf my office and rid me of their blasphemy. With the whole basis for my group's existence disassembling in front of me, my hopes had now been forced to pin themselves on Erin, whom I had instructed to re-run Brian's experiment and get us out of this mess.

Unfortunately, there was no mistaking the new nightmare I could now, literally, see staring me in the face. One glance at these mice was enough for me to know that Erin's initial report was right. I didn't have to check the aggression scores in her lab book, just the look of them, the way they gathered themselves with their backs arched into the air, the tautness of their whiskers, the pattern of their breathing. They were mad as hell.

The protocol she was using had been tried and tested, and guaranteed to induce aggression in a highly predictable way. The whole thing normally took six or seven weeks to run, with the mice exposed to an, essentially, hostile environment in a controlled manner that slowly encouraged alterations in their behaviour. We made sure it was to their advantage to change. We gave them no choice but to become mean. We used 'scenarios' in which aggression was the only way to get out of a maze or the only way to ensure the next batch of food (this despite the fact it bore a striking resemblance to their droppings). And then with drugs or genetically modified animals like the knockouts we could evaluate the importance of a particular mechanism like SNF. Standard stuff.

The only problem was that the experiment hadn't started yet.

'Someone's definitely cocked up.' I heard myself saying to an innocent pair of pink eyes in one of the cages they had stacked on mobile trolleys in an otherwise bare, white room. All the rooms were like this. It wasn't just the air that was conditioned, it was the temperature, the light, the food – each mouse, rat or rabbit guaranteed to receive precisely the same amount of each. Even the animals were genetically bred to be indistinguishable from each other, so that nothing could interfere with our experimental objectives. At least, that should have been the case. Because something had gone wildly awry with this particular batch. The only cause for optimism I could see was that, so far, I had managed to moderate the tone of my voice just enough to conceal the true mix of dread and desperation I experienced upon seeing them.

'Are you sure these aren't the mice left over from Brian's original experiment?' I asked, vainly.

Erin's eyes pleaded before her mouth. 'I checked and double-checked, Daniel, honestly. I've been in here every day for the past two weeks. And anyway, look at the size of them.'

She was right of course; the mice were far too small to be the ones Brian had used. We began every experiment with a fresh batch of young mice, only a few weeks old, which then grew considerably, almost doubling in size, by the end of a typical aggression study. But the ones I was looking at were still tiny. There was no way Erin could have confused them with Brian's mice, which would have been much bigger by now. These rodents could only have been at the beginning of the conditioning process. In which case, it was difficult to explain why they were behaving as if they were at the end. It was as if they had come into the world inexplicably programmed for belligerence.

'Well Christ knows what's happened with this lot,' I said, eventually, feeling less than profound.

The unexpected in science can make for the most exciting or the most wrist-slitting of results, and this was either a triumph or a disaster of monumental proportions. Was it possible, I wondered, that someone was playing an elaborate trick on us? God himself, perhaps?

'I'm glad you said that,' said Erin peering into one of the cages. I can't bloody figure it out either. It's nuts.'

'Well they certainly are.'

Neither of us could bring ourselves to laugh.

I bent down next to Erin, catching a delicious pheremonal breeze from her skin, despite the queasy odour of animal bedding. 'And you're absolutely certain they haven't mixed the cages up with any of the other colonies?'

'Definitely. For a start, there aren't any other cages to mix them up with. We're the only ones in the building using this strain. I couldn't even order any more, the suppliers have been out of stock for weeks. The only way Brian managed to get enough for his study was by breeding the mice from his last experiment, which is what I ended up having to do.'

We would never normally have used mice from a completed experiment to breed mice for the next. Animals that had been through the aggression protocol would clearly be tainted by their involvement. Brian was an imbecile, but I was surprised the technicians in the animal facility hadn't tried to stop him and Erin from using old mice as breeders.

I didn't say anything. I needed time to think. I merely resumed my intense examination of the cages as if the occupants might reveal their secrets to me in the twitch of a whisker.

Well,' I said, 'whatever happened, this experiment is over.'

Erin sighed. 'I'm not going to argue with you.'

'What the hell have we done to deserve this?' I asked the oblivious rodents. 'First the anti-sense data and now a bunch of psychotic mice to contend with. You're not supposed to be angry yet you bastards! You're supposed to be calm!'

Erin was laughing. 'Just like us, you mean?'

'Baxter will have a field day.'

'Perhaps we should just go out and get drunk with the rest of them?'

'Yes,' I said. 'I think perhaps we should.'

...

In spite of a relatively poor sense of humour, we scientists are still capable of occasional fun, albeit condensed into a few select evenings of excess. For my part, I have always maintained a healthy interest in the unhealthy. There were my Thursday evenings with Adam, for a start, and my avid patronage of the Sunday Times Wine Club. I had even scored a little weed from one of the more enterprising post-docs on the sixth floor from time to time. However, there remain many amongst us who strive more earnestly to embrace the white-coated, bespectacled image of scientists the rest of the world holds so dear. There are no shortage of dour spinsters and high-browed curmudgeons to be found within the whitewashed corridors of our institutions. But just like our mice, given the right environment, some of them can be persuaded to shed their erudition long enough for any scholarly pretensions to be drowned. For their more trivial-selves to be unleashed.

Stepping down into the wine bar, I felt an absurd clench of anticipation as I read the handwritten sign that announced 'Reserved for Private Party'. At the nod of a waitress, we moved out into the darker recesses of the bar. We didn't really have the place all to ourselves, of course; had we invited the whole of the Medical Department we couldn't have filled it. Instead, our group was to be cordoned off by a long table in one corner like a sociology experiment.

They sat me at the head of the table, I think more to isolate than honour me. Erin and Brian were soon similarly banished. Brian no doubt for the same reasons as me, but Erin, I assumed, because of her late arrival, as we'd been sure to take separate routes to the party. We waited an age for the first course of a set meal to arrive while the waitresses all too eagerly re-filled our glasses, challenging the toughest of resolves toward restraint. As usual, I entered a preparative phase of quiet contemplation, leaving the rest of them to chatter anxiously amongst themselves. Such occasions, I was only too aware, could present a significant danger to the unwary: the blurring of professional boundaries that is apt to follow a blurring of vision. One has to pace oneself to avoid the alcoholic candour that might threaten friendships and careers alike. In other words, you had to watch your mouth. Women know this instinctively, whereas men seem to seek out these avenues of self-destruction unashamedly.

I noticed Erin gazing off into the candlelight and, utterly failing to heed my own advice, I leant towards her and asked if she had ever tried to find out who her real parents were. She didn't flinch. Either she was good at hiding her annoyance or she was used to the question.

'I tried once, but not very hard. It's never been like that for me. I don't think I ever really wanted to find them.' She threw me an embarrassingly tender look. 'Your father died recently, is that right?'

'Just before you started.'

'Sorry,' she said.

I took a jerky swig of wine. 'It's OK, he was seventy-two.'

'That's not that old these days.'

'True, but at my age parents are more like people you once met on holiday.'

'I bet you miss him really?'

'I'll take that bet.'

I was surprised to find myself a little angered by the exchange. It was none of her bloody business. I knew she didn't mean any harm; she was just naturally inquisitive. Good for science, bad for dinner parties, directness only ever a stray question from rudeness. I covered my mouth with the wineglass and took a series of small breaths to calm myself.

The starters arrived. Lettuce like damp tissue paper and a pile of stunted shrimps that should have been smothered at birth. It took no more than two mouthfuls for us to clear our plates and get back to the wine, and I signalled a change to white for the main course. Brian was still trying to fill my ear with talk of work. I managed to look directly at him while ignoring every word he said, training all of my resources, instead, towards Erin and the conversation she was attempting to hold with Leo.

Leo was another doctoral hopeful, short, spikey hair, expensive footwear, and advertising hoardings for clothes. To be an academic was to embrace a certain level of poverty and I couldn't see him hacking it for any longer than was absolutely necessary. He was destined for a job with the Pharmaceuticals the second the ink on his PhD was dry. It didn't sound as though he and Erin were discussing anything of great interest. Something about Leo's brother and a crappy rock band that was playing the Town and Country Club. I think he was trying to persuade her to come to the gig.

Brian, meanwhile, was still buzzing, drone-like, next to me. As predicted, he had picked his moment to make the case for getting his hands back on the mice carefully, and he continued his pitch over the arm of the waitress as she poured the white to taste. I sniffed the puddle at the bottom of my glass. The wine tasted sweet for a Pinot, but it was more than adequate for a house, and I indicated as much to the girl, who looked wholly unimpressed. The main course quickly followed, which was, thankfully, enough to turn Brian's attention from mice to sirloin and gave me a few moments respite from telling him repeatedly that he would be better off sticking to the cell work because the mice weren't going anywhere.

Mid-mouthful, I found one end of a Christmas cracker hovering over my plate with Erin clinging expectantly to the other. I dropped my fork, took hold of it, and yanked, but the banger failed to bang. By the time I'd fished the hat and key ring out of my food Erin had already secured her crown by pulling another cracker with Leo, and I went back to contemplating the myriad reflections in my ever-replenished glass.

The music grew louder and louder, and by the end of the meal had reached a level high enough to drown out most of the conversation around the table. People started to drift away towards the main bar, and just as the volume rose another few decibels, Erin suddenly leapt from her seat and almost dislocated my shoulder trying to prise me from mine. She dragged me over to a clearing where some of our lot were already gyrating to an ABBA number. There was no official dance floor, but with the crowd, understandably, giving us a wide berth, we comfortably carved out our own, providing a cabaret of sorts for a wall of smirking onlookers.

After a couple of tracks it became difficult to distinguish my encirclement of Erin from the room's encirclement of me. Everything turned kaleidoscopically in a nauseating excess of movement that seemed quite entertaining at the time. But I had no idea how inebriated I really was until I caught Erin and Sarah raising their eyes at me, at which point I mouthed the words 'off for a pee' and left them to it.

To reach the toilets I focused on a point approximating the place I believed them to be and then drilled my way through a squirming, jabbering mass of bodies towards it. The whole crowd seemed to be dressed in black, the experience much like riding a ghost train with monstrous faces lurching up from the shadows and bodies sprung from the underworld in billowing clouds of smoke, all of them infected with an insane, cackling laughter. One look at me, though, and most of them moved out of the way quick enough. A few of the more burly suits tried to hold their ground, but I just kept falling towards them until they had no choice but to let me pass.

I didn't think I was going to be sick by the time I reached the cubicle, but I was, and felt a little better for it. I washed my hands and rinsed my mouth, though I couldn't face the mirrors, the vision there too awful to contemplate. Before I had the time to think about throwing up again, I was staggering back to our hole in the crowd, only to find it had been filled in by strangers decidedly more contemptuous of me than the students from the lab. Eventually, I discovered most of them had reconvened at the dining table, though Erin was still nowhere to be seen. I probed Gavin for information, but he was even more vague on the subject of Erin's whereabouts than I was, and there were only puzzled looks from the rest of them.

I decided to cut my losses. A final shot of wine, a lunge for my overcoat, and I was staggering up the stairs, the night, I feared, already lost.

The bitter air circulating at street level, coupled with the blinding, brilliant angles of a thousand water-flared lights, did their best to try and sober me up, but only left me feeling a little nauseated again. Cars emptied rain from the gutters. Shoes slapped and clicked on the glistening asphalt. I patted my cheeks a few times, drew a lungful of exhaust fumes, and set off, more with purpose than direction. Yet, by chance, I still managed to catch up with Erin and Leo just as they were approaching the entrance to The Underground, and I was able to follow them on to the northbound platform with ease. Familiar territory.

I paid rather less attention to shadowing Erin the second time round. In fact, initially, most of my energy was spent trying not to doze off, despite the jolts of the carriage. Then at Wood Green, having politely dismissed Leo a few stops earlier, Erin made her way through the backstreets at quite a pace (although speed is another one of the many things about which one loses objectivity when drunk), and I almost lost her any number of times before rounding a corner just in time to see her dart into her driveway.

The house was dark. My appreciation of time was weakening, but I presumed that if the tubes were still running it had to be before midnight, and certainly not late enough for a house full of students to be asleep. Which meant an empty house. I waited until Erin had made the top of the steps before heading up the pathway, approaching as confidently as I could with the thought that any suggestion of stealth might worry her unduly.

'Erin? Hi!' My words seemed to come from someone else's mouth. From the stranger inside my head.

'Jesus!' Erin twisted violently towards me with a hand to her chest. 'You scared me. What are you doing here? How did you know where I lived?'

'I remembered the address on your CV, knew it was around here somewhere.'

My lips were rubberised. I hoped, at the very least, she would understand what I was saying, and only at the very worst realise how utterly pissed I was. Then again, being drunk might also form the basis for some sort of excuse, should it prove necessary.

'Did you follow me?' Erin smiled nervously, trying to convince me that she would merely think it humorous if I had.

'Of course not!' I said as emphatically as a litre of cheap house would allow.

An awkward pause followed. Given that everything appeared to be happening faster than it really was, I can only guess for how long we stood there not speaking, with Erin jangling her keys and her eyes skittering anxiously from me to the front door.

'You left the party without saying goodbye,' I said. 'I thought maybe you were upset about something. I just wanted to make sure you were OK.'

'I'm fine, honestly. I didn't know where you were. I had to catch the last tube.'

She knew damn well where I'd been.

'I was in the loo,' I said, pointing somewhere behind me.

'Sorry,' she said. 'I didn't realise.'

She turned to place a key in the lock. I lurched forward and took a firm hold of her elbow.

'I'm very fond of you, you know.' My voice was hoarse from the cold and the booze.

'I think we're both a bit pissed.'

She was being kind. She was as sober as a jury.

'I couldn't say it if I wasn't drunk.'

Erin glanced towards the door. 'There's nothing I can do about it, Daniel, not now.'

'You're an intelligent woman. I know that. It's what I like about you. Those arseholes, they...' The sentence stalled. I moved against her, placing my arm around her waist. I was on autopilot. The worst was over; and the worst wasn't too bad. Erin looked a little nervous, yes, but who wouldn't have been? It was to be expected; she was young, after all.

'Could we go in and talk, at least?' I said. 'It's bloody freezing out here.'

There was no place for her to go. I was close enough to smell her cosmetics, to feel the warm intertwining of our breath.

A light. Footsteps inside.

Erin pushed herself away from the door and I, in turn, fell away from her, stumbling down the stairs, only managing to steady myself after three or four.

'Andy, hi,' she said.

A familiar shadow stood in the doorway. There was no detail in the man's face, just the outline of his evenly combed hair – short at the sides – across a square forehead. Rather an old fashioned styling, I remember thinking. He was even larger than I'd expected. If this was Erin's boyfriend, there would be no winning her by duel. Pistols, perhaps, but at a distance significantly greater than forty paces.

'Hello,' he said, looking only vaguely in my direction. He seemed to be finding it as hard to locate me in the darkness as I was he in the light. He was a thick caber of a man. *Scot's Oats*-weaned.

He turned to Erin. 'Who's this?'

I leant forward into the light. 'I'm Daniel,' I said and began climbing the steps again.

'Daniel's my Boss,' said Erin. 'Daniel, this is my Dad, Andrew.'

'Dr Hayden?' said 'Andrew' with evident surprise, his accent broader and rougher than hers – a highlander, at a guess.

'Hello,' I said, offering my palm.

'Daniel was just seeing me home,' said Erin.

Erin's father reached for my hand with all the willingness of a politician. His shirtsleeve drew back along an expansive forearm to reveal the thick, ugly ink of a tattooist's scrawl.

'Well,' he said, 'thanks for looking after her.'

'Andrew is my adopted father,' said Erin.

'Of course!' I said, beaming inappropriately.

Then nothing for a moment, just our eyes dancing and the cold biting.

'I should say goodnight,' I said, eventually.

Andrew offered me the open doorway. 'Do you want to come in for coffee?'

Was he bluffing? I had half a mind to accept. I certainly had half a mind.

'I'm fine, thanks,' I replied. 'I'll miss the last tube.'

Erin smiled awkwardly. 'OK, well, I'll see you when you get back from Chicago then? Thanks again for seeing me back.'

'Not a problem at all.' I slurred.

A further round of clipped goodbyes and I was staggering back down the path with the ghost of Erin's smile still haunting the air. Behind me, on the other side of a closed door, I could hear muffled voices exchanging frank views.

The last tube had long gone. I could have rummaged the High Street for a cab but decided to walk home, instead, hoping I might sober up. I kept thinking about Erin's choice of words. "Not now" she'd said. Did she mean not now, but later, or not now, and not ever? Though why should it have mattered? Why such an overwhelming feeling of loss at the thought it might be the latter of the two? In what way had I been in a position to 'lose' Erin anyway? It was ridiculous. I had never possessed her in any sense of the word. Whatever had passed between us was at best unspoken and at worst wholly imagined on my part. Erin was a colleague, perhaps even a friend, but no more than that. Witness how keen she'd been to brush off the pass I'd made at her. It was a foolish, tactless move on my part and Erin had rightly demurred. I should have been hoping for the whole sorry incident to be quickly forgotten about, and for us to be joking about it after the holidays, laughing the way we had before at the pub beside the invisible river. But all I wanted was to be with her, and I'm not sure, now, how far I might have gone to make that happen. Perhaps 'Andy' had done her more of a favour than he realised?

Somewhere near Shepherds Bush, I climbed a concrete bridge spanning a dual carriageway and watched the lone cars slide underneath, their headlights scanning the road. An uneasy sense of certainty settled over me, foreign and unwanted; that the answers to questions I had previously been unable to voice were out there waiting for me, their slow-creeping ciphers hidden in the white lines and the road-signs and the pin-holed sky. An experience all the more unsettling because, although I had no idea how at the time, I knew some vital element of myself was about to be revealed.

CHAPTER NINE

That Christmas my mother chose to stay with her sister, Beatrice. My Aunt had a retirement cottage on the Suffolk coast she shared with a vicious Yorkshire Terrier, and I suspected my mother had her eye on a place nearby. Plus, Beatrice had family. Proper family. Family that visited. Family that spent Christmas with family.

My mother's departure was a relief. It left just the one set of relatives to endure. Nevertheless, I had my flight to the meeting with *Quintex* in Chicago timed for an early retreat from even this, the briefest of festivities. There may only have been twenty-four hours for me to last, but it was still ample time for unpleasantness to flourish.

Jane's parents resided on the hinterlands of the upper class. Their house had an electric-gated driveway and a garden that went all the way round. Every item of furniture in the house was older than they were. They drank medium-dry sherry before dinner. They even had 'staff'. I had met them only twice before: the first a dyspeptic luncheon in an austere London Hotel, the second a christening for the son of a minor peer, both events brief and constipated. The father was in business, the mother in rehabilitation, although I was only supposed to know about the former. One can only mourn the fate of secrets left to the discretion of drunks, but this poorly concealed flaw at least made her more interesting in my eyes. I have always admired worldliness in any form, and there was certainly an unspoken knowledge behind those neon lips and bruised cheekbones, frightful and challenging in equal measure.

If I'd had much more of the *Cote de Roussillon* I might not have noticed it, but halfway through the day I realised that Catherine and Graham spoke to each other almost solely via Jane. Barely acknowledging each other's existence, they seemed as remote as the house they were trapped in together. And I thought how odd it was that Jane and I should share so much in the temperature of our parents and the isolation of our upbringing, and yet they were similarities that only seemed to exaggerate rather than lessen our plight.

Looking at the parents, it was certainly easy to see why Jane had become Jane, and why Jane did not in any way hold them responsible. Being parents was simply beyond them. They had pretensions to a house full of servants and a box at the opera, but in reality all they had was a part-time housekeeper and a collection of dubious antiques. It seemed unfair, like being born poor and being no good at sport. It wasn't fair for them to have to cope with offspring when they had so many self-preoccupations to contend with. And that evening, as we sipped our aperitifs in the wavering flame of a burning tree trunk, I even found myself wondering whether Jane had been a surprise to them in more ways than one. The mother I could believe readily enough, a suggestion of the Mediterranean beneath that bleached hair, a fiery temperament, and a skin that bronzed with ease, she was Jane all over. But the father, a stolid, creased type, I was less certain about, and my mind filled readily with images of Catherine, her string of young lovers, and their ill-matched passions.

'Share the joke, said Jane, breaking the silence.

'Oh, nothing,' I said and quenched a smile.

Jane's brother, Michael, joined us later in the day. Tall and built like a cereal box, it appeared he spent most of his time playing Polo. Dinner consisted of me chewing overcooked beef whilst the men of the house exchanged equine statistics. There was much talk of 'hands'. Jane's father did try to involve me, but I must have appeared so dumbstruck by his early attempts to haul me into the conversation that I succeeded in putting him off for the rest of the evening.

The exchange of presents was a charade, an exhibition of familiness I was all too familiar with. And then we played charades. The constant flow of wine brought a few snipes and grudges to the fore but all in all it was a surprisingly civil affair, observed closely throughout by Jocelyn the Irish housekeeper who, like me, had been forced to suffer this pantomime. She was a young woman, I imagined, for such a position, more the age of an *au pair*. Attractive in a bland way, she took looking bored to the heights of an art form. With most of the meal clearly pre-prepared there couldn't have been much for her to do, and I suspected that she had been asked to stay on for my benefit, and to make sure she looked the part, too, right down to the black pinafore and white apron. Yet, as I continued to observe our hosts' strained interplay, a theory regarding the role of the serving class began to take shape in which the purpose of servants, far from being just the running of a household, was to ensure restraint amongst their Masters and Mistresses. To help maintain a cool air of civility whereas, unguarded, debauchery and bloodshed might ensue. They were the umpires of the upper class.

Jocelyn's hold on the game didn't last. Her stifled yawns and constant shuffling became too uncomfortable even for Jane's parents to endure, and following her mid-evening dismissal I found myself cast in her place as surrogate peacekeeper. The role didn't come easily. I was having to bite down hard to avoid confrontation myself, let alone avert theirs. A saintly aptitude for appeasement and an uncommon interest in the banal appeared prerequisites for the post. The effort was enough to put me off the port altogether, which, like the atmosphere, grew dusty in its crystal decanter.

It was in liquor, however, that I found my keenest ally. With its support the company did at least become more placid as the evening wore on, which, in turn, meant less of a need for any reasonable interjections from me. It also allowed me to find a new intermediary in Michael, who was so pissed he couldn't conceal his frantic look of distress as Jane and I excused ourselves sometime after midnight and left him to close down for the night.

Our room, at the far end of a long corridor on the third floor, was Siberian, which made undressing an oddly vigorous event. Jane was particularly drunk.

'You quite fancy my Mum don't you?' she slurred through the body of a nightdress half-pulled over her head.

'She's OK.' I said benignly.

'Don't blame you. She's attractive for her age. Still has her figure, dresses well, and she's worth a bob or two.'

'Sure.'

'Well, then you can admit you fancy her.'

'I could. But I don't.'

'You couldn't keep your eyes off her.'

'Jesus!' I tossed my shirt melodramatically to the floor. 'OK, I fancy her! I want to drag her up here right now by her split ends and fuck you both on the four-poster!'

'We're not quite the toffs you'd like to think we are, Daniel.'

'Today has made that abundantly clear.'

'Us in twenty year's time,' she muttered, sliding beneath the bedclothes. 'That's if you give us that long.'

I found myself isolated on the far side of the room wearing just my socks. 'Why are you playing with me? Why is any of this my fault?' I asked of the bedding Jane had now buried herself in.

'Why is what your fault?'

'Fancying your mother, not fancying her, what's it go to do with anything? I pretty much stopped your parents from killing each other tonight. You should be thanking me.'

'You're a liar,' she said

I took a deep breath.

'You can't admit it, can you?' she said.

'I told you, she's not my type.'

Jane twisted violently towards me. 'Now that I can believe.'

I made a gesture of confused capitulation towards the ceiling and edged myself, shivering, between the iced sheets. I rearranged the pillows loudly and then lay there staring at the ornate turnings of the uprights on that ridiculous bed.

'And what does that mean?' I asked, slowly.

'It means she's not nearly young enough for you, is she?'

'Christ's sake.' I muttered.

'So how is Erin?'

I just managed to avoid saying: 'Erin who?' but it was close. 'You mean Erin from the lab?'

'Yes, 'Erin from the lab'. Who the hell else?'

'She's twenty-two for fuck's sake!'

'And?'

My face burned. '*And* I don't know what the hell you're bringing her up now for. She's just another PhD student.'

'Well, if not her then someone else.'

'Do you honestly think I'm having an affair with Erin? How come you even know about her? You never normally take any interest in anything I do at work.'

'I just do. You talk to Adam, Adam talks to Clare. Maybe you mentioned her. It doesn't matter. There's always smoke, Daniel. I just can't always be bothered to find the fire. And you know damn well why we don't talk about your work.'

'Because you're convinced I think you're too stupid to understand.'

'Too stupid to bother with, anyway.' Jane's voice was growing tired, less defiant. 'All the clever bastard things you do with your cells and your rats in your little white coats. I wouldn't dare waste your time by having you explain any of it to me.'

At that exact moment the bulb in the light next to my bed blew. For some reason, the sudden darkness turned my voice to a whisper. 'I don't know how you can accuse me of having an affair for no other reason than I don't fancy your Mum. Hardly bloody fair, is it?'

Jane turned away from me again. 'No,' she said, 'hardly bloody fair.'

She was comatose within minutes, whereas I entered my usual cycle of half-sleep, half-wakefulness. At some point there was a stumbling on the landing, followed by the repeated slamming of too many doors. I could have guessed Jane's parents didn't sleep in the same bed, but that didn't mean I would be taking advantage of that particular arrangement, no matter Jane's florid imagination.

I woke in the night, suspended in complete darkness with only the weight of the sheets to remind me of my corporeal self and its connection to the world. Gradually, a soft light from an unidentified source bleached the curtains (we were far from any city), revealing feint lines and shadows as if offering me a new way to appreciate the room, its contents made visible by virtue of some previously hidden band of the electromagnetic spectrum. Images, too, from my encounter with Erin drifted into my consciousness like an amorous hangover.

Jane flinched the first time I touched her, then slackened again almost immediately, though too late to disguise the instincts of her flesh. Even so, I dared to let my hands wander her skin, rediscovering once-familiar crests and falls. She turned towards me and we lay side by side, my hand resting on the edge of her pelvis. I felt a curious desire for normality, without knowing what that might turn out to be. A rare shiver of tenderness, perhaps? A fugue? A capitulation? There were so many forms of physical encounter, so many states of mind, but all I wanted was the right one. Part of me wanted to talk them through with her, to summarise our options. We might have stated our preferences and our points of view and then devised some campaign of mutual satisfaction. But this had never been our way. Instead, we fumbled blindly through a menu of desires, an account of lovemaking that, as usual, came to nothing beyond a string of excuses with their sorry foundations set in tiredness, alcohol and anger.

I tried again later on, prodding clumsily in the dark, trying to conquer her dry cavities. But after a high-pitched noise that sounded too close to a scream I fell away from her, rigid in all but groin. And in the silence that followed I held my breath and listened for further sounds that failed to materialise.

CHAPTER TEN

I arrived in Chicago late afternoon as weary as if I had carried the plane. I'd briefly thought about flying Business with a little help from *Lloyds*, but that would have meant acknowledging the existence of my father's account and, so far, I had been reluctant to give it life. The money itself meant little more to me than it apparently had to him, though there was scarce comfort in this uncommon convergence of opinion. I still hadn't mentioned the money to Jane either; wary of how she might respond. The mood I was in, nothing she could have said would have pleased me, and I didn't need another reason to be any more pissed off with her than I already was. Our relationship couldn't afford the distraction, even if the *Lloyds* account could.

Quintex had booked me into a hotel by the lake. I threw my suitcase into the room, drained my bladder and cut my face with a razor blade. The half of me still stranded in England wanted to fall asleep to the sound of CNN, while the half of me stateside wanted to get lost in the sprawl. In the end, it was this more childish of yearnings that took me out into the cold Chicago night.

Along the waterfront Lake Michigan lapped a thin lip of beach like an oil slick. The shoreline was deserted, the only movement a distant flicker of car headlights between trees in a lonely echo of London. A harsh wind moved across the sluggish surface of the water, trying to bully me into submission. But all it did was numb my face and bring tears to my eyes and leave me feeling a stranger to the world, as if I had come to rest here momentarily like a solitary snow flake – an ephemeron – a sensation more disconcerting than it was liberating. Freedom or belonging, independence or comfort: one of the more clichéd of crises.

The cold eventually found its way through the meagre defences of my overcoat, and despite pocketing my hands and pulling the waist closer around me, I still couldn't make a tight enough seal. I turned, shivering quietly, and gazed up at a city now decapitated by low cloud. From nowhere, a bicycle streamed past me in a sudden rush of air that left me far more startled than I should have been, my pulse and my pace unnecessarily quickened. I can't tell you precisely what thoughts continued to submerge themselves in my consciousness, only that I was thinking like a drunk – mistrustful and confused – and all I could think of to lose the feeling was to drink.

For someone who hadn't, as a rule, made a habit of drinking to excess with any real frequency, the there was still some purpose to the process, particularly its capacity for the temporary misplacement of oneself. Reference: my fumbling on Erin's doorstep. It still had its uses. And I believe it's only when this benefit is lost that it starts to become a real problem – an insight I graciously imparted to 'Kyle' as he slouched behind one of the dimmer bars along Chicago Avenue.

Kyle turned out to be as unlikely a barman as I was a drunk. An economics student with torn jeans and dreadlocks thick enough to keep the Titanic at berth, he looked as though he should have been trying to wrest tracts of precious woodland from the clutches of unscrupulous developers, or waving a placard at an anti-Vietnam demonstration, rather than serving a middle-aged Brit in a dive like that.

We were both amateurs and we both knew it. I had a stab at my self-pity and he at his downbeat sagacity, but the conversation only exposed the privilege of our upbringing, the comfort of our lives breaking through the thin veneer of melancholia we had tried to shroud ourselves in to remind us of our fundamental good fortune. Our arguments were too well informed, too cogent and, at least to begin with, too sober, which made for a wholly unsatisfying experience. I wasn't at all surprised when he left me for better fare, – a thin, mean looking man in a baseball cap and raincoat at the wrong end of the bar. Just what the young man needed, a professional, a seasoned hand to show him the ropes, to teach him about real misery and not the diluted variety I was trying to peddle. From the corner of my eye I watched their hunched shoulders and collusive nods, but could only catch an occasional word. Of course, an occasional word may have been all they were saying. The way it was meant to be.

Back at the hotel bar and a fair way towards oblivion, I became aware of a young woman sitting next to me. Chewing. Soon, whatever it was that had engaged her jaws so successfully began to preoccupy me as well, and I placed my short drink down on my frilly mat to take a closer look. The woman didn't seem to mind the attention and remained hunched over the granite bar. She was dressed like a warped LP, a black leather number that revealed more of her own hide than was decent. For a moment I thought the bar might actually be her place of 'business', but she would have been expensive because, even with the state I was in, I could sense something about her that smelled of too much money.

The woman continued to chew. Normally I would have hated the sight of a woman chewing almost as much as I would a man. For women it conveys a lack of style, for men an air of thuggery, but there was something oddly alluring about the way she managed to carry it off – jaws like hips, a certain seduction in their movement.

Despite her obvious state of intoxication, she possessed a curious poise, a dynamic equilibrium in which each part of her was toppling in equal and opposite directions. It suggested breeding, which only entranced me further. And I watched slightly open mouthed as she took a slow draw on her cigarette then let her hand fall down to a cocktail the colour of chemotherapy, sensing a stirring in me that I could only vaguely place somewhere between solar plexus and groin.

I said, 'Hello,' and gave the woman an angled smile.

'Hi.' she replied flatly, gawping at the optics, the half-expired cigarette dangling limply from her fingers like she'd learnt how to hold it from the movies.

Her voice was well mannered and sounded local. I asked her if she was at the hotel on business and she said she was a Stock Market Analyst, and for a sip I actually believed her. She mumbled something unconvincing about 'Futures', but my attention was consumed by her high cheekbones and the perfect arc of her nose curving up towards its tip before sloping seamlessly downward to that small cup of flesh where perspiration can gather. Her lips were unashamedly full and rich in colour, her soft skin soaked in an expensive mid-winter tan.

Perhaps aware of the direction my attention was going, she began to probe me for information about my line of work, and I told her I was a Doctor and let the ambiguity hang (I knew enough to carry it off with most people).

For a while we returned to the faint tinkle of muzak and the muted collisions of ice and glass. During the lull I attracted a well-cut youth who placed fresh mats onto the bar and waited silently for our order. Our drinks arrived without the passing of time, and with a fresh dose the woman seemed to revive. She sat more upright on her stool, wrestled the folds of her dress down to a more modest level of thigh, and bent forward to take a sip from the liquid rainbow in front of her by leaving the glass on the bar and bringing her lips down to it. With her head still curled over the surface of cocktail she turned to look at me.

'What sort of Doctor are you, anyway?'

'I'm in medical research.'

'Oh, a PhD.'

'Yes,' I confessed, adding: 'I work on the brain,' as if the mention of that most mighty of organs might help recapture some of my lost ground.

'Spooky!' she giggled girlishly and waved her hands in the air like an amateur ghost. 'I dated a lab technician once.'

'We have those in England too.'

'England! God, I knew it!' She slapped her hand on her thigh like calamity Jane. 'Are you from London?'

'I am, as it happens.'

'Cool!' she giggled.

Her eyes alighted her drink and on to my hand. 'Married?'

'No. You?'

She made a face.

'So, what do you do?' I said.

'I already told you that!' she screamed and leant over to smack my arm.

'I know, but what do you really do?'

She grinned furtively.

'Honestly, I'd like to know. Somehow you don't look the Wall Street type.'

'So just what type of a girl do you think I am, exactly?'

I narrowed my eyes. 'I think you're a character from a Film Noir.'

'Or a Chandler novel?' She seemed pleased by the allusion.

'You're smarter than you look,' I said.

'And you're dumber than you sound!' Her head fell back and another laugh unhinged her jaw.

Slipping her moorings on the stool, she placed gum into an ashtray and stood over me, head cocked, hand on hip, and her body twisted like a question mark. I had to suppose she was either very tall, or standing on very high heels, in which case she was good at hiding it because she remained quite still. I glanced down at the kidney imprint she had left on the soft leather of the barstool. It must have been warm to the touch.

'Come on,' she said, 'I have a room.'

A long elevator ride to the forty-first floor and I was standing by an open door, aggrieved to consider the extent to which this woman (I did not yet know her name) had already managed to usurp my manhood. Not just because I was being taken back to her room rather than to my own, but because her room was far superior to mine. It most definitely fell into the 'suite' category.

'Shit,' I observed as the door swung open.

She left me almost as soon as we crossed the threshold. I moved aimlessly about low-slung furniture, aware of ice falling in another room I had yet to discover. The suite was partitioned by a long leather sofa, beyond which was an accommodating surface I hoped was a bed. I staggered over and slumped down on to the edge of it. I took a deep breath and felt dizzy for a second. The woman reappeared with glasses and suddenly everything went quiet bar a distant ringing in my ears like a recent rock concert. Usually I found women by accident, but this pick-up business was a new experience, and I felt pissed-off that I was too pissed to take it all in. Of course being pissed was the only reason I had made it that far.

She found a spot next to me on the bed and we both sipped at our drinks. Some clear variety of alcohol, that was the limit of my perception.

'Kim,' she said softly, holding out her hand.

'Daniel.'

There seemed barely the resource between us for speech, and we drank in silence, growing distant from the world, heading back to our cocoons. After a while I lay back on the bed and watched the lights turn above me like a constellation of stars. A breath of thick air set my mind afloat like an anaesthetic, threatening to carry me off into those synthetic heavens, and with the sweet, narcotic scent of her soothing me all the while.

In the small hours I woke to a drumming in my head and a hush of traffic just audible beyond the hotel double-glazing. I rolled over and found her again. The softness of her skin made the covering of my hand seem coarse and brutish by comparison, no matter how gently I tried to apply it. I cast my fingertips down onto her leg as far as they would go, but still failed to reach the end of her thigh. Edging upwards, I moved out across her stomach and found a small mound of flesh beneath her navel like warm dough that I cupped in my palm. She turned and came to rest on her back, her legs parting imperceptibly. My hand set to work again, experiencing the fine sensation the softest of her hairs had to offer.

A paroxysm – a neurosis – gripped me, reminding me of the last time with Jane and how much of a debacle that had been. The blood drained from me, and I fell away from her, cursing under my breath. But she said nothing. She just laid there in the darkness, waiting for me to begin again, and somehow knowing that I would.

Taking hold of her small but perfectly rounded breast, I teased its proud nipple between my finger and thumb. I bent forward with my tongue, and she began to moan just like a woman is supposed to. I sucked harder on her, my erection reforming, and my mind filling with an image of her, and with the images of a thousand women like her.

The sex was short, ending as it had begun with me on top trying to ignore the exaggeration of my headache. I came with a loud, dull moan of pleasure I could do little to suppress. Later, my muscles still warm with exertion, I opened my eyes to find her smiling at me. Only it wasn't the kind of smile that one easily returned.

Next morning the world had turned yellow. A blinding sun filled the room. Light sprang from the mock antique furniture, the scattered garments, and the empty glassware, the whole place a still life of infidelity. In one obvious sense, at least, I had prevailed (I tried to remember the last time I'd managed it with Jane and couldn't), but even this small victory was curiously tainted by a lurking sense of betrayal. I knew that Jane and I had been clinging to our particular piece of the wreckage for long enough, but the guilt still came as a surprise. I almost wanted to phone her and tell her the good news: Guess what? I've just fucked someone else and I feel guilty about it, isn't that fantastic? Guilt was not an entirely shameful sentiment it struck me, but something to be grateful for. Guilt at least implied the existence of a moral code, even if it was buried deep in my subconscious like a forgotten time capsule.

I pulled the bedclothes tight up around my chin as if someone had already walked in and caught us at it. My body rolled towards Kim and my stomach followed shortly afterwards yielding a grumbled belch. The small ball of cotton and skin lying next to me seemed hardly to be alive, just the rising and settling of her gently cambered shoulders, and the dark waves of her hair flowing out across the pillow like spilt ink. I watched her for a while before deciding to heave myself to the bathroom to empty a few hollow organs. I drew back the sheet and swung my legs over the edge of the bed. A glass on the table beside me toppled over, leaking its contents onto my feet in a tiny, clear waterfall. Untroubled, I looked up from the darkening carpet and toured the quasi-expensive furnishings, thinking it was possible yet that money might be demanded of me by this slumbering damsel. My wallet lay half-open on the table and I was bored enough to be mildly suspicious. I fumbled with endless credit cards and receipts but couldn't easily find my way around its myriad compartments. Either the cash I'd been hoping to count really was missing or it had been temporarily hidden from me by the rusted, groggy cogs of my overhanging mind. I only realised my true error when I came across the photograph on Kimberley Twain's High School library card.

...

'How old are you, exactly?'

'How old do you want me to be, asshole?'

Sobriety had soon rid us of all grace. I pinched clothing from about the room, struggling to recall having taken any of it off, and listening like a Harlem pimp for the Vice Squad in the hallway. Though silhouetted against the sunlit curtains, I could see that Kim was young. I already had an idea about how old she was from the date of birth on her ID card, but I couldn't bring myself to believe it. Mathematics wasn't my strong point, of course, a shortcoming repeatedly proven to me by my father. I might have gone over a problem with him a dozen times and yet with precise and unimpeachable logic I could produce the same perfectly incorrect answer every time. And all I could hope for now was that I was still as confused in matters numeric.

I recalculated, only this time counting back the years. 'Seventeen!' I answered myself aloud, glaring at a shirt cuff that stubbornly refused to be buttoned.

Ignoring my outburst, Kim continued to dress, almost luxuriously it seemed, enjoying the sport, the humiliation, a half-hidden smile beneath her scowl that made me wonder if I was part of some form of revenge she was trying to exact? For the parents that ignored her, perhaps, or for the men who had already handled her at such a tender age, whose eyes had been allowed to drip across those precious curves?

'I assume you have the same laws as the rest of the planet with regard to underage sex?' I growled.

'With regard to underage sex…' she mimicked in a fair crack at an English accent. 'Stop worrying, for Chrissakes. I come here all the time.' She put a hand to her mouth and laughter spewed between her fingers. 'Chill out! Nobody's going to say a word. I tip too heavily.'

'I'm afraid it is somewhat less than reassuring to be told to 'chill out' by a bloody Prom Queen!'

Her eyes caught me in the dressing table mirror. 'Oh, I'm still too young to be a Prom Queen!' she laughed.

'You're certainly too young to be fucking middle-aged men in hotel rooms!'

'You didn't seem choosy last night?'

'I was drunk.'

'So?'

She sounded more childish with each utterance, regressing in front of me, deepening the horror. I watched with reluctant admiration as she pulled a brush through her long and sumptuously conditioned hair, although I was still less transfixed by her beauty than she was.

I sat on the edge of the bed to pull my trousers on. 'I didn't know you were this young,' I was muttering. 'All that crap about the stock market. Is that where Daddy gets his money? I assume he's the one paying for all this?'

'Daddy's long-gone I'm afraid, but he did leave me a nice trust fund to play with.'

The absurd parallels with the *Lloyds* account might have been funny if I hadn't felt so disgusted with myself. 'Well, you'd need it for all that make up and hair, you stupid little girl!'

'For your information, I hardly wear any make up. You older guys seem to like it better. And for another thing...' She lifted a clump of hair and let it fall back onto her shoulder. 'This is no fucking dye-job.'

She was right, of course. She required no enhancement. Her lascivious style and smooth architecture had been enough to entice me the night before, but all it did now was provoke a slow-grinding nausea that made me want to run to the bathroom again.

'You tricked me,' I said quietly.

She picked up a pillow and thumped it down onto the bed. 'You fooled yourself. Why is it you guys only get worried after you've screwed me?'

'Spare me the analysis, please!'

She lifted her coat from the chair, clutched her clutch bag, and strode past me at full pelt. My instinct was to go after her, despite the absence of any good reason to do so, and I did shuffle vaguely in her direction for a yard or two before my un-zipped trousers fell to my ankles and slowed me to a laughable pace.

I reached the open door a few seconds behind her and shouted: 'You forgot your money!' in the hope I might transfer even a small fraction of the guilt that had, by now, engulfed me. But there wasn't even an echo in response, and I was left teetering on the threshold to the room, the empty hallway suddenly a deep well into which I might fall and drown.

CHAPTER ELEVEN

In a cramped diner across the street from the hotel I struggled to find my reflection in a decidedly matt cup of coffee. Around me, a weary clientele occupied cracked vinyl booths in ones and twos, eating silently from tables strewn with sugar as if they had been gritted for snow. My room rate at the Hotel included breakfast but I'd been unable to face the staff for fear they had seen me going into Kim's room the night before. Neither had I stopped to wash and I could still smell her on my lips and my hands. Without daring to look up, I summoned a waitress and asked for directions to the restroom where I washed with a rigour Pilate would have been proud of.

Back in the booth, my coffee had grown cold, staring back at me as black as a baby's eye. The waitress was taking an order at the next table. A network of veins ran like river deltas across the backs of her legs, and I began to think that, from behind, she looked a little like Jane, which only made me wince again at the thought of my hollow victory the previous night. My hangover was starting to make its presence felt, too, as if to remind me of my excuses. Had I been too drunk to notice, or just too drunk to care?

My heart thudded in my temples and my mouth was painfully dry, further drained of moisture by endless refills brought to me by the waitress with the marbled legs, and which I drank partly to extract a decent dose of caffeine and partly to please her, the kind-treatment of whom I hoped might have some redemptive quality. There was certainly no comfort in my blaming "Kim", even though she'd known damn well what she'd been about. I wished there had been an exchange of money, which might have helped to ease my shame a little. It would have branded her an opportunist and me a… a 'mark', wasn't that the word for it? But a far more complex transaction had taken place, and one not so easily decoded in the dazzling wall of light that poured through the Diner window that morning.

I pushed my untouched plate into the middle of the table and threw down a shamefully large tip. As I walked towards the door, the waitress gave me an innocent smile that managed to reach inside and scoop out what little remained of my innards.

I tried finding a pharmacy I'd seen somewhere near the hotel, to relieve the various pains I was experiencing. But I must have ended up passing it by, because, soon, I was wandering aimlessly, that desire to be lost again sending me to the places people lived rather than to the places they made their living. The buildings in those streets were low rise and awkward, echoing with the strained sounds of an inner city: a child crying, a television channel in another language, a lone motorcyclist bringing fear into the homes of the hard working. At intervals, shabby tenements gave way to strip malls, more liquor stores than I cared to know existed, small bars that looked seedier than sex shops, and sex shops that looked more like barbershops used to look with coloured ribbons fluttering in the doorway. I passed street after street of similarly grim outlets before I abandoned the sidewalk and followed a glowing neon arrow down steep stairs into a basement.

At first there seemed to be very little inside the shop I had entered, save a few magazines arrayed forlornly along blank wooden shelves like lost gloves on a railing post. Their covers bore open orifices and varnished nails about big pricks and dildos, and they were numbered – some into the eighties – their publishers clearly having run out of the usual profane permutations. Beyond them, the shop branched out into further neon-lit recesses, chambers identified only by cardboard signs that announced 'S&M' or 'Lesbian', the walls covered with a wood laminate that looked ripe and ready to peel.

The place was as quiet as a monastery. My first thought was that it might benefit from a serious re-branding: a cappuccino machine, some steel furniture, a few Yuccas. No wonder the men of the world had turned, with relief, to the Internet for their titillation. And yet, despite its crude anachronism, I felt a confused excitement. My guilt seemed to have abandoned me as quickly as it had come, my conscience perhaps deciding that I had fallen as far as I could fall, that there was nothing more to lose, and I began to burn again at the thought of Kim's perfect skin and my re-discovered potency unbound.

It was some time before I noticed a tall, wide man with a fluorescent crop of blonde hair standing behind a wooden counter in one corner of the shop. In other circumstances, my middle class prejudices might have sent me fleeing for my life at the sight of him, but I was oddly reassured by the ceramic smile he flashed me. I could almost believe he was there to protect me from something (though likely not from whatever compulsion had brought me there in the first place). With my lingering hangover enough to deter me from more alcohol and my room at the hotel waiting scornfully for me, it actually felt better to be out there amongst the pornographers and perverts.

A shadow hovered next to me. 'Looking for anything in particular?'

He had read the script. I was as nervous as if it were my first time in such a place, even though I could remember the first time cycling with Keith Jarvis to a sex shop in Canterbury he'd been told about by a sixth former; an outlet so discrete it took us three hours to find. Having extracted the nerve to go inside from a litre of cheap cider, we managed to pass ourselves off as something approaching eighteen for no more than ninety seconds before being told to 'fuck off out of it' in a voice that didn't appear to have it's origins in Kent.

Keen to avoid offence, I allowed my eyes to drift in the direction of the…salesman I suppose I should call him. He wore a tight, silk T-shirt in dark grey that bore no detail beyond the outline of his pecs. He was a man who worked out. Disturbingly well groomed, too, his gelled hair and polished fingernails glinted beneath the buzzing neon strips. I could have talked to him at length about his repressed homosexuality, but demurred.

'Not really,' I replied, calmly, hoping he would grow bored and leave me alone.

He only looked at me with heightened interest. He seemed to be waiting for the right moment to make me an offer, though judging by the graphic and varied literature in front of me I couldn't imagine he was keeping anything from me in the way of porn.

A noise at the shop entrance turned our heads. His impending sales-pitch delayed, my host moved at some speed to greet the new arrival, possibly because in his line of business two customers at once was more likely a prelude to a robbery than a sales bonanza.

My respite was short-lived. The new man was a regular. A vigorous shaking of hands, an exchange of plain packaging, and he was back out through the doorway, the coloured streamers lifting gently in his wake.

'These are good,' said the salesman, back at my side and pointing to a particularly graphic copy of Cumfest 15.

I thanked him (God knows why) then made a point of picking up an entirely different magazine – any magazine – which I studied like an ancient manuscript.

I continued to be the undivided focus of his attention. I browsed blindly while he pulled long, slow breaths into the imposing muscle of his chest.

'Magazines are OK,' he said, 'but there's nothing quite like the real thing, right?' He folded his arms. 'You know what I'm saying?'

I knew what he was saying, but I wasn't at all sure why it was he was saying it to me.

'Sure,' I said sheepishly, back in Canterbury again with Keith.

He dipped his head slightly as if he was trying to get a better view of me over spectacles. 'You want to see something?'

Before I could answer I was being led by an arm on my shoulder towards the back of the shop through a series of interconnecting rooms cluttered with more magazines and videos in vast sky-scraping towers. We crossed a doorway into a narrow passage where the sides – a once-whitewashed brick – were now heavily layered with grime. Light bulbs dangled by their flex at irregular intervals throwing us into alternating light and shadow and I had to concentrate hard to avoid slamming into the walls as we moved at speed, my fear and my excitement mounting in equal measure.

Rounding a corner, I ducked beneath pipes edged with frozen drips of an unknown chemical. The passageway began to narrow, giving the illusion of even greater speed, and threatening to wedge the man in by his not inconsiderable shoulders. Then, at the last minute, he twisted sideways and pushed on into a wider stretch beyond. I hadn't noticed when, but at some point we had moved outside, and now the air was icy and laden with brittle, distant noises. Above us, tower blocks loomed like observers at an operation.

An unmarked door resolved dead ahead. The passageway continued on to the right but we came to a halt in the semi-darkness.

'What are we doing here?' I asked.

He knocked and waited. Only silence came in reply, but apparently this was sanction enough because now he was turning a key in the lock, pressing a hand to the door, and pulling me through it with him. Why, at that moment, I didn't turn and run for my life is a mystery that haunts me to this day. They are wrong about fear, if that's what it was. It doesn't paralyse, it compels.

What I saw inside was unexpected: a room – an almost perfect square painted camouflage-green – with a standard-lamp on a bronzed base and stem in one corner illuming a single bed along the far wall. Over the window a thin excuse for a curtain pulsed gently in a draft.

Then I saw the girl. A part of me must have noticed her the moment I entered the room, but for some reason my mind had refused to acknowledge her presence until now. I sobered instantly. There was no mistaking this waif for a woman. Everything was too big for her: the room, the bed, the lamp. Even her makeup had run out of space and ran over the edges of her lips and eyes like derailed trains. With her short bob of jet-black hair and her ice-white skin she had an almost oriental look, a spectral beauty.

The man gave me a broad smile that seemed to assume satisfaction. 'Welcome,' he said.

I began to notice how warm the room was. Sweat pricked my skin. 'Why have you brought me here?' I asked him.

'Don't worry. She's clean. And I won't be charging you top dollar either.'

'But why?' I asked again.

My man looked a little puzzled. He smiled. 'You mean why her or why you?'

'Either of us, for fuck's sake, you know what I mean!'

'Come on! I saw you looking at those magazines. I've been in this business long enough to know.'

The girl was smiling at me. Maybe she'd decided a smile was what I wanted. For her to be a 'happy' girl. She could barely have been thirteen years old. Or less. Or more (I couldn't think about less). Chubby, pale arms poked out from beneath a plain silk nightshirt. She was without blemish.

'First time?' he whispered up close.

'You've made a mistake.'

'Now listen,' he said, a sudden edge to his voice he was trying hard to polish. 'Why don't you go on over and sit by Debbie?' He looked at the girl. 'Debbie, take the nice man's hand and let him sit next to you, that's a good girl.'

A hand pressed down onto my shoulder and now I was sitting next to her. It must have seemed easier not to resist.

'Hold the nice man's hand, Debbie.' He looked at me. 'What's your name?'

I couldn't speak. The man pointed to his chest and said: 'my name's Jason. Now, what's you name, Mr Nice Man?' His eyebrows arched expectantly.

'Daniel,' I said, surprised to hear myself answer. Who was I trying to please?

'OK, Daniel, now you take Debbie's hand.'

A smooth ball of flesh came to rest in my palm.

'Good. Now, I'm going to leave you to get to know each other. I'll be next door if you need me.'

Jason flicked his head at me. I put down the girl's hand (it troubles me now to think of her name) and stepped back across the room.

'Three hundred,' he whispered.

'What?'

'Three hundred. Three hundred bucks.'

'I don't think I have…'

'You touch, you pay. Whether you play on or not is up to you. I want three hundred.'

He rose to full height, as if I needed further convincing of his physical superiority.

'I didn't ask you to bring me here,' I said.

'But you're glad you came, right?' He threw a look towards the girl. 'You didn't exactly put up a fight.'

'Jesus Christ! I thought perhaps more magazines. I don't know what I thought. I want you to let me go, please.'

'Listen, you're gonna have a fine time, so be a good boy and give me my money.'

'I don't have it.'

He grabbed my jacket and reached into the inside pocket. 'Don't fuck with me! I can get the money one way or another.'

He definitely had all the lines. Someone should have said 'cut' right there and put us both out of our misery. I took hold of his wrist and tried to pull his hand away but, unsurprisingly, failed. His time in the gym had been well spent.

We paused for a second – arms and eyes locked – before he pushed me back against the wall.

'OK!' I shouted. 'I have money, just not on me. Not that much anyway.'

'How much have you got?' he said, whispering again as if he didn't want the girl to hear how much she was worth.

He let go of my wrist and we moved apart. I felt for the bulge in my back pocket and produced my wallet. I showed the man a hundred and twenty dollars.

His stale breath swept across my face. 'That isn't enough.'

'It's all I've got. What am I supposed to do? I didn't want to be here in the first place.'

'Why don't you just figure out what the fuck you want and stop wasting everybody's time, you fucking pussy?'

He snatched the bills, twisted my arm behind my back, and frog-marched me out through the doorway. I glanced back at the girl, but she wasn't paying us any attention, preoccupied instead with a magazine, and chewing gum in a frighteningly reminiscent manner.

The air in the passageway was thin and crystalline, emphasising the oppressive snugness of the room we had just left behind. We moved slowly, Jason pushing me from the rear while I struggled to find an evenness to my step. I wondered if he was the type of man that bothered to shoot people like me? We reached another door hidden in the brickwork. Either I hadn't noticed it first time round, or we were in a different part of that iniquitous maze. Jason fumbled with his free hand and I heard a padlock fall. The door opened. But before I could make out what lay beyond, I felt a heave in my back and I was launched into the void, landing hard on the ground with rubble and concrete tearing at my skin. I lay still, face down, trying to find my focus. Then my side became a dull penetrating ache as moccasin collided with spleen. I creased in agony, my breathing stifled and shallow, and the warm taste of iron in my mouth.

Jason's shadow reared over me again. Another kick landed. I couldn't tell where, only that it brought a fresh surge in the intensity of the pain. I curled tighter into a ball, listening for any trace of movement above me. But now there was nothing, and I wondered if he was waiting for me to expose myself again before carrying on?

Not daring to move, I lay coiled on the bare ground – I'm not sure for how long – until eventually, slowly, I had the courage to put a hand to my mouth and found the blood where I had bitten through my tongue. I rolled over on to my back and stared up at the city-glow. I managed to lift my head just enough to see that I was now alone amongst the discarded trash cans and spiralling fire escapes of an alleyway. A quick survey suggested most of me was present and, essentially, intact, though I did wonder about a broken rib or two. And that was when I started to cry, each sob the blade of a knife slicing into my chest.

I may have lost consciousness. The alleyway that dissolved slowly back into view was dark and desolate, and I quickly realised I might be in more danger out there than I had been in the passageway with the pimp. I lifted uncomfortably to my feet, the movement bringing a new dimension to my pain that caused me to freeze, half-risen from the ground.

A flash of light at the end of the alleyway – more than one light and of more than one colour – casting a swirl of shadow against the surrounding walls. The whoop of a siren, and within seconds, a wide-chested policeman crouching by a squad car threatening me with a gun. In the passenger seat, another cop had a radio to his mouth. The one by the car told me not to move. I wanted to run, and might have tried if I'd had even a fraction of the strength required. Instead, I stumbled a little and tried pulling myself upright again. My lack of coordination seemed to reassure the man and his revolver slipped down a notch. The thinner cop sloped from the car, similarly grim and armed, and now they both edged cautiously in my direction as if it was a wild animal they had trapped in the alleyway and not an English academic.

It was the thin cop that frisked me. The other waited with his gun aloft and a spare hand ready to catch me in case I fell. I still had my wallet (now cashless, of course), which the skinny cop inspected with a flashlight.

'Bridish?' he grunted.

I nodded and saw the lines on their faces smoothen. Britons were obviously too polite to be criminals. They must also have seen that I was hurt.

At the police station, I was forced to go through all the motions the string of lies I'd told them demanded. A long wait in a holding cell, a weary filling out of forms, and then me staring blankly at a computer screen as a parade of Chicago's criminal denizens flickered by, searching for my non-existent mugger. It's difficult to say the man's face didn't pass me at some point, but even if I hadn't been too dazed to be certain of my own name anymore, shame would still have kept me silent. I couldn't help thinking that 'Jason' (if that was his real name) might only have been preying upon instincts I had revealed to him. The eyes the policemen gave me said it too: that there was no such thing as an innocent victim.

...

A squad car returned me to the hotel sometime after one am. The Night Porter ushered me into the glittering, vacant lobby where I stood shell-shocked by the brightness and clarity of it all. Hotels have a nightmarish quality at that hour, their empty corridors and hushed elevators sumptuous but sterile like a last meal on death row.

Morning arrived in the middle of the night, a first stirring at four, and then a robotic call from the front desk at six that left me flat on my back, scouring the rippled ceiling for answers that refused to come. There were certain physical preoccupations too, with the pains in my head, mouth and chest melding into a single dirge, and a dense tiredness like concrete setting behind my eyes. With no obvious source of relief beyond a bottle of codeine tablets I had found at the bottom of my toilet bag, there was little else I could do except lie there motionless and mute, trying my best to wish the previous day's events away as just a series of unfortunate misunderstandings and not anything more sinister.

The front desk rang again at seven thirty. It was the only reason for me to be in Chicago, but I had no stomach (literally, it felt) for a meeting with *Quintex*. Nevertheless, (and with the ongoing aide of the painkillers) I prepared for my performance to come by pressing and preening to a ludicrous degree in the poky hotel ensuite.

A car had been provided for me, a black ogre of an automobile that sat grumbling and gleaming outside the hotel as I broke cover into daylight. The chauffeur tipped his hat and held the door open as I tumbled onto glistening leather. We crawled through the Downtown traffic, the ice-light of winter struggling to find us between the ominous buildings. Along Michigan Avenue I spotted a payphone and ordered the driver to pull over. I called 911 and anonymously revealed the location of the girl as best I could remember, doing my utmost to assure an indifferent-sounding policewoman of the terrible danger 'Debbie', and possibly others like her, was in. I cut the conversation short on the rather absurd notion that I might risk giving them enough time to 'trace the call'. This belated act of half-decency at least allowed me to pass the rest of the journey in a welcome daze, dappled by sunlight and soothed by the soft growl of my motorised coffin, so that by the time we reached the mirrored matrix of the *Quintex* building I could begin to suppress the foreboding that had so troubled me in the early hours.

At the front entrance, more doffing of caps and opening of doors ensued as I patted my overcoat for a tip the driver and I both knew was stillborn in my pocket. The meeting room on the eleventh floor was plush. Carpet piled higher than Aylesham corn and a PA that made the ones at the institute look like gargoyles. *Quintex* were not the largest of biotechs, but they were rich. They focused. They avoided over-diversification. They knew their limitations and they knew their market. They weren't trying to cure cancer. Psychotropics were their forte. If leisure was to be the boom business of the twenty-first century then madness would be its disease. If you believed the statistics, the whole planet was ill in the head. And every nut would surely need its cracker.

Though my work was of a more behavioural nature, SNF was a key target for *Quintex* Inc. One man's aggression is another man's psychopathy, and with the venture capitalists snapping at their heels, *Quintex* needed the results of the SNF knockouts almost as much as I did. They had compounds ready to go into man if the data looked strong enough, and for that reason alone it was to be a disappointing morning.

Frank Powell was their CEO, greying and proud of it, and important enough to come to work without a jacket and tie. Ties were what the drug-reps wore.

'Daniel, you know Ulrich?' he said, indicating Professor Ulrich Braun, a German with a mind even sharper than his dress sense, and the person who had originally introduced me to the *Quintex* crowd. Silver-haired and tanned in a blue-checked jacket and trousers he looked more international playboy than scientist. Despite being an elderly statesman of the behavioural sciences he was still an opinion leader the biotechs respected. He was a friend, too, but he would be looking to impress Powell and I knew I'd have to tread cautiously.

Struggling to respond to Powell's introduction, I realised my tongue had been gradually swelling since I'd bitten through it and sent off searing pains at the slightest of movements. I decided to nod, instead, with pronounced enthusiasm.

Post-handshake Powell had us straight down to business at a long table lined with men in matching haircuts, adding: 'I think everyone else here knows you, Daniel.' And apparently they all did, even though I could not distinguish any one of them from another.

They introduced themselves, smiling and nodding in series like a Busby Berkeley routine. At the finale, Powell resumed his seat and signalled for me to begin. I went straight for a bottle of Evian on the table, which might have appeared a pathetic attempt to create dramatic tension but was actually a desperate attempt to unglue my tongue. Despite the relief it brought, together with the mounting effects of the codeine, it was still very much an anaesthetised slur with which I opened my presentation.

The data, I confessed immediately, was going to be preliminary. The mouse work was at an early stage, but it looked promising and would likely be ready for their consideration within the next couple of months. We had had trouble with the import licenses for the knockouts, I told them, and then there were the viral infections in the animal house and the poor quality probes...they seemed to swallow it readily enough.

I had too many introductory slides, but distracting them from the rather obvious paucity of data to follow was the priority, which meant the first half of my talk was effectively spent telling them things about SNF they almost certainly knew already. Irritated glances started to pass amongst the clones, but just as Powell looked ready to cut me short, I skipped a few slides and would have braved the first northern blot if a glass door hadn't swung open at the far end of the room to interrupt my flow.

The *Quintex* CEO gave one of his famous power-smiles. 'Brian! Hi! Good you could make it at such short notice.'

Technically, Brian was funded on *Quintex* money, but I'd been careful to keep any direct contact between him and them to a minimum.

Powell turned earnestly towards me. 'Daniel, I hope you don't mind but I thought that with all the hard work Brian's put in on the project he at least deserved to get in on a trip. Might give you bit of support against all us hard-nosed Industry types.'

The men of *Quintex* chuckled synchronously. Brian was smiling like an arsehole.

'Hello Brian,' I said flatly. 'I was just getting to the data.' I looked at Powell. 'Although, strictly speaking, this isn't Brian's data.'

Powell's face tightened. 'No?'

'Some, but I've recently re-run the basic wild-type experiment with a new PhD student of mine, and we're well on the way to sorting out some of the earlier problems.'

'Re-run?'

'We're just being thorough, Frank. And just as well as it turns out. You'll have to meet Erin; she's quite a star.'

I smiled at Brian. My antipathy towards him was proving to be something of a motivator, and in the next thirty minutes or so that followed I imagine he wished he'd stayed at home. He couldn't say anything in front of Frank – they were paying his wages – so he had to sit there quietly as I proceeded to contradict his last 6 months output. The experience might have brought out some of the Swede in him, the diplomat, but that wasn't the way it turned out.

'What the hell was that?'

It was later, outside the conference room. Brian's face was burning.

'Calm down, Brian. Remember where you are.'

He was trying not to shout. A vein like a sewage pipe throbbed on his neck. 'We need to talk about this.'

'We can talk later. And then you can explain why you didn't tell me you were going to be here today.'

Powell approached sipping a mineral water. I quickly drew him towards a rubber plant.

'Frank, a quick word.'

'Looked good in there.'

'Thanks, but I think Brian's nose is a little out of joint with me not showing his data.'

Powell shrugged. 'He's got his pride, I'm sure, but that's a good sign. He cares about what he's doing. But he knows that, in the end, it's a team effort.'

'I think a word from you would help…' I glanced towards Brian. 'To help him see the bigger picture. It might settle him down.'

'Sure, I understand. By the way, what happened to your mouth?'

'I bit my tongue.'

Probably because he thought I was being ironic, Powell didn't seem able to respond and set off on a glide path towards Brian instead. I drank cold coffee as the two of them talked – Powell with a fatherly hand resting on Brian's shoulder – and waited for a sign, a smile from Brian perhaps, no matter how contrived, to suggest he had been persuaded to swallow his integrity. I was relieved when they came out of their huddle all handshakes and backslaps.

Brian and I took separate cars to the ludicrously early dinner Powell had arranged for us to wrap up the day's discussions. The restaurant was an allusion to some indistinct European culture that excelled in gaudy art, ornate furnishings and a vulgar smattering of gold leaf in the most unusual of places like toilet handles and coat hooks. Waiters in waistcoats were thin and dark and full of grins.

Everything went smoothly enough to begin with. Brian and I had been set a cautious distance from each other and kept busy listening to the banal treatises of the *Quintex* execs on every aspect of neuroscience from axonal regeneration to tau proteins. But as we progressed through the bland meal, Brian's voice grew louder from the far end of the table and I knew he was drunk as confidently as I knew Frank Powell was sober. Fresh off the plane, the alcohol must have been near neat in his veins, and in true Lindgren style he chose an awkward time to challenge me, stalking me into the restrooms.

'That wasn't my data.' he said, closing the door behind him.

'Of course it wasn't your data. I told them it wasn't.'

We were both pretty tight and in a tight space too. There was just enough room to swing a punch, and Brian's body language suggested he was of a mind to test the dimensions.

'It wasn't Erin's either, he said. 'She showed me the re-runs of the northerns she did for you.'

'There are bigger wheels turning, Brian. I was trying to save us both from looking like idiots. You didn't actually think I would present that crap you showed at the lab meeting? I had to make up something while we figure it all out.'

'I've repeated those experiments over and over again, and so has dream girl Erin...'

'And you've both made a mistake. I'm not saying it was your fault, but whatever it was the sense probes are binding better than the antisense, for God's sake! It was a duff experiment. There's no point breaking unnecessary bad news. When we get the right result it'll be good news for everyone.'

'Not for *Quintex* if you keep telling them porkys.'

'Brian, are you feeling OK? Because at times, today, I thought perhaps I'd been losing my mind, but you've definitely left yours on the plane. Your salary depends on *Quintex* funding too, remember.'

The vein on Brian's neck was fast recruiting tributaries.

'You might want to consider this your last post-doc with us,' I told him. 'Maybe you should get out there and put your tongue back up Powell's arse and hope he gives you that job.'

'What job?' he flared.

'He offers everyone a job, Brian. You don't have to bullshit me, I know how they operate. They're as desperate as you are. You'll be perfect together.'

Brian went suddenly quiet and, for the first time, started to unnerve me. I became wary of the limits the jet lag and the booze might push him to.

Then his voice cooled considerably. 'So, is that the data you showed Baxter?'

'What do you mean?'

'At the Research Assessment Exercise meeting, did you show them the same data you tried to palm these lot off with?'

I sighed. 'Brian, why don't you leave the running of the Department to me. You may already be as good as fired, but I could still knock the shit out of you.'

'Baxter's not the fastest brain on campus, but some of the other department heads must have picked up the problem with the probes.'

'Well *you* didn't until I pointed it out.'

'That's assuming, of course, you showed them the real data.'

I laughed. 'What now, blackmail?'

'Only if there's something to blackmail you with.'

Clearly, Brian was beginning to hold his own out there in the big bad world of science. I even felt a little proud of the contribution I had undoubtedly made to this sudden budding of maturity.

'I don't have to explain myself to you. I think you'd better cool off or you might as well take your P45 now and put us all out of misery.'

'You need a verbal and two writtens.'

'Read your contract. It says: 'as long as funds are available'. And guess what, Brian? We've just run out of money. And I don't suspect you have too many grants of your own under consideration at the moment, am I right?'

Brian was beyond sullen.

'You're pissed, Brian. Go home. I don't have time for it.'

Brian kicked the door, opened it, and walked out. How much the *Quintex* crowd had overheard I could only guess, but once I'd calmed down enough to go back into the restaurant I found the atmosphere had relaxed significantly. Ties and tongues had been loosened. Brian was back in conversation with Powell and the clones had been re-distributed around the table and now there was nowhere safe from them.

I made straight for Ulrich and pulled him up from his chair. 'Are you staying at The Nelson?' I asked hurriedly.

'Yes, awful isn't it?'

...

Through a wall of tinted glass, I reassured myself of Kim's absence from the hotel bar. Not that I really expected to see her back there for the pleasure of my company, but for the sport, perhaps, that was possible.

I ordered brandies. Ulrich didn't waste any time in asking me about the results.

'So, you have conflicting data from the northerns?'

'Unfortunately not.' I replied.

'Brian was saying something different in the restaurant. What happened between you two? He told us you fired him.'

'It'll give him something to think about,' I said, knowing I wouldn't be letting Brian out of my sights that easily.

I took a gamble and told Ulrich the truth about the northerns. I had to hope our friendship was stronger than his ties to *Quintex*. Afterwards, we sipped thoughtfully together, our brandy glasses catching the light; and with the burn came memories of the *Chivas* my father had kept hidden under the kitchen sink. Not that he was, in any sense, the drinker I seemed to be fast becoming. Alcohol in our house was always strictly reserved for births, deaths and marriages, none of which came with any reliable frequency.

'I couldn't show those data without some sort of an explanation,' I concluded.

'You think it's just a technical problem?'

'I had hoped, but we seem to have exhausted all the options.' I paused. 'And there's something else. We've had some bizarre data from the animal model.'

Ulrich settled back into his chair and began a low frequency nod while I told him about the oddly pugnacious mice Erin had shown me.

'Let me be clear,' he said, finally, drumming his hairy fingers on the arms of the chair. 'The mice bred from parents that had already been through the protocol displayed aggressive characteristics from birth?'

I confirmed.

'Interesting,' he said and delayed again. 'The whole thing almost sounds Lamarckian.'

'Lamarck?'

A slow smile from the German. 'It's an old idea, perhaps, but it would seem to fit the data.'

'No offence, but I was hoping for a rather more up-to-date solution.'

'If you are telling me you believe this is a genuine result then you have to face up to it. You know very well, that error, not necessity, is often the mother of invention. Or chance, depending on your point of view.'

'And what about Occam's razor?' I asked him. 'What about the simplest solution being the most likely, which in our case would be some sort of technical glitch?'

'But you have just told me that you have accounted for all possible sources of error, and yet the problem remains.'

'I hate to be agreeing with you…'

'Then you must be prepared to look for alternative explanations – of which the Lamarck hypothesis is one. Crazy, but it's there. I don't know what else to say.' He gave an uproarious laugh. 'Perhaps you could put Brian onto it. He seems immensely interested in the project.'

'I think I'd sooner have my mother work on it.'

In my room that night, beached on the hotel duvet two arms-lengths from the mini-bar, I wrestled with Ulrich's ludicrous suggestion. By the window, a ghostly gauze of curtain swayed to the ebb and flow of the lakeside air, while around me the confused furnishings – trapped somewhere between extravagance and subdual – seemed to mirror my own uncertainty. We were certainly beyond the first flush of romance that room and I. The relieved excitement of our first encounter had long since passed, the promise of fresh occupancy turning quickly to acceptance and then complacency. I had neglected to fold my towels and clear away my clothes, and, in return, the room had revealed the chipped corners of its aging veneers and the bubbling edges of wallpaper that seemed to curl and laugh at me for even considering that our data could be explained by the discredited theory of a two hundred and fifty year old Frenchman.

I knew Ulrich had only been half-serious about the idea, but I was already convinced there was something to it. In science the greatest of pitfalls is when, no longer the pursuit of truth, it becomes the pursuit of happiness. When we seek only the answers we wish to find. When, for a moment, we believe we can exert some control over our small corner of the universe, an undoubted pleasure in such solutions when so little else in life can offer the same. And I can only imagine that it was a similar self-satisfying logic that enabled me to see the potential in Ulrich's idea. Jean Baptiste Pierre Antoine de Monet, Chevalier de Lamarck, a grand name indeed for the man who might yet turn out to be my saviour.

CHAPTER TWELVE

Adam's mother and I were both at thirty-seven thousand feet when she finally took her leave of the World.

Separate planes.

Rashly, Adam's family had decided to fly her to Corsica for one last holiday but she'd thrown off a blood clot into her lung on the return journey and had passed away rather less than peacefully clutching an airline oxygen mask and her husband's startled hand. While I had persuaded *Quintex* to upgrade my ticket for the overnight return to Heathrow and had spent the night in the clutches of the airline champagne, trying to sleep as best one can at an angle of forty-five degrees. This coincidence of altitude meant I was spared the news of her demise for an extra seven hours. I think if I'd known before leaving Chicago, I might have stayed there decaying slowly with the rest of the furniture, whereas, jet-lagged in London, I almost welcomed the notion of death. It was suitably lacking in complexity. It was manageable.

Jane sat on a patio chair swathed in dressing gown, clutching a mug of tea. Around her the garden glistened in a peach dawn. It was the first thing she said to me, 'Adam's mother died,' bleakly, as if it was her own mother who had just passed away. But beyond that it was difficult to extract any additional information from her, bar the fact no time had been lost in arranging a funeral, the only slight delay due to the Coroner's referral required of any death aboard a passenger airline. It hadn't taken long to pronounce the obvious, which was that she had succumbed to a pulmonary embolism, a not uncommon mode of death amongst the chronically sick – especially those who choose to fly.

The news barely absorbed by my sluggish senses, I walked back into the house, reached for a ringing telephone, and was mildly surprised to find Adam's voice at the other end. He started babbling ghoulishly, trying to relay funeral details while I continued to be muddled and slow. I hoped at least a few of my long silences might be interpreted as empathetic, despite it being one of the many sentiments long-haul flights do little to promote.

Adam was quick to express regret over his mother's death (for reasons only he could comprehend), and then he started apologising to me too. He seemed overly preoccupied by how I was feeling about my father's death, as if the recent bereavements we had both suffered might somehow reinvigorate our relationship, allowing us to break through the emotional barriers we had struggled so hard to build up over the years.

A dreamy indifference began to seep over me – a codeine moment – reminding me of times sitting drowsily with my mother in Dentist's waiting rooms and Head Teacher's offices, not yet able to appreciate the enormity of the punishment that was about to descend. I fell back against the woodchip wallpaper then slipped down onto the floor, my mind swimming in a warm red ocean.

Someone kicked me.

I looked up, startled.

'He hung up.'

'What?'

Jane crouched down and picked up the receiver whining next to me. 'Adam?' she said, brandishing it in my face. 'He hung up.'

'Right,' I said.

'Go to bed for goodness sake, you look buggered. Blues bars, I suppose?'

The strength for rebuttal deserted me.

Jane stood over me. 'Erin phoned earlier. She wants to talk to you.'

She waited for an answer then added: 'Sounded cute.'

Ignoring her, I managed to haul myself to my feet. Jane continued to mutter something inaudible at my back but I was already concentrating on trying to make it up the stairs. I grabbed hold of the railing. If I was going to reach the landing it would have to be at the first attempt. Either that or I risked falling where I was and being found days later clutching the banister like a live power cable. The briefest of naps was all I needed, a few precious moments of sleep to gather my thoughts in preparation for labours to follow.

The next morning I woke with a body clock in the Azores and a hangover in gross disproportion to the half bottle of Chianti I had consumed alone the previous evening after another pointless row with Jane. It was only the beginning, but already Nature was trying its best to fool me. The early morning sun played its part faultlessly, bursting through every window in the house in all its effulgent glory. More than enough to cruelly raise my expectations of the day when, in reality, a stinging cold waited for us outside, a cold that frosted glass and cracked lips. The roads sparkled and the cars moved slower than canal barges as Jane and I rolled slowly free of the city, heading for a Dorset burial.

Neither of us could have anticipated so much traffic, nor so much ice. We might have used the time to talk, but I saw nothing in Jane to encourage dialogue, and I gazed at the city scrolling past the window wondering how much longer we could rely upon cool indifference to get us through the days? Perhaps forever, if our respective parents were anything to go by. How eerily familiar it must have been for both of us, the many such trips we had endured as children? At least there were no offspring of our own to inflict these tortures upon. For certain no child could have broken the deadlock.

Our late arrival meant we had to park at the end of a long line of single-filed cars at the bottom of a steep hill, and we were embarrassingly breathless by the time we reached the imposing uprights of the graveyard gates. We were in the arse-end of nowhere as far as I could tell, and yet everything about the church was surprisingly grand in scale – if a little dishevelled. Broken stained-glass windows set in vast grey-stone walls towered over us, surrounded by a cemetery plucked straight from the pages of The Doomsday Book where untamed grasses explored lilting, fissured headstones.

I spotted Adam flitting between two groups of mourners and, even from a distance, detected an unfamiliar, nervous energy about him. It was a worrying sight. I wasn't sure I could handle ebullience from Adam.

He saw us and raised a hand. 'Guys,' he said, trotting over, grinning feverishly in only a shirt and tie, while Jane and I stood shivering in scarves and overcoats like a pair of arctic explorers wondering how he was managing to tolerate the cold. He certainly looked well enough. He had shaved, I noticed, and closely for once, and his hair had recently been cropped too. The greater changes, however, were to his mood, which was wild and excitable. I could only marvel at the transformation. We hadn't really spoken to each other since our last Thursday night out together, and I had to confess our separation seemed only to have done him good.

As neither Jane nor I had met any of Adam's family before he decided, somewhat impulsively, that we should be introduced to every last one of them. And, while he attached himself to Jane, I was led round by a myopic uncle, an irritable war-veteran bent double under the weight of his impressive decorations. I found his relatives to be curiously infused with the same cheeriness as Adam, the gathering more summer fete than winter funeral. I even summoned the nerve to say 'so this must be the Addams Family' to one group of aunts and uncles, but as their laughter quickly died, I knew I had exposed an immense unease, and that I was not the only one playing along with Adam's born-again disposition.

A few minutes later, as I scoured the various tufts of dark tailoring for a sign of Jane, I recognised the lone figure of a man who, by then, I knew to be Adam's father. True to form, his eye caught mine and our conversation opened in a series of half-shouts as we wove our way through the gravestones towards a patch of open ground, the bottom of my trousers drawing moisture from the long grass like litmus.

A short man, he reached forward with a stocky hand. 'Thanks for coming, Daniel,' he said breathlessly in a West Country accent softer in tone than expected. 'It's John,' he added. 'Adam's told me all about you.'

At a guess, John was considerably older than his wife had been – the hair white and plentiful, the skin liver-spotted – but there was also a vigour, a tautness, an air of constant preparedness about him, the locked spine and pigeon chest of an Army man. He made Adam seem sickly by comparison, and I imagined him being a little disappointed in his son, the academic who would never know how to tie a boxing glove or form a scrum.

Somewhere across the churchyard, Adam let out a shriek of laughter.

'He's been like this since his mother died,' said John following the noise.

I pressed my lips together.

'I suppose it affects everyone differently?' he said.

'I suppose it does.'

I renewed my efforts to locate Jane. The crowd was thinning as people began to move inside the church but she was still nowhere to be seen. I presumed she'd sneaked off for a cigarette.

'You've known Adam a long time?'

'Since university.'

'Ah,' he said with a fond grin, 'he was a right terror in those days.'

Adam, I am certain, was more teacher's pet than terrorist, but perhaps 'those days' really had been wild compared to life in a Dorset backwater.

'We had our moments,' I said, trying to indulge the old man's fanciful notions of college japery.

'He's a good lad,' he said and looked away to where Adam might have been but no longer was.

'And a good friend,' I replied earnestly with the sense that, the way we were talking, it might easily have been Adam who had died and not his mother.

'She was a good woman. She did a good job with Adam and Joan.'

'It must have been tough.'

He sighed. 'It still is.'

Jane arrived, sucking on something.

'I can still smell them,' I said and smiled.

She looked at me with a cold stare. 'We should go in.'

It seems we were not the only ones to have been duped by the weather. After an absurdly short service, we returned to Adam's parent's house and discovered a whirl of activity in which grey-haired women were attempting to retrieve plates of speared sausages and cheese from a trestle table in the back garden. Clearly an outdoor event had been planned, but over the course of the afternoon the sky had bleached, the temperature had fallen, and now the first drops of rain were beginning to spot the doilies.

We ascended a gentle slope to the front door. Adam's parents had moved into the bungalow for the final years of his mother's illness and every feature of the house had been adapted for wheelchair access and ease of transfer. I wondered if it was caring for Adam's mother that had kept his father so lean. There would have been less of her to lift as the disease progressed, of course – as her muscles melted on the bone – but still enough to test his strength, and in more ways than one.

In contrast to the weather, the wake was a depressingly dry occasion. I worked hard to procure a sherry and then Jane reminded me that I had offered to drive home. I was glad when she finally decided to brave the cold for another *Marlborough Light*, even though it was clearly a ploy designed to remove herself from the dullest of company, which undoubtedly included my own.

I, too, bored of the mantelpiece and wandered off into the hallway where my attention was immediately seized by the soft thud of something heavy falling in the far reaches of the house. Tracing the sound to one of the bedrooms, I found Adam's father straining under the weight of what I could only make out, at first, to be a large black box. The curtains were drawn and it took a moment before I could see the initial alarm in his face subside into relief and then the old-fashioned suitcase with rusted locks he was in the process of hauling from the top of a wardrobe.

'No time like the present,' he muttered setting his burden down onto the accommodating springs of an old mattress.

Though awkward to watch, I could neither tear my self away from the doorway nor offer him help as he proceeded to open drawers and wardrobes, and then efficiently and without ceremony lift handful after handful of clothes into the gaping case. I was reminded of the shoebox my mother had given me, mundane and secretive. Posterity's end.

'I can't remember the last time she used any of this stuff,' he was saying. 'Always liked to turn herself out nicely. We spent quite a time of it each morning getting her ready, but there were only a few clothes she really wore often.'

He paused to gaze at the mountain of material. 'I could never throw any of it out before. But now it seems like the right thing to do.'

Though I was barely cognisant of it at the time, packing his wife's clothes away so quickly after the funeral was not only an acceptable thing to do, but also an entirely appropriate one. Her death had not been sudden or calamitous but, rather, the slow ebbing of a tide. And as she had faded from them, so their resilience and stamina would have emerged. Order and routine would have become necessities, each of their small, every-day chores stacked one on top of the other, filling the days and the weeks, and helping them to pass with as little anguish as possible. A pragmatism all too obviously reflected in the embarrassingly brief service we had witnessed at the church. There had been no need for any final release of emotion that day because it had marked an end to their grief rather than a beginning.

Adam's father looked anxiously at me. 'You don't think Adam would want any of it, do you?'

'I shouldn't think so,' I said, wishing there was someone else on hand to provide the appropriate words of reassurance..

'I'll check with him later,' he nodded to himself and resumed folding a tatty-looking shawl. 'Adam says you lost your father recently?'

'I did, yes.'

'Then you'll understand.'

(Of course, I could do nothing of the sort.)

'We've always been a close family,' he continued, 'especially Adam and his mother.'

I wanted to ask him why, then, had Adam barely mentioned her to me in all the years we'd known each other?

He looked at me again. 'Were you close to your father?'

'Not really, no.'

He nodded. 'It's always harder for men.'

Gauging this to be the opportune moment to make my exit, I turned towards the hallway.

'Sorry,' he said, 'I wasn't trying to pry.'

'It's fine, I replied. 'I'd better head back.' I glanced at the case. 'Assuming you don't need a hand?'

'Oh, never mind all this,' he said, looking suddenly bewildered by the accumulation of skirts and jumpers in front of him. 'It's the rest of what they leave behind that matters.'

I left him to shift the rest of the mothballed knitwear. The moment stayed with me, though, and arriving home that evening I had trouble suppressing instincts that would have sent me straight up to the study in search of the shoebox my mother had given me. I felt drawn to it for the first time since it had come into my possession. Instead, I walked into the Kitchen and started to help Jane with the previous night's washing up, prepared for a discussion on the banality of funereal chit-chat but finding her in a more serious, fragile mood, as if she had been shaken – moved even – by the day's events.

But I couldn't stop thinking about it. I knew that boxes like the one waiting for me upstairs almost always contained junk, the worthless accumulations of a lifetime. I had one myself filled with bubblegum cards and school swimming medals in the loft, and I suddenly wanted to know why my mother had taken the trouble to pass any of my father's things on to me? One man's junk is another man's heirloom, I supposed, and yet I knew enough of my father's disdain for material wealth to be sure there would be little of historical or financial consequence inside. It was what made the money in the *Lloyds* account so unusual.

Jane made her way to bed while I, on the pretext of urgent revisions to an article long past its deadline, sat silently in the study, gazing into space and waiting for the light under the bedroom door to disappear. I didn't want to risk being disturbed. Not that I expected there to be anything worthy of being kept a secret, more that it was something I felt had to be done alone, if for no other reason than for the fear of appearing foolish.

I opened the box and immediately felt foolish. There, neatly piled, were dozens of family photographs, all monochrome and white-rimmed. I leafed through them, the faces of one appearing from behind the landscape of another, with no specific theme or narrative to tie them together, and no obvious chronology either. Images, it seemed, with all the coherence of a dream.

At the very bottom, however, something different – a series of newspaper cuttings held together by a paper clip. I scanned them briefly. Local newspaper nonsense from *The Kentish Gazette* and its ilk, each story with a vague connection to my father or the surgery: the opening of a new birthing pool in Aylesham, a run for charity my father had organised to raise money for an electrocardiogram at The Cottage Hospital, an award ceremony from *GP Monthly* with a cheesy promotional shot of my father and the other doctors from his practice in poorly-tailored suits. But the last clipping in the pile was immediately different, a single column of newspaper print the colour of a smoker's fingers, folded once and undated. It was a brief account – the length of an average journal abstract – concerning the alleged sexual assault of a young girl in Aylesham, the identity of whom had been withheld. A police investigation was underway, the article concluded, and that was it. A casual summation of an obscene act. No names, no places, no mention of my father, his practice, nor anything connected with him. In fact, nothing to indicate why that particular piece should have been there amongst the otherwise trivial collection of media highlights.

Had I known the girl? I considered the stupor in which I might have spent my youth to have missed something like that going on around me. Could I have been so preoccupied with exams and erections? And things like that rarely remain a secret for long the way children are wont to press their ears to doors. If it was someone I had known, surely the news would have spread amongst the playground eavesdroppers like measles?

At first, I tried to dismiss the idea that my father might have been connected with the assault in anyway, other than in a professional capacity. Likely, he had been required to examine the girl afterwards, to provide a medical report. I remembered his poorly paid stints as Duty Doctor for the police in Aylesham, and I assumed this article was related to such a task. But why keep a record of that one case when all the other articles were so comparatively benign in nature? Why hold onto that particular clipping?

A shiver ran through me. If I had been a smoker I would have taken a long, hard draw, but I was not and never had been. Even my burgeoning appetite for alcohol deserted me, and I was forced to contemplate the implications of my find alone and unfortified. I tipped back on two legs of the chair. How to resolve this? Might anyone else have remembered the incident? My mother was the obvious answer, but hers was a company I wished very much to avoid, and if she had wanted to tell me something she could have done so to my face without resorting to a pile of cryptic cuttings in a shoebox. No, if there was anything more to this I would need to tap an alternative source.

CHAPTER THIRTEEN

Consumed by some higher principle, I convinced myself that the Internet was not an appropriate place for enquiries of such potential significance, any more than I should look for the answers I needed between the covers of *The Sun*. The British Library, on the other hand, seemed to posses the gravitas, the austerity, that my investigations demanded. My imagined vastness of the place – its discrete corners and hefty tomes – offered the real possibility of first knowledge, of a footprint in fresh snow. But I was no pioneer; it was another man's ideas I had come for.

Getting into the Library was not as straightforward as I had anticipated. Appointments had to be made, sessions had to be booked. However, with the last drips of friendship duly squeezed from the hands of the requisite Professors and their Administrators, by mid-morning I was signing a register at the main reception and pinning a nametag to my lapel.

The library's innards, thankfully, bore little resemblance to its hideous outer shell where all attempts at artistry had been supplanted by random proportion and the mere juxtaposition of angles. The main reading room, by contrast, was airy and well lit, dispelling any remaining preconceptions I might have had of a Dickensian gloom. I found an empty desk, slipped my jacket over the back of a chair, and looked out across the rows of faceless heads inclined towards their hidden texts. Utter silence prevailed. Just the occasional scratch of paper, a cough, the scrape of a chair, and then a face rising randomly to yawn and send its eyes about the room. I felt completely alone.

The location of the documents I required had already been established via a short conversation with one of the Librarians on my arrival. Now I simply had to wait for the two translations of Lamarck's original work to arrive. Where better to hear the news than from the original text? Eventually, an assistant pushing a heavy trolley sidled over to my station and, without word, offloaded the four dusty volumes comprising *Philosophie zoologique; ou, exposition des considérations relatives à l'histoire naturelle des animaux*. After one last glance around the room, I began peeling back the brown pages of the manuscript as if dissecting fragile layers of tissue.

Viewing the original text was an indulgence, I knew, and, given my low level of French, more about gaining a feel for the science than for the detail. Lamarck's theory of evolution as outlined in the *Philosophie Zoologique* has been well recorded (and reviled) in countless biological texts since its original publication in 1809, but I wanted to rediscover it for myself, as best I could, free from any post-Darwinian influences. The translation I couldn't change, but the interpretation was another matter.

I had already gained something of Lamarck's history from a brief session in the university Library. Born in the village of Bazentin-le-Petit in 1744, the youngest of eleven in a military family, Lamarck had entered the Jesuit seminary at Amiens. Yet no sooner had his father died and he was off to join the French Army. Injury eventually forced him to resign his commission, but that was not before he had been distinguished for bravery under fire. Then, after only a brief sojourn in the dusty offices of a bank, our man was all set to study medicine and botany. From cleric to academic via Napoleonic warfare, now that was an education! It was a peculiarity of the times – the way a man might move amongst the professions – and how unlike the drudgery of modern schooling.

After only a short period of study in Paris, Lamarck was quick to publish his seminal work on the plants of France – Flore Française – which was an academic success (though a limited financial one) and also earned him the admiration of Buffon, a senior academic and would-be mentor. Buffon, like many of his peers, was a gentleman in the age of gentlemanly science at a time when intellectual pursuit and wealth were so closely aligned. Perhaps the freedom to think beyond the travails of daily living was what the money permitted?

Somehow Lamarck continued to raise funding for his work. Not, I suspect, via the interminable grind of grant writing we now have to submit to, but perhaps by virtue of an eloquent dissertation over brandy or a few mockingly kind words across an auditorium. The tug of a wig might have been enough for any up-and-coming scientist of the day to gain support from a suitably flattered benefactor.

The text was long-winded, and in places difficult to follow, but after an hour of reading I was convinced that (bar the odd pandemic and a distinct lack of dental hygiene) Jean Baptiste and his like had it made. The manuscript reeked of freethinking. Dissenters might argue that without the control over science we now have in the form of peer review and our undignified struggle for subvention, men such as Lamarck might have been prone to the undiluted forces of ego and economics. But reading his work, I couldn't believe that for a moment; his calling was that of the true aesthete. Today, such a voice would have drowned in the torrent of mediocrity that is the bulk of modern scientific literature, but back then he was one of the lone hunters, roaming wild and free. A fact borne out, if by nothing else, than by the sheer diversity of subject matter Lamarck was able to tackle. Publishing a series of books on invertebrate zoology and paleontology, he was the first to separate the *Crustacea*, *Arachnidia*, and *Annelida* from the *Insecta*. His classification of the mollusks was far in advance of anything proposed previously and he even anticipated cell theory by stating that:

No body can have life if its constituent parts that are not cellular tissue or are not formed by cellular tissue.

Scientists of his era were more like artists, possessed of a creativity all but a few madmen have lost. Lamarck found time to write papers on physics and meteorology, including annual compilations of weather data. But of all of his works, it was the *Philosophie Zoologique* I had before me in which he had most clearly stated his theory of evolution. Simply put, it proposed that the characteristics we pass to our children are those we have acquired during our own lifetime. Our offspring inherit the very physical and mental adaptations the environment forces us to make in order to survive, rather than be at the whim of some random genetic event when an unsuspecting ovum is ambushed down a dark fallopian alley. Survival of the fittest, yes, but in a Lamarckian world the fittest are those who respond most quickly to change, those who, by definition, demonstrate the greatest capacity to evolve. The son of a blacksmith will inherit the enlarged biceps of his father; the giraffe will pass on the neck – strengthened by a life reaching for the highest branches – to his progeny. And this was what Ulrich had seen in the data from our mice. They were born with aggressive tendencies because their parents had been trained that way. Because they had been forced to adapt.

My mind erupted. I had previously known something of Lamarck's theories, but I had been exposed to them only as a pretext for Darwin – so that I might better appreciate the superiority of his work. I had been asked merely to accept Lamarckian theories as implausible and without a credible, scientific basis, and yet the observations in the animal house seemed to revive such unfeasible notions.

Lamarck's works were never popular during his lifetime, gaining neither the respect nor the prestige enjoyed by his patron Buffon or his colleague Cuvier. Despite appreciating Lamarck's work on invertebrates, his contemporaries had no use for his evolutionary theories and, instead, used their influence to discredit him; whereas I had been given the chance – no, the responsibility – to restore the man's honour.

I stepped out onto the crowded pavement in a state of near-shock. The temperature had dropped and a few of the cars had brought snow from the suburbs. People hopped on and off the backs of buses and dodged each other in a scene so ordinary, yet so laughably surreal, that I wanted to stop and shake them and tell them all what goes on inside the minds of our greatest thinkers! But there was no one for me to share the news with, of course. I had already accepted the fact that loneliness would be my ally, hardening me to the task ahead, and ridding me of any unnecessary distraction.

Unfortunately my next port of call, The British Library Newspaper Archive, had been moved to Colindale, which necessitated a further round of booking before I was able to make the long tube ride north from Euston Station. It was already late afternoon by the time I emerged from a tunnel into the light of a sun already losing its grip on the sky. The carriage was empty for the final few stops, reminding me of my anonymous late-night journeys shadowing Erin. Since that time on her doorstep I'd thought of her only fleetingly, an indication, perhaps, of the level of concentration I was able to apply to the matter in hand, a relentless energy driving me forward to the exclusion of everything else. Thinking back, I couldn't possibly have known how an article from *The Kentish Gazette* would come to so intimately bind my experiences of past and present. All I felt at the time was an unwavering conviction to see the work through, and that this was merely the period of chaos that ultimately precedes the coming of order.

The Repository at Colindale certainly had them all, every copy of every edition of *The Gazette* from 1952 onwards. A fact as depressing as it was uplifting. That we should find so much to say about such a small corner of England's green and pleasant, and that we should go to such lengths to preserve it. Yet there I was, at the mercy of that exhaustive archive, and grateful for the retentiveness of the few.

I had underestimated the task. Even microfilmed the archive presented me with a football pitch of plastic to get through, and no possibility of combing every issue. As determined as I was to get answers, I knew I would almost certainly miss my tiny snippet amongst all the irate columnists and bleating councilors; a fact brought home to me, all too readily, by the struggle I was having to keep my grip on the slippery bundle of film I had just been handed by the elderly curator of the establishment. She wore a knowing smile that spoke of the many such misjudgements made by similarly optimistic clients she had witnessed in her time. Reluctantly, I passed the sheets back across the counter and saw them accepted with a discernible sneer that said: who in their right mind would imagine they could scan fifty years worth of newspaper for an article the size of a cigarette packet? Television detectives, perhaps, but not people like you.

In a side street I found a public house with tables and chairs scattered by the roadside, and still a glimpse of the sun's dying warmth, where I sipped at a pint of something dark and local. It had been a day of varied success. Lamarck had been a hit. So much so, I had yet to absorb the true implications of my rediscovery of his work and its possible connection to Erin's data. As for The Gazette, it was distressing not being able to dismiss or affirm the importance of the newspaper article as easily as I had the Frenchman's theories. Tracing the background to the story would be impossible without a date to go on. I had no friends in the Kent police that I knew of, though I did have an old school friend or two, and one in particular had been on my mind since first reading the article. She might have been the only real friend I'd had or maybe she was just the only one I could remember? Might I be able to track down a telephone number, talk to her, I wondered? And even if she did still live at her old address, would she wish to be exposed to the past so clumsily after all this time? Speaking to her might force her into a corner, her instinct to bury the past, to say nothing. Whereas a letter would give her time to reflect, to get used to the idea. It was decided: contact first by letter and then visit later only if absolutely necessary. It was something of a wild idea that a friend I had chased in a school playground over twenty-five years ago would even consider helping me, but such was my mood.

The house lay still and empty on my return, the rooms derelict in the darkness. Upstairs, I warmed my laptop and teased a single malt. I had to hope she was at the same address. I moved the mouse towards the word processor icon but then hesitated. A personal touch was required. Nothing too officious. Nothing that might discourage her from replying. I closed the lid of the computer, found an unopened pad at the back of the desk drawer and began to write quickly as if my nerve or my faculties might fail before I could finish. And, as I drafted the letter, I saw Sheila's face again and wondered if she had grown up to be as old as her name in the years since we had, briefly, been allowed to become friends.

The next morning I woke with a new mission. There was much to discover and much to protect. In the kitchen, Jane sat veiled in newsprint, the outer leaves of *The Guardian* enveloping her like the walls of Jericho. I gazed in from the hallway, but she made no sound or movement of recognition so I slipped the letter into the pocket of my overcoat and exited the front door quietly.

In town, random gusts of wind were playing games with the coat tails and the umbrellas on Bolsover Street. A low sun stretched pliant shadows along the pavement. To avoid a Chiswick postmark, I slid the letter into a mailbox outside one of the sandwich bars proliferating around campus.

Baxter caught me fifty paces from the institute. 'Daniel! Good holiday?'

He could be annoyingly jovial at times.

'Meeting.' I corrected.

'Ah, with *Quintex*?'

I nodded impatiently.

An earnest look came over him. 'What's all this nonsense I hear about Brian? Says you've fired him'

'He's a sneaky sod.'

'Seems shaken.'

'So he should be. He almost ruined the collaboration.'

'So how are things going with *Quintex*?'

'Brian was pissed off that I didn't show his data.'

'I thought his stuff looked pretty good?'

'I'm afraid Erin's is rather more convincing.'

A tall man in a raincoat passed us by. He turned and beamed at Baxter. 'Charles!'

Baxter responded. 'David!' He bent towards my ear and whispered: 'Up for Vice Provost.' Then, turning to the thin man again said, 'Hang on a second.' Now back to me: 'Sort this thing out with Brian, will you? Good post-docs are hard to come by.'

'I know,' I smiled. 'That's how we ended up with Brian.'

With an uncertain laugh Baxter left me to pursue politics with The Man Who Would Be Vice Provost.

The heating in the institute had failed. Sweater-bloated white coats crossed me in the corridor. People huddled in scarves and hats at their benches like asylum seekers. Erin must have been waiting for me because she was at the door to my office before I had a chance to lower my briefcase. Her clothes were more dowdy than usual, and no make-up either. And she seemed to be making a point of looking at the floor, the walls, or the windows – anywhere, in fact – rather than at me.

'I needed to ask you something,' she said.

Straight to business. I had not underestimated her in the slightest.

'I'm fine, thank you.' I said. 'And did you have a good Christmas too?'

She blushed. 'Sorry. Yes. Fine thanks.'

We both hesitated.

'Listen,' I said, 'I'm sorry about that stuff with your father.'

'Don't worry about it, everyone was hammered,' she said as if 'everyone' had made a clumsy pass at her that night.

I smiled awkwardly. 'Sign of a good party.'

Erin's face signalled relief. Maybe she had been more drunk than I'd realised? Maybe I'd got away with it?

'Do you want a coffee?' I said. 'I need a small barrel.'

'I'm not sure it's coffee you're thinking of,' she laughed. 'You do look knackered, though.'

'Thank you very much. For that, you can make the drinks.'

The atmosphere in the lab was subdued, and not just by the temperature. The students' return to work after the holidays was always a gradual process, and now, at such an early stage, I was surrounded by the weakest of my brood: the newcomers and the poor-performers returned early on the off-chance I might be there to witness their sacrifice, to see them 'upping their game'. They even tried to look surprised to see me as I ambled between the benches, which was both heartening and pitiable. It wasn't my intention to be overtly cruel; I've just found that a touch of fear tends to get the best out of people.

Back in the office, Erin perched on the window ledge. I sat at my desk, both of us trying to draw heat from our cups.

'Have you been working much over Christmas?' I asked her.

She suddenly looked anxious – wary, even.

'A bit, why?'

'You didn't do anything more with the mice?'

'No, of course not.'

'But you crunched the data again?'

She nodded. 'Same result. I don't suppose you got any bright ideas from the *Quintex* crowd?'

'Not from *Qunitex*, no.'

She smiled. 'And…?'

I had been wondering how much of my discovery would be covered by the contract with *Quintex*? We certainly shared the rights to any data I generated around SNF, which meant they probably had the power to bury or benefit from Erin's data, and suddenly telling anyone about the Lamarckian hypothesis felt risky. It wasn't a matter of trust, merely one of practicality. The fewer people who knew about my theory, the easier my chances of protecting any claim I might have to the intellectual property. It was for her own good, too, I reasoned. No need for her to be caught up in any of this. Not yet, anyway, while my thinking was at such an embryonic stage.

'*And*,' I replied, 'you can't tell a soul about these data.'

Erin shrugged her shoulders. 'Who would I tell? Baxter?'

'Why don't you put all the mouse data together so I can go over it again?'

She looked at me in puzzlement. 'Shouldn't we just get rid of those bloody mice? They only seem to be giving us grief.'

'You're almost certainly right. But let's review the results one more time, just to humour me, before we make any final decisions.'

'Only if you tell me what you think is really going on?'

'It's probably all nonsense.'

'Well I haven't managed to come up with anything better, so "nonsense" sounds pretty good to me right now!'

'Later on, maybe.' I smiled. 'When I've had a little more time to think it over.'

'Sure, if that's what you want,' she replied, clearly unconvinced.

She rose from the windowsill and offered to take my cup. Drinking the tepid remains and passing the empty mug into her hand felt like the first real contact we had made that morning.

'By the way,' she said, 'did you really fire Brian?'

'Yes, I really did fire him. Will he stay fired for long? I'm not sure.' I checked my watch. 'Actually, I should have a quick word with him. Is he in?'

'Oh yes, he's in.'

Brian was pipetting in the lab. Despite being such a prick, he was proving to be a worthy adversary, and under different circumstances I might have relished the challenge. But his presence was just an irritation to me now, and confronting him too much of a distraction at a time when, more than ever, I needed to keep my focus. Appeasement would be the key.

I took him back to my office and pointed him into a chair.

'Listen Brian,' I began.

'I think I was a bit jet-lagged,' he blurted. 'I'm really sorry.'

I sighed. 'Well, we were both under pressure. And I don't imagine the booze exactly helped matters either.'

Brian was mute. Crestfallen. Taking it like a Swede. I went on to give him an official verbal warning for his outburst in the toilets. I also made it clear that he had a chance to make amends if he could start behaving more as if he was part of the team and less like one of our competitors. We have to work together if we're going to crack the big papers, I told him. I couldn't allow individuals to dictate the scientific direction of the group or put our chances of high impact publications at risk. There would be enough glory to go round etc. etc.

All in all, a not an unsuccessful morning; a few loose ends tidied up, a few wounds on their way to being healed. I even tried tidying my office for once. I threw out a small forest's worth of old journals, tried and failed to fix the blind, and finally put my Red Barrel Cactus out of its misery (Nevada itself couldn't have provided a drier spot). Pointless distractions, of course, and I can only wish now that they had been more successful, because beneath that purposeful exterior lay an immense weakness like a fault-line ready to crack and swallow me whole.

CHAPTER FOURTEEN

For a week I cursed The Post Office and all its subsidiaries. Should I have hand-delivered the letter? I thought not. I might have been spotted, and that would have defeated the whole purpose of writing, which was to avoid scaring her off. Would she have recognised me, though, even if I had gone to see her? And would it have mattered? And now I had written, how might she choose to reply? By letter? Had I given her my address? Of course I had. And my telephone number at home, and at the institute. Or might she turn out to have more courage than I myself had demonstrated and try to visit me in person? Again, unlikely. The clear advantage of a letter is that it gives the recipient time to think, to absorb the details, to account for subtlety, and only then to craft an appropriate response, rather than risk being revealed as a tongue-tied clot on a stranger's doorstep.

This, a kind of cerebral confetti, fluttered amidst the drafts and currents of a mind still struggling with the events of the previous few weeks. In reality, the only thing I could do about the letter was wait, so I ended up brooding, instead, over the one conclusion I had managed to reach regarding Erin's data that seemed irrevocable; that the young mice in her experiments had shown convincing evidence of Lamarckian inheritance.

It was evolution on fast forward. In a Lamarckian world, a species didn't have to wait for the wheel of genetic fortune to spin in its favour, to throw up the chance mutations that might promote survival. Instead, an organism could adapt within a generation. It could change as fast as the weather.

But how was this possible? If I was to convince anyone: *Quintex*, Baxter, even myself, I had to have a biological mechanism. How, within our understanding of the apparatus of inheritance, was it possible for an environment – aggressive or fear inducing, or any other for that matter – to alter genes themselves, to alter the immutable lexicon of life? As far as even I could understand, such a system would require the appropriate cellular tools, and yet science had already described the inner workings of a cell in such shocking detail that there didn't seem to be any room left for the machinery required of Lamarck's 'rapid-response' genes. How could we have missed something so fundamental?

A better mind might have reached the solution more quickly, but the answer didn't come to me for several days. I was reviewing an editorial on the SNF gene for a journal with a discouragingly low impact factor, Jane peacefully asleep on the sofa, and my thoughts suitably softened by a mid-quality Beaujolais. In the opening paragraphs, the structure of the SNF gene had been described in typically unimaginative detail. Like all genes it is composed, broadly, of two main regions: exons and introns. The exons carry the code that will eventually be translated into the RNA and then to protein – the real meat of a gene. Sprinkled amongst them are the introns. As far as we knew, these other pieces of DNA did little to directly affect the structure or function of the proteins they made; they were there simply to fill in the gaps between the exons. Various theories existed regarding their possible function, if indeed there was one. They might, it was proposed, influence the folding of DNA – its three-dimensional structure – and thereby change the activity of a gene. It had also been suggested that they might control a gene's activity directly, by acting as accelerators or brake pedals to determine how much RNA was transcribed from it. But hard evidence for these functions had been difficult to find, and so introns remained, to a large extent, an enigma. What's more, as regards useless sequences of DNA, introns were just the tip of the iceberg. Each gene itself is usually separated from its neighbours by even longer stretches of often-repetitive DNA, which together with the introns, means that – in theory at least – the majority of human DNA serves no obvious purpose whatsoever.

Nature's white noise.

Practically, or rather chemically, this might make some sense. You couldn't have all the genes sitting right next to each other; there wouldn't be enough space for the mechanics of a cell that produced RNA to get to them. Crowding genes together only increased the chances that mistakes would be made. Yet there was so much of this 'noise' in the system. Did we really need it all? Wouldn't it have been sensible for evolution to have eradicated at least some of this chromosomal stuffing if it was all so redundant?

Its existence suited my purposes perfectly. This unwanted genetic debris, I was sure, held the solution to Lamarck's (and now my) theory. But I wasn't quite there. Not yet.

I should make it clear that even I didn't believe such a mode of inheritance was of sufficient impact to, say, alter the length of a Giraffe's neck as Lamarck himself had suggested. Complex features such as those result from the interaction of hundreds of genes, and not via subtle variations in the activity of a few. I could not (and did not) extrapolate Lamarck's theories that far. But perhaps a handful of genes, if subjected to sufficiently powerful environmental stresses might be controlled in the way he proposed. A pattern of behaviour altered, a physical trait enhanced – that much seemed possible.

So why hadn't we seen evidence of it in humans before? Because, until my discovery, there had been no reason to look for the effects of Lamarckian inheritance. And even if we had thought to look, the effects would have been subtle, and the experiments might have taken decades to run – whole generations, even. That's why we'd been so lucky with the mice. They live for a year – two at the most

– with many of the experiences of a lifetime compressed into just the few short weeks it took to run our experiments. With mice we could skip rapidly through the generations in a way it would have been impossible to achieve in man.

My theory remained far from complete. Even if it were true, I would have to explain how these regions of junk DNA were able to influence the function of a gene?

In the middle of the night Jane came looking for me in the kitchen and found me hunched pensively over a coffee mug.

'You look tired. Are you feeling alright?' she said.

I nodded without catching her eye.

'Is everything OK at work?'

I shrugged.

'I don't suppose you're going to discuss it with me anyway, are you?'

'Sorry, I've been a little preoccupied.'

'A little!' She gave a short laugh. 'Is it something to do with your father?'

'Partly,' I replied, and it was partly true.

Then I remember standing rather dramatically, flinging my chair to the floor and, to Jane's utter mystification, shouting 'Coding!'

'You've cracked it then?' she said. 'I'm so pleased for you.'

I brushed past her into the living room and from a corner of the sofa began an intense watch over the fireplace. The answer suddenly appeared so simple, so frustratingly obvious. Those apparently random areas of the genome were able to code. They could produce their own form of RNA. But this RNA wasn't destined to produce a protein. Instead, it interfered with the function of the RNA from real genes, preventing their translation into protein. Anti-RNA binding to normal RNA, anti-sense binding to sense!

But what else? These anti-genes would have to be highly susceptible to change if they were to fit the purposes of my theory.

Their sequences had to be able to mutate, somehow, in response to the environment before being passed on. For regular genes, structural alterations of that nature would be a disaster. An organism simply couldn't have its genes and proteins liable to change so easily. Even subtle changes in the structure of a protein can have disastrous consequences: cystic fibrosis, haemophilia – the list was endless. But these anti-genes had a more subtle purpose. Perhaps they could afford to be more adaptable?

It all seemed to fit: the mouse data, the northerns, dear Brian and his tedious perseverance. His data had been right after all, the answers buried deep in the shadows of his northern blots so meticulously executed and so alarmingly contrary to anything I could possibly have understood before. Erin had even managed to corroborate his findings, and yet, still, I had failed to recognise their significance. There was nothing wrong with the probes we were using. They weren't lying to us. The sense probes we had designed to act as controls weren't meant to bind to anything but they were binding to something, true enough; they were detecting one of Lamarck's anti-genes – an anti-gene for SNF!

Everything began to slot into place. As always, Nature was one step ahead of us. It had its own antisense at work, changing the people we are and turning us into the people we had yet to become. We had done everything one could possibly do to exclude technical error from our experiments. We had repeated them. We had re-analysed them. And we should have believed them. We should have stopped trying to fit the data with our feeble preconceptions and concentrated, instead, on finding new explanations, new hypotheses to take us forward. What fools we were. What a fool I was!

The theory might have more disturbing consequences, I realised. Man had always adapted – and would always continue to adapt – to his environment. But now our environment was, itself, so much a product of our behaviour, so much controlled by us, that more and more it had come to reflect our own drives and ambitions.

And with Lamarckian evolution in action wasn't it possible that the world we were busy creating for ourselves would become truly self-fulfilling because it would reinforce the behaviour that originally created it – our own. In evolutionary terms, at least, perhaps we had already peaked as a species, destined never to change, fundamentally, again, doomed to an evolutionary loop of war and greed and desire, confined by the Mobius strip of our genome to a future apparently endless and yet utterly finite, utterly predictable?

I must have fallen asleep because the next thing I knew I was lifting my thick head from the sofa to find morning had arrived, stretching its brilliant canvas across the horizon, dusting the sky a pale orange and the rooftops a gentle ochre. My stomach knotted as the night's meanderings returned. But running through the arguments again I couldn't convince myself of any major flaws. Gaps, yes, but this was still a hypothesis after all, and these theories of mine still just that: theories. To overcome the scepticism of my peers I would need something more than a psychotic mouse for evidence. The ultimate experiments would have to be performed in man. But I didn't live in the age of Lamarck. I couldn't begin to test the hypothesis of an eighteenth century botanist in humans so lightly without more data to support my claims. This, then, was the first of my dilemmas: how to carry out the necessary experiments when the need to conceal my discoveries was as vital as the need to prove them?

I'd need money too. Science was expensive. Modern molecular biology couldn't be conducted in palaces, or basements or garden sheds. It required infrastructure. It required people. Even if I could have brought myself to use the *Lloyds*'s money, it wouldn't have been anywhere near enough. And raising funds for the research would have meant exposing my ideas to outside scrutiny and almost certain ridicule when they were at such a fragile stage in their development. Yet to deny them the means for rigorous scientific testing would consign me to the life of a crackpot. There was *Quintex*, of course, but they already had millions invested in the SNF programme and had so far seen precious little for their money in return. In the long term, what I had discovered had the potential to cause a scientific revolution, but long-term investments were not what either of us needed. More immediate results were required to satisfy the company shareholders and the review boards of the Research Councils alike if we were to capitalise on my discovery, and I had no idea how fast I might be able to deliver. Plus, if I went to *Quintex* they would almost certainly end up owning the rights to the research. I was a lone academic, not a businessman, and there would be little I could do to prevent them swallowing me up and all the intellectual property to-boot. It also wasn't beyond the realms of reason to suppose *Quintex* might quash the data. It was a potentially dangerous idea I had stumbled upon, and its full implications, though staggering, I was only just beginning to explore myself. It's translation into new medicines was an obvious possibility, but if there were no 'quick-wins' *Qunitex* might consider it more of a threat than a boon and bury the whole damn lot.

I crept into the bedroom and dressed quietly, sensing Jane following my movements from beneath the duvet while she pretended to be asleep. She had every right to keep an eye on me, though she couldn't have known half the reasons why. I collected my overcoat from the hall, slipped out into a brisk spring morning and paced the silent streets trying to avoid annoying the insomniacs and the sleepers alike. The sharpness of the air did just as I'd hoped it would, shaking off the last of the tiredness and rousing me to fresh insights.

For example, there was also the small matter of Charles Darwin to contend with. Though as I walked, I grew more confident that he presented no significant obstacle to my idea. In fact, his and Lamarck's theorems, far from being at odds with each other, were in many ways complementary. They might even form part of some Grand Unifying Theory of Evolution, my ambitions no different to those of the physicists in that respect. If it could work for quantum mechanics then why not biology? If interactions between matter and anti-matter were fundamental to the fine balance of nature, then why not genes and anti-genes?

My mind was swollen with ideas, but I knew I had to focus on the more immediate issues first. Like Brian. I could keep him close to me in the lab, and I could keep him busy, but I couldn't control the conversations he might have at seminars and conferences nor the e-mails he might exchange with Ulrich & Co. And the likes of Ulrich would surely find it impossible to maintain their silence forever on the basis of friendship or integrity alone? This was the stuff of Nobel prizes and of less-than-noble profits.

It was clear. No one was to be trusted when there was so much at stake. I had to keep my Lamarckian fantasies to myself. These ideas had waited over two hundred years for recognition; they could wait a little longer. Yet even as I told myself this, I also knew that knowledge is not so easily silenced. It is eager to be heard. If something is scientifically possible, no matter the technical or moral hurdles, I believe we will eventually make it so. From the Spinning Jenny to cloning; scientists know they have only to wait long enough and any furore their discoveries might cause at first will inevitably fade with time. Society soon accustoms itself to innovation. It might be possible to contain my findings for a few months, even a few years, but eventually someone would figure it out, just as I had done, and they wouldn't hesitate to explore its potential in every conceivable way. I had to find the means to conduct the necessary experiments whilst maintaining strict governance over what I was sure would be their startling consequences. A controlled detonation.

CHAPTER FIFTEEN

The letter arrived unannounced, revealed to me like a chosen playing card amongst the minicab leaflets and the double-glazing flyers on the hallway floor. A small, square envelope I might easily have discarded for recycling with the rest of the doormat junk had I not noticed the address. Most of the mail I received at home either demanded or offered me money, but from its outward appearance this was immediately a different proposition. A real letter. With real handwriting. And it filled me with real dread. Nobody I knew wrote letters anymore. They e-mailed or they phoned or they ignored, but never ink to paper, not for a long time.

I slit the envelope. Despite its diminutive proportions, I had to search hard for the contents, which comprised a single sheet of white writing paper. I walked from the hallway into the kitchen and sat at the table with the letter propped against the teapot and me staring anxiously at it.

She was still there.

The note was brief. She was well, she wrote, and it was nice to hear from me again after all these years, but unfortunately, she knew nothing of the story and she was very sorry she couldn't offer me any further help. She also pointed out that 'this thing' could have happened at anytime in the past 30 years, which was true enough. Without getting hold of the original article I had no way of dating the event for certain. She wished me well, and that was the end of it, barely a side in total.

It was foolish of me to feel disappointed, but I did. Could I really have expected her to solve all my problems with a few strokes of a pen? But as I read the letter a second time, I began to think its apologies were perhaps too profuse, its denials too robust. She didn't sound at all curious about how I'd come by the cutting (I had made no mention of its origins in my letter) nor did she even begin to speculate as to the identity of the girl, which would have at least been in-keeping with a certain feminine curiosity. If the incident was news to her she didn't appear at all interested.

She was lying. Her dismissal was too cool, her prose too perfunctory. She had almost fooled me. I had even contemplated going back to Colindale again – God forbid – but my letter had served its purpose well enough. It had drawn a response from Sheila so ordinary as to be brimming with insight.

I had to speak with her. If it turned out she really didn't know anything about the incident in the article then the worst I would achieve would be the rekindling of an old acquaintance. But I would have to be tactful. If there was any information to be gleaned, it would have to be teased delicately from her.

Barely dressed and barely awake, I was soon driving through the dark and bleary streets of South East London again. I hadn't bothered to ask Jane about borrowing the *Megane*; she hardly ever used it, probably because it was a gift from her father, a pay-off for some forgotten birthday or another holiday ruined by rows. Sheila's response had undoubtedly been intended to push me away, and yet there I was, eagerly motoring through a light rain towards Aylesham with absolutely no idea what I was going to say or do when I got there. I caught my dishevelled reflection in the rear view mirror. I might prove a shock to my old friend yet, I thought, letter or no letter.

The rain turned from drizzle into a harder form as I slid the *Megane* into the narrow mouth of Drovers Lane. A strong curve and dip to the road meant only the nearest houses were visible from the top of the laneway. I brought the car to halt, turned off the engine, and sat listening to my heart rocking in my chest and to the rain, a wall of noise like the sound of so many genes firing.

Another childhood image was with me. I was eleven years old on a bicycle skidding into the laneway. The tyres threw water from a summer puddle. A warm breeze skimmed the cornfields nearby. The bicycle was a second-hand model from *Jackson's* in Aylesham that I coveted like a Krugerrand. Three frame-sizes too big for me, it was a bike to be grown into like a school uniform. In the garden of Sheila's house were the remnants of a makeshift castle, its blanket-roof caved in and the Morrison's Alsatian chasing an empty squash bottle menacingly about its perimeter. I slowed. The dog lifted its head then dismissed me as unworthy of prey. I slipped from the saddle onto tiptoes, my knackers barely clearing the cross bar. Then, by virtue of what appears to be the sheer power of my expectation, the front door to Sheila's house opened, and with the cries of unfinished chores chasing her into the garden, she appeared, running.

She stopped as abruptly as she had arrived, examining me, trying to find something in my eyes. Unspoken plans passed between us, a nod perhaps but no more. In my memory, Sheila was an amalgam of all the girls I had seen before or since: pigtails, a summer dress, white socks, and single buckle shoes, with the sun in her face and a hand forever pinned to her forehead for shade. Nothing more precise than that. It was an impression of childhood, and one that I couldn't even be certain was mine.

Sheila was younger than me, and, worse, she was a girl. Had we lived in Canterbury our relationship would never have been tolerated, the teasing and taunting more than either of us could have endured. We went to different schools – me to The Grammar, her to The Middle – and at that age the three years separating us was virtually a generation. Yet we became friends. Necessity played its part, of course – we were both stuck in the middle of nowhere – but there was also something quite natural about our being together, a matching of personalities, and each of us an only-child, content to loose ourselves in silent activity. So much so it was difficult to recall what, if anything, we had ever said to each other. Even when we had spoken it had probably been more in character than as ourselves: as Doctor and Nurse, Indian and Squaw, Boss and Secretary.

It was an innocent summer we spent together before our friendship seemed to vanish in a cloud of pollen. Had advancing youth imposed its customary divisions upon us? My recollection was of something more dramatic, more catastrophic. New images now: Sheila jerked back into her house by a hidden hand, front doors slamming, her mother's face frozen behind netted curtains, Sheila's diary suddenly as full as Gatsby's. Solitude again in my own garden fortress, hospitals without nurses, tepees without squaws, no one to tend or cook or take the memos...

The engine of the *Megane* had been off for some time and the car was losing heat. Rain obscured the windscreen, melting the houses of Drovers Lane into thick rivulets of water. I peered out into what was, by now, virtual darkness thanks to a low blanket of cloud, the landscape a montage of flat, colourless shapes. A slatted fence opposite the small terrace of houses separated a newly ploughed field from the rough surface of the road. Trees swayed in the distance like the masts of storm-tossed Man-O-Wars.

I gathered my raincoat from the back seat and ran from the car, uncertain if speed would heighten or lessen the impact of the downpour. Instinctively I came to a halt at one of the front doors, the rain cracking onto my waterproof. I leant purposefully on the doorbell, but when no sound came in return, for a moment, I didn't want anyone to answer. I was almost relieved at the thought of there being no one inside. Then a slim column of shadow began to form as the door drew back into the house. A face emerged. My first thought was how badly Sheila had aged. Her skin was like paper folded too many times, her hair a mix of reds and yellows, sparse and brittle from bleach, and she was much thinner than I'd imagined she would be. The eyes, though, were familiar.

'Sheila?'

There was no reply, only a restless shadow shifting in the darkness.

'I'm sorry to turn up like this,' I went on. 'It's Daniel. Daniel Hayden. I got your letter?'

I produced the envelope.

'Did you now?' came a voice, craggy and catarrhal.

The door opened wider. I could just make out the towelling cloth of a dressing gown and then an arm reaching out for the letter. After what must have been a cursory glance she handed it back to me.

'She isn't here.'

It was the mother. A teenager when she'd had Sheila, she was more older sister than parent.

'Sorry,' I said. 'I thought you were Sheila. It's hellishly dark out here.'

Apparently pleased by the confusion she had caused, a fractionally softer look fell across the woman's face that was almost a smile but was really just a series of ripples around her mouth.

'I told you; she's not in. You're wasting your time. And you're wasting everyone else's time writing her stupid letters.'

'Do you know when she'll be back?'

'Could be anytime. Never sure with her.'

'I just need a few minutes. Would you be able to give her a message?'

'Why don't you call her instead, like a good lad?'

'I don't have your number.'

'Well that's just a shame isn't it,' she said, and slammed the door in my face.

I stepped back from the house, unable to pull my eyes away from it, prescient of the answers it might hold. I was intrigued, too, by the instinctive bitterness Sheila's mother had shown towards me, the doctor's son come to put ideas in her daughter's head, perhaps, the letter a part of Sheila's world beyond her control?

I had given in too easily. Women like Sheila's mother know only too well how to expose a man's weaknesses, and she'd done a pretty good job reducing me to an apologetic pulp. But at least I had found Sheila; there was some comfort in that. And, unlikely as it seemed that the only girl I had ever really known as a child was the one from the article, it started to make frightening sense. Would I have been so viciously dismissed from the doorway if my presence had not so obviously revealed the pain of the past? Shouldn't I have been sitting in their front room at that very moment, refusing my third cup of tea and exchanging old school stories, rather than listening to the rain beat down on the roof of the clapped out *Golf* in their driveway?

The door flew open the second time, dragging the wind and the rain with it into the house. Sheila's mother bore down on me, fierce and formidable. 'Leave us alone, you little fucker!' she was screaming. 'She doesn't want to see you, so why don't you fuck off!'

I peered past her into the hallway. I could hear a television game show coming from the back of the house. 'Sheila?' I shouted. 'Sheila, I just want to know about my father. It's important!'

I must have sounded pathetic, but suddenly I didn't care anymore. I had to know what they knew. I pressed against the door, trying to force it open, but Sheila's mother had anticipated the move and it was closed before I could put the necessary weight behind my shoulder. I tried yelling and pounding my fist on the door like a psychopath. But all she had to do was stay locked inside the house with the television at full volume, and wait for my anger to weaken and subside. And I was left standing there in the rain like a fool, staring at the house and breathing hard for I don't know how long, until, eventually, the last of the lights went out, and I had no choice but to trudge back to the car with my head aching from the running of too much blood.

As I reached the main road, above the rhythm of my footsteps another regular pattern of sound arose from within the soft roar of the rain. I turned to see a figure following me down the laneway. As it drew closer, I could make out the shape of a woman, her face a pale beacon in the darkness, and, even allowing for the unnaturalness of the light, her mascara, I surmised, had run by more than the power of rainfall alone.

'Sheila?'

Standing in front of me, she looked lost, uncertain what to do next, as if she had come to me only for the sake of running away. A white blouse clung translucently to her skin. She was almost as tall as I was ('big-boned' my mother would have said), and I tried picturing her again as a young girl, trying to match her damp features now to those dimples and pouts I could only dimly recall.

'We can talk in the car,' I told her and pointed to the *Megane*.

Sheila looked back towards the house. The point of no return.

Inside the car, I suddenly realised how cold I was. Sheila, too, sat shivering in the passenger seat like a cobweb. I reached for the ignition key and drew a frightened look from her, exaggerated by the network of hair and make-up criss-crossing her face.

'The heating,' I said, nodding at the vents.

I started the engine and twisted the temperature dial into the red. We sat in silence as the air slowly warmed, while outside a terrible darkness continued to close the sky.

Sheila's voice startled me. 'I'm sorry about my mother,' she said with a familiar estuary edge.

'And I'm sorry for turning up out of the blue like this,' I replied. 'I must have been a bit of a shock to you both.'

'I thought you might come. But as you probably guessed, my mother didn't know anything about the letter.'

'Yes, more apologies from me, I'm afraid. I didn't realise who I was talking to.'

Her head lifted. 'I don't know what you expect me to tell you, Daniel.' She paused. 'I heard about your dad.'

I reached for the glove compartment and Sheila flinched like a wounded bird. 'It's OK,' I said, slowly reaching inside. 'This is the article I mentioned. It was with some of my father's things.'

I handed her the clipping, which she read blankly.

'It's just like you said in your letter. So What? I told you I've never seen it before.'

'I know this is difficult, Sheila but I need to understand why my mother gave it to me. Believe me, I wouldn't be here if I thought there was any other way. It's just that I have all these theories running around inside my head…'

'And what's that got to do with me? Why can't you just leave us alone?'

Writing to Sheila in the first place might have been a trick of my subconscious, but everything she and her mother had said or done since I'd arrived in Drovers Lane – the very fact she was sitting here with me now and not slumped in front of the television set at home – had convinced me beyond all doubt that she was the girl from the article. It was too early to express such an idea so brazenly, of course. It wasn't something one could easily approach head on. Which meant we had our game to play, Sheila and I.

'I realise it was a long time ago,' I said, trying to calm us both. 'I even mistook your mother for you, for goodness's sake, that's how good my memory is!' A smile flickered across her lips, but still no eye contact. 'You're the only person I could think of to ask. I know it's upsetting, but if you can remember anything about it at all, something someone might have said at school? I tried finding the original article but it was virtually impossible, so I don't even know for sure when this happened. I just need to find out if and how my father was involved.'

Finally, she turned to me with eyes as black as coal. I could still see her in there somewhere, that little girl, incomplete, frightened.

'Funny, you always wanted to be a Doctor like him,' she said.

'Really? Some people might say I went one better, a "proper Doctor".'

A knock at the window. The passenger door swung away from the car and, before I could react, Sheila being wrenched out on to the road. I leapt from my seat and ran round to the passenger side, but I only saw the lights of an oncoming lorry just in time and fell back against the bonnet as it thundered past. By then Sheila was already halfway towards the house, dragged, crying and stumbling, by her mother's determined hand. And by the time I had reached the other side of the road, Sheila had righted herself, and now they were running together, heads buried beneath an anorak, disappearing into a wall of rain.

CHAPTER SIXTEEN

I left Chiswick at a ridiculously early hour. Travelling to Aylesham each day was going to be impractical, so I packed a case and booked myself into the Abbeyford Hotel. My early departure made for a quick exit from London but put me in Canterbury just after sunrise, where there were only birds to be seen rummaging through engorged dustbins at the roadside, courtesy of a wildcat dustmen's strike. After driving around for the best part of an hour, I found a café open along the A2 packed with lorry drivers fresh from The Channel and labourers with yesterday's mortar barely dry under their fingernails. Unkempt and unshaven I blended with ease.

I had an hour or more to kill, but the minutes seemed loathe to pass, hanging mercilessly about the clock above the deep fat fryer as the headlines and heart attacks came and went, a profane banter merging with the steam and grease overhead.

At seven I headed out to Drovers Lane, but the *Golf* I'd noticed the day before was missing from outside Sheila's house and I suspected Sheila had gone missing with it. Early risers meant early workers, which meant I would have to suffer twenty-four more hours in Canterbury before I'd have a chance to tackle her again.

Out of sheer agitation, I phoned the lab. Gavin answered. He told me Erin was on a course, that Baxter had been stalking the corridors in search of me, and that 'The Man From *Quintex*' had been in touch but had left no message. I felt a jealous pinch at the thought of my much-secretaried colleagues in the institute with their telephone messages prioritised and their unwanted callers politely rebuffed. With a Nature paper under my belt, I felt I deserved a little more than Gavin, who prattled on about the latest in a series of misguided experiments I'd decided to let him run with, honestly, to keep him out of harms way while I attended to more important matters. The call did nothing to calm me. Quite the opposite, it reminded me of my petty responsibilities to the institute and to *Quintex*, and only left me more agitated by the sense of a duty-shirked – the kinds of mawkish ties I could ill-afford. And why, in particular, I had bothered to enquire after Erin, I will never know. I can only assume that despite my best efforts to push the women in my life away there was still a part of me apt to seek feminine reassurance. And now she was on my mind again, along with an absurd desire to be with her, and, perhaps more disconcertingly, to confide in her. I knew I was doing the right thing protecting her from all this, but that didn't mean it was an easy thing to do.

I even came close to calling Jane. She hadn't come home the previous evening, but by then neither of us were bothering to inform each other of our whereabouts, and I didn't think it anything unusual, those basic courtesies already lost. We had become cohabiters, unable or unwilling to champion anything but our own cause. Making contact with her would only have compounded my earlier mistake with Gavin. Best not to let sentiment mist the lens too much.

I spent the rest of the day watching a 24-hour news channel, it's stories and my fitful periods of sleep cycling endlessly, the natural disasters and the political commentary woven into the fabric of my dreams. Being awake didn't improve the order of my thinking much either, with my mind continuing to scour the broken ground of my encounter with Sheila for some shred of hope: a word, a look, any small detail I might have overlooked at the time that would help bring our dealings more swiftly to their conclusion. But there was only one aspect of the whole incident that gave even the slightest cause for optimism. She had come after me. She had followed me to the car. And that had to mean there was a part of her willing to confess.

By five the next morning I had concealed the *Megane* behind a tall hedge at the entrance to a field a few hundred yards from Drovers Lane. Slouched down in the seat for warmth and anonymity, I was still able to spot Sheila through the windscreen of her battered *Golf* shortly after six, though I allowed some distance to develop between us before daring to follow her along roads still desolate at that hour.

The plan this time was simple enough. For my interrogation to have any hope of success I knew it had to be conducted far from the mother's tug. Divide and conquer. And in a public place, somewhere Sheila would have to talk me and not cause a scene. From the outskirts of Canterbury we drove in discrete tandem to the central shopping precinct, an edifice in smeared grey. Sheila deposited the *Golf* in a small multi-storey but I avoided the intimacy of the car park and left the *Megane* on a single yellow, confident it was too early even for the wardens.

Now I was back on foot, a far more familiar mode of pursuit. I waited for Sheila to descend a gusty stairwell and then trailed her out on to the pedestrianised area where only a handful of flannelled shop assistants roamed the concourse. After a few hundred yards she turned into a gap between a shop selling crap for a pound and a shoe-repairers and we entered a less than glamorous aspect of the precinct. It was the business end of the retail trade: enough cardboard for a hundred homeless cities, skips frothing with polystyrene, and coat hangers jutting from tall plastic bins on wheels.

By a loading bay a lorry set to self-destruct was reversing nervously into place. The driver waved at Sheila and she returned the gesture. We were close. Using the lorry for cover, I watched her ascend a ramp leading to a doorway marked 'Staff Entrance' at the back of British Home Stores (of all places!). The driver started to eye me with suspicion in his side-view mirror so I rose and smiled and retraced my steps back out onto the precinct. It was going to be at least an hour before the first somnambulant shoppers arrived, and there weren't many jobs that required such an early start. Cleaner was my first guess, or shelf-stacker – both possibilities equally depressing.

Bloated by grey coffee handed cheerily down from the hatch of a burger van, my first few minutes inside BHS were spent weaving between clothing carousels in pursuit of a urinal. It was a search that led me not only to relief in the toilets but also to Sheila. Emerging to one side of the restaurant, I caught my first glimpse of her at the checkout through a line of fresh sandwiches in plastic cartons. I slid a damp tray towards the coffee machine and waited for my drink to trickle into a china cup. Sheila didn't flinch as I approached her. She tapped my order into the till and took my money without looking up. I tried catching her eye with an earnest look of reassurance, but it only seemed to strengthen her strict focus on the register. I then proceeded to make a series of gentle, but irritatingly persistent, enquiries as to the accuracy of my change, which drew impatient snorts from a group of sturdy women behind me in the queue, but had the desired effect on Sheila, who jerked her head towards a nearby table.

I barely had the time to stir my coffee before she was standing over me, hairnet in hand. Her heavy makeup barely concealed the pockmarks on her cheeks, and her hair, drawn into a tight bun behind her head, made her seem suddenly unfamiliar to me. I felt strangely despondent, as if I would have to begin all over again with this new incarnation, this other Sheila, a Sheila far more resilient than the one I had sat shivering with in my car. But perhaps this was the real Sheila, Sheila without the mother standing guard?

'Why are you following me?' she said.

'Well, for a start your mother wasn't exactly keen for me to speak to you the other day.'

'Look, this may be important for you, Daniel, but what about the rest of us? We've already had to live through it all once.'

Did she realise what she was saying? The skin between my shoulder blades felt cold with sweat.

'Why don't you sit down?' I said.

Cautiously, she pulled a chair out from under the table.

'It was you then,' I said, unable to contain myself, 'the girl from the newspaper?'

The slightest flicker of her eyes was the only answer I needed.

'It was my mother who gave me the newspaper cutting,' I said, perhaps trying to shift the focus of her resentment. It's not my fault, I was really saying; there's nothing I have to reproach myself for. I'm just here to lay the matter to rest, for all our sakes.

'Why don't you ask *her*, then?' said Sheila.

We were talking in code. I might have spared Sheila this ordeal if I'd had the courage to face up to my own mother, was what she meant.

'I don't trust her,' I said.

'But you trust me?'

Yes I do. And you, me, I hope. There's no need for anyone else to know about this, Sheila. We can keep it between ourselves.'

'Just like your mother did, you mean?'

Tears fell over her lids and cheeks onto the tabletop, and she had to dab her eyes with the cuff of her tunic like a scullery maid caught lifting the silver. I knew I had only to wait for the machinery of torment to do its work, for its silent advocates to press my case. Eventually her muffled sobs subsided and she took a long, shuddering breath.

Listening to her recount the story of that summer we spent together was like listening to the story of someone else's life. Every moment was a new revelation, and only once the words had left Sheila's lips did they begin to form some plausible part of my own history, like silt thrown up from a riverbed settling slowly back into place. It was my life, but a part I had chosen largely to forget, which meant, unknowingly, Sheila was forcing me to live, rather than relive, my past.

Being a Grammar School boy, my term finished a little later than the comprehensives, and by the time I was able to make my dash for freedom across the cornfields near our house, Sheila had already made serious headway on the treehouse. She had chosen a remarkably good spot for a girl, providing an excellent vantage point over the small copse at the edge of the largest of three fields, yet with enough foliage to ensure its secrecy from our foes, even if they were largely imaginary.

The tree had all the pre-requisites for a successful build. A little more than two feet from the ground arose the first in a series of thick branches that was almost a stump in its own right. This was the much-needed first foothold. Many of the nearby trees had suitable nodes and branches higher up that would have accommodated the house admirably, but almost all lacked this vital point of access. Of course, one had to accept that easy access for us also meant easy access for anyone else that might care to share the view and our supply of biscuits and cordial, but at our height we had little option.

By virtue of gender and age (I was thirteen, Sheila was nine) and despite my late arrival on the project, I took immediate control of both the construction and the stocking of the house. Sheila seemed marginally put out by my commandeering, but she didn't show it for long. We were mostly happy in our roles and the arrangement soon had all the comfort of a well-established hierarchy.

With the small added strength of my pale and sinewy limbs, we quickly had the main shell of the house in place, the wood and nails pilfered from every possible source: an old go-cart disassembled, my father's toolbox raided. The rest of the preparations we managed to spin out for almost a week. Sheila made curtains while I scoured the forest floor for ammunition, but eventually we had to accept that our task was complete, and we sat in our leafy tower, wallowing in success, listening to the birds gossip in the trees and to every cracked twig that might signal an impending attack from one of our many unseen adversaries.

It didn't take long for us to get bored. Our spirits, like our supplies, were soon consumed. The comics we read and re-read, and there was little going on in the fields below to distract us. We became the victims of our own meticulous attention to camouflage. Nobody knew we were there. We couldn't even rely on our parents to come looking for us, reassured, as they were then, of our safety roaming the Kent countryside for days on end. Occasionally we might have caught the odd car roof above the hedgerow on the Aylesham road, and once we watched a couple stop to picnic in one of the fields left to fallow, but it was hardly excitement.

Inevitably, we began to squabble just like all the adults did, except in that ludicrously vicious manner only children are capable of. Retreating to the corners of class and culture, we came out name-calling and spitting, and I have to admire the fact that not once can I remember Sheila crying the way other girls might have done. A stoic little creature, she put up with some pretty shitty behaviour from me, I recall. But perhaps because we were each other's only hope of company during that endless, oppressive summer, or because neither of us were keen to spend more time with our parents than was absolutely necessary, we always found a way to make up and become the best of friends again.

I looked up to find Sheila had fallen self-consciously silent, relating intimately to her coffee with that *Upstairs-Downstairs* look on her face again.

'I'm not sure what this has to do with my father.' I told her.

'I'll be late getting back for work,' she said suddenly, glancing up at the clock and edging away from the table.

I was so desperate for the truth, I wanted to grab hold of her and pin her to the chair until she told me everything. This despite my growing contention that truth is just the knowledge we possess at any one particular moment in time and not a fundamental dimension of nature. Judging by recent experience, I knew it was likely anything Sheila did tell me would only be a hypothesis, which like all good hypotheses would be verified or rejected and then, ultimately, replaced. But that didn't seem to matter to me at the time.

'Can we at least talk again, at lunch?' I said.

Her story half-told, Sheila looked resigned to divulging the remainder, and three interminable hours later she was waiting for me by the front entrance to BHS, transmogrified again, looking far younger than her forty-three years in chocolate brown trousers and tan leather jacket. Her hair had been loosed from its netting, and her lips bore a more strident application of colour. She might have smiled at me as I approached, or perhaps she was just struggling to see me against the low-set sun, a hand raised to her forehead, just as I remembered.

We walked in silence through cramped, winding streets towards the Cathedral, its imposing structure catching me unawares as we stepped into the shadow of its Western Facade. We found a bench and sat next to an elderly man who smiled patiently while a group of children agitated and screamed, and made the small dog he had on the end of a leash yelp and snap at them. A pang of distant innocence seized me.

From her bag, Sheila produced two polystyrene cups, each with a ring of cold tea in the lid. 'Perk of the job,' she smiled.

She seemed more relaxed in the open air, less confined. Was the worst over for her? Or had she merely summoned new strengths to resist me, re-evaluating her position, perhaps, and realising that there was nothing to be gained from telling me what had happened, whereas silence might be a weapon wielded in the name of revenge?

'I need you to tell me about my father?' I asked her.

She looked curiously at me. 'You seem pretty sure about all this. I mean, you find a newspaper clipping from thirty-odd years ago and suddenly it's all about me and your father.'

'I wish I could explain why I wrote you that letter. I honestly didn't know who else to ask. I guess I must have known something about what happened, but I'm still not sure what, exactly.'

She took a sip of her tea. 'Show me the clipping again.'

I gave her the – by now – much-folded and frayed slip of paper.

'It could have been anyone,' she said with no real conviction.

'Sheila, there doesn't seem much point in trying to pretend it didn't happen. You look traumatised, and I can understand why. And your mother is obviously incensed by the very sight of me. I'd have to be an idiot not to think you're the girl they're referring to. But if that's not the case, or if this really has nothing to do with my father then just say so and I'll leave you alone, I promise.'

'You never liked him much did you? Is that why you're here? Trying to get back at him because he wouldn't buy you a new train set for Christmas or something?'

It was an unexpected show of malice, the pain inside lashing out.

I shook my head. 'I don't know what to think of him, because I'm not in possession of all the facts. I can't understand why you don't just get it over with?'

'Because I'm not sure you'll be any better off knowing,' she said. 'And because you can't just come waltzing back here after all these years and expect us all to roll over.'

'Do you think I'm here for the fun of it?'

'Probably not,' she replied coolly, 'but that doesn't mean you're not looking for something that isn't there. The state of you. You look terrible.'

I suddenly felt light-headed. I thought I might need to lie down to stop from passing out. Had I eaten that morning? Was the temperature in the Cathedral grounds rising or falling? My sensations were confused. A sudden rapidity of breathing. My lips tingled.

'Are you OK?'

I nodded and tried to reassure us both that I was going to be alright by taking smaller breaths and forcing a smile. Yet, strangely, my little show of anxiety must have gone someway to weakening Sheila's resolve because she started to talk again. And though her voice was cool and indifferent – as if reading lines for which all the words required of her were their shape and timing – her eyes bore the unmistakable glaze of memory.

'We were playing in the treehouse,' she began. 'It was hot and you were being a particular prat, teasing me, being a real boy, a real teenager. And I said something back to you and it must have been pretty risky because the next thing I was running out of the treehouse and you were after me. Getting down a tree was the only thing I could do better than you, but I was in such a hurry I almost twisted my ankle. I kept going, though, and I ran off towards that little clump of trees between our wood and the road – that funny one right in the middle of the field we always used to wonder how they managed to get the combine harvester round it. You came up on me from behind and pretty much fell on top of me, sent us both flying. You had me pinned to the ground – you'd done it loads of times before – but I remember that time you were a bit more heavy-handed with it. But I reckon once you'd got me down there you didn't know what to do. The corn was digging into my back and I got loads of cuts, but there didn't seem much point me resisting, you weighed a ton compared to me. So I just lay there. And then I felt your wotsit digging into me.'

I turned to her with the blood fast-cooling in my veins.

'You started rubbing yourself up and down a bit and getting all hot and sweaty. But I didn't really mind. I sort of went along with it.'

Tears welled, the sensation of them taking me by surprise. I couldn't speak. Was this somehow my fault? Had I been too eager to blame the father for the sins of the son? I wasn't sure I wanted her to go on. It wasn't what I'd expected to hear. But this was science, I told myself. You had to face up to the data, wasn't that what I was always saying to my students? Wasn't that what Ulrich had said to me? Have the courage to see what it was trying to tell you and then use it, learn from it.

'I'm sorry,' I managed to say.

'We didn't do it or anything, if that's what you're worried about. Funny, but I can't actually remember it that well. You're supposed to aren't you? I mean, things like that, you're supposed to remember them really clearly, aren't you?'

I'd listened to everything Sheila had told me in that endearing, rambling way of hers, and yet I was still as much in the dark about what had happened as I'd ever been. I clasped my polystyrene cup as tightly as I could, shivering but transfixed.

'Anyway,' she said, 'I'm not sure we were going for long before we got interrupted. It was me heard him first, coming at us through the field, moving bloody fast as well. We both tried to keep dead still, but I knew he'd seen there was someone there. I was crapping myself. Angry farmer, I reckoned. I couldn't tell how close he was until he was right on top of me. His shadow was right there.' She put her palm to her face. 'But you'd already made a run for it by then.'

'I ran away?'

Sheila had no time for my insecurities. 'It wasn't exactly a stupid thing to do when you think about it,' she said. 'On my own, I was just a little girl mucking about in a cornfield, but with two of us there we had to be up to something. It would have been much more suspicious us being found together. And you weren't to know what would happen.'

'It was my father.'

She nodded.

'Was that when he attacked you?'

'No. He just asked me a bunch of questions, really slowly, like I was some kind of nutter or something. He kept asking me if I was 'alright', and that I didn't need to be scared. But I was scared. I didn't think you could get so scared that you threw up like they do in films. It always seemed stupid to me because I never saw anyone do it in real life, but I felt like it then.'

Where then, I wondered, had my father taken a child's life and tortured it into miserable adulthood? The surgery? Of course, where else but the place in which the powers of his profession could be most keenly wielded, the hushed discretion of the examination room.

'Was it you who threw the stone?' I asked.

Sheila started to cry again. I wanted to console her in some way, but didn't dare touch her, so I just sat there awkwardly as she pressed one tear-soaked ball of tissue after another into her coat pocket.

'It was a stupid thing to do,' she sobbed. 'I don't know why I went to the house. And when I got there I didn't have a clue what I was doing. It was just the nearest thing I could find.'

'You caused quite a stir.'

'I bet I did.' She tried to laugh, but just ended up squeezing her swollen eyes more tightly together. 'I didn't think I'd even hit the bloody house. I ran off down the road like a right yob. Some fat bloke came after me for a bit, but then he just stood there watching me, and I kept on running. I don't reckon he fancied chasing me much, looking at the size of him. I didn't mean to upset anyone.'

Why should you feel sorry, I thought? We had just buried the man that destroyed your life.

'If you don't mind me saying,' I said, 'you actually seem relatively calm about the whole thing. I would have wanted to kill him if I'd been you. I think it would have been perfectly understandable if you'd broken every window in the bloody house. You must have hated his guts.'

Her crying slowed. 'I did, once,' she said. 'But it goes away after a while. You can't keep it up for long. It wears you out. You just want to get rid of it.'

'Well, I'll hate him for both of us then. For what he did to you.'

'And to you,' she said, examining me more closely, as if searching for traces of my father in the lines of my face. As if she knew to look for something of him there.

'I'm not sure what you mean?'

'I mean, you're pretty calm yourself considering I've just told you your father was a child molester?'

I hesitated to reply, but then, from nowhere, found myself saying: 'I think I already knew.'

We walked around the Cathedral a few times, not saying very much, until the light began to fade. Then we braved the laneways again, now thrumming with heavily-laden patrons fresh from the shops, swapping bags from hand to hand, and trying to quell their rampant offspring.

'So how come you didn't go to the police?' I asked her.

'We did. Mum took me as soon as she found out.'

'But no prosecution, no court case?'

'We dropped it.'

We came to a halt, forcing shoppers to flow around us.

'Because my father paid you off?'

'My mother. He paid *her* off, not me.'

'Sorry, yes, but it can't have been much. I mean, you're still...'

'Still what?' she laughed. 'Still living in Drovers Lane? Didn't you know? We pretty much own it. Just three of the houses to begin with, but with the profit on the rent, we ended up buying most of them. Well, my mother did.'

Finally, it dawned on me. Her mother was not angry with me or with Sheila; she was angry with herself. Because she had sold her daughter. Because she had watched my father stroll the country lanes a free man, knowing he was back in The Surgery handing out vaccinations and lollipops to the brave little girls of Aylesham after all he had done to her daughter. It must have taken a certain depth of hatred to keep her family there just to spite him.

Then Sheila said the strangest thing of all. 'In a funny way your father did me a favour.'

'Jesus, I find that hard to believe!'

'I mean, with us having all those houses. I've got one a couple of doors down all to myself. You've seen my mother. Can you imagine being cooped up with her all bloody day? I don't think I'd have got away from her otherwise.'

'Two doors down is hardly getting away. Why don't you sell it and move away properly now he's dead?'

'Because they're not mine to sell, are they? They've given me a sort of freedom, but I'm still stuck here really. I can't afford a mortgage on what I earn.'

We reached the front of British Home Stores. House prices seemed a mundane note on which to end the conversation, but before I knew it, I was shaking Sheila's hand, exchanging goodbyes, and wondering whether I was ever going to see her again. She was right. I had got what I'd come for. But there seemed to be so many things left unspoken between us, our history incomplete.

As she turned to go inside I caught her by the arm and told her how sorry I was. A random token of regret, perhaps, but it felt better to say the words in the hope Sheila might tell me everything was going to be OK, and that none of this was my fault. Then she looked at me and said, 'it's not your fault,' and I didn't believe her for a moment.

CHAPTER SEVENTEEN

There is an undoubted calm in the sanctuary of knowledge, in the absence of contradiction. It had been a cruel victory to finally wring the truth from Sheila and have my father's weaknesses revealed. To find out that he was as flawed as the rest of us. An imperfect number. And I held on to this fleeting sense of satisfaction for as long as I could before the darker consequences of what Sheila had told me began to take their inevitable hold.

I sat in the *Megane* with my head drooped forward onto the steering wheel, asking myself why my mother had held on to that incriminating article for so long? Because it was the only proof she had, the only evidence that anything had ever happened to Sheila, my mother – to any of us. Without it there would only have been the echoes of their damaged minds to rely on. But she needed a more reliable record, the foundations of her loss wrought within those few sombre lines of print.

That she had kept the clipping, with its cryptic allusion to such a wretched period in our family's past, also convinced me that there were no other articles to discover. There had been no reprimand for my father, no court appearance, no charge of professional misconduct, no shame-faced media intrusions outside the cottage, because there was nothing else to report. As far as the outside world was concerned, it had begun and ended right there with that seemingly inconsequential by-line.

But what about Sheila and her mother? The mother was surely not the kind to have let the matter rest so easily. She was beyond serfdom, and the depth of her enduring rage no more obvious than if it had been my father knocking at her door the previous night and not his rain-soaked son. She had ample recourse to the law and the venom to use it. She could have sued my father for damages and made many times the money he had paid her off with. I had to suppose she'd kept her silence to protect her daughter from the anguish of a trial. No one could have walked away from such an ordeal unscathed, and she would have known the price it might have carried for them both. And what good would it have done Sheila, anyway, with so much of the harm already done?

Rising from the wheel, my head was dense with thoughts of the deal my father and Sheila's mother had struck. What must that conversation have been like? Whispers shared in the veloured snug of a public house or the still of a country lay-by at night, his guilty proposal, her grudging complicity…

Or was there another side to the story? If for no other reason than to uphold the principles of my profession, I felt bound to consider every aspect of the case against my father. Had I been too quick to blame him for what had happened, with little or no tangible evidence against him bar Sheila's tainted confession? Perhaps there were no more articles to discover because there had been no crime for anyone to answer to? There was no scandal, no trial, only the fabrication of a confused child, her pushy mother, and their blackmailing intent. The threat to my father's reputation might have been reason enough for him to go through with the payment, the mere implication of his guilt enough to destroy his reputation, his career, and, along with it, the trust of his colleagues, friends and patients. If the allegations had been made public, he would had to have relied upon people coming to the right conclusions by themselves, balancing his sober denials with the impassioned charges of a mother and child, which surely would have been too much to expect?

Viscerally, I felt this was not the case. I might have come to my conclusions with little or none of my supposed scientific objectivity, but sod objectivity, this was instinct – a far more powerful means of discrimination. And this was genetics – the warped misfiring of Nature's gun. I knew my father had done this to Sheila as surely as if I had raped her myself.

I was lucky to reach the hotel alive given my state of turmoil and my inexperience behind the wheel. Staring out over the vivid green of the hotel garden, I waited for a small kettle I had found under the television set to boil. I dissolved brown granules from a packet and gave the resulting solution every opportunity to scorch my throat by sucking it down in almost a single shot. I noticed a feint but discernable spin to the décor. Too much codeine or caffeine I supposed (I'd had a few of each that morning) and suddenly that image of my mother's face was there again, staring out from the kitchen at my father and I playing with our numbers. Something in her eyes. Something familiar but hidden. And I could see now that she wasn't looking at me. She was looking at him. And it was a look of hatred. It was a look of loathing.

Later that evening, I sat on the bed fresh from a shower, my back still damp, and a monogrammed towel half-open around my waist. Somewhere in the hotel a large scotch was being prepared at my behest, while I tried to concentrate on more practical issues of science. A series of patents would need to be filed to cover my theories on Lamarckian inheritance, for a start. The College would have to be involved (the experimental work had been conducted on their premises), and there was *Quintex* to think about too. Just how much of this did they really have a claim to? Perhaps not as much as I'd first thought, if I remembered the terms of our agreement correctly. The money they had given me was for 'blue skies research', which, to anyone that knew, meant the funding wasn't bound to any specific programme of work, which would have incurred a substantial overhead from the university. Rather, they had chosen to fund me through a 'charitable donation' and had saved themselves a few tax dollars at the same time, so there was a good chance the patent rights were still mine, or at least mine to share with the university.

Such considerations were motivated not by greed, you understand, but by pride. As an academic, one gives up all hope of financial reward; but intellectual honour, to be remembered, to become eponymous, this is our recompense. And to achieve that I knew I would have to protect my legacy both by and from the law.

I also knew I had to try and avoid linking Lamarck with our discoveries in the lab too closely. His name was not exactly a byword for credibility. I wasn't trying to be disingenuous – he had paved the way, of course – but our post-Darwinian Universe is far more complex than the one Lamarck had inhabited. Besides, I had not only extended Lamarck's, frankly, wild theory substantially, I had also given it a mechanism, and thereby the plausibility, it had so critically lacked during his lifetime. Lamarck's problem was that he had tried to apply his theory too broadly, to explain all aspects of inheritance by this one system. Whereas Mother Nature, as we constantly discover (and as Lamarck should have known) is a far more complex creature.

I hadn't even begun to contemplate the therapeutic potential my discovery might have, either. That the experiences of a lifetime could be imprinted upon the very stuff of our inheritance meant the prospects for medical intervention were immense. But there were issues. Such as, were genes susceptible to Lamarckian influence throughout the life of an organism or only at specific phases of development? And which of all the many pressures had the power to shape our future in such a way? How strong did the environmental forces have to be? Surely one couldn't have all the every-day trials and tribulations we go through shaping our genetic code? The influences that mattered would have to be substantial or repeated over time. It was nurture shaping nature.

I was ahead of myself, and thankfully the scotch arrived to slow me down. I drank it in the doorway and sent the man back for stiffer reinforcements. More work was needed to fully expound my theory, but I was tired and losing concentration. I can't remember eating either, the alcohol and the codeine granted unhindered access to my bloodstream. I lay down on the bed. My eyes closed, and suddenly I was aware of a strange medley of songs looping endlessly in my head. At first I could almost enjoy chasing the tunes as they skipped randomly from one to another. Then I realised they had been with me at other times during the day, perhaps for most of it, and when I tried blocking them out they wouldn't go away. In fact, the more I tried to silence them the louder and more incessant they became.

I opened my eyes and sat upright in the bed. I turned on the television, reached for the phone and ordered yet more alcohol. But I couldn't banish those sounds anymore than I could the vision of that girl in Chicago locked away for the pleasure of perverts, or Sheila could the memories of a summer that still haunted her. Memories I now felt very much a part of.

...

Another suitcase in another hall. A Don Black lyric, I believe, and part of the constant musical backbeat that continued to accompany me where ever I went, the songs changing but never a pause between the tracks, each one segueing remorselessly into the other.

Another suitcase in another hall. The image before me was such a terrible cliché. How long had Jane waited for me that day, I wondered, so I would come home to this sight? To the sight of her leaving?

Staring at the luggage, all I could think of was how little she had to take with her, how little she had acquired during the years we had spent together. I'm not sure we had ever been shopping as a couple. To look at those cases, she might only have been going on a week's holiday, and yet there was an unmistakable completeness to the task.

Jane rustled to life, standing at the doorway to the living room with a flattened expression. We exchanged hellos. Mine heavily affected to dampen the most anticipated of surprises; her's tinged with suppressed annoyance.

'So,' I glanced behind me, 'where are you off to? Or should I say, to whom?'

It was a clumsy bluff, but to my surprise Jane blushed, possibly the first time I had witnessed the phenomenon.

'A tour,' she announced theatrically, with even a slight toss of her hair. There was an air of re-invention about her, prideful though far short of confidence. For certain, something momentous had happened. She was sober.

'Where?' I asked absently.

She looked puzzled.

'Where are you going on tour?'

'It doesn't bother you then?'

'What do you mean?'

'You don't really give a toss about me, do you?'

A part of me wanted to tell her about my father, but I was still digesting the facts myself, his disgrace a burden I wasn't yet ready to share.

'Let's sit down for a moment,' I said, 'unless you have to go right away?'

We went into the living room.

'Why don't you stay?' I said, 'I'm sure we can live under the same roof without killing each other. I'm going to be pretty busy, anyway. I'll hardly be here.'

'You're hardly here now.'

'I have my reasons.' I said, knowing I must have sounded as though I was trying to be mysterious, but really I was feeling terribly distant from it all. I'm not sure I had the faculties left to take anything else in.

'You still look like shit,' she said.

'Thank you.'

She regarded me more thoughtfully: 'You know, I've had all this time sitting here on my own, trying to work it through in my mind, but it's only just occurred to me this very second what we've been doing all the time we've been together.'

I waited.

'We've been learning to live without each other. That's what it's all been about. And guess what, Daniel? We made it. Congratulations! It's been a hell of a fucking lesson! I hope you're as thoroughly used to being alone as I am.'

My mind was empty. The walls of the house seemed to draw in a little closer.

'I can drop you somewhere, if you like?' was all I could manage.

Jane looked incredulous, trying her best not to cry. And I hate myself now for living up to all her expectations of me, for not screaming at her or kicking her out the door or begging her to stay or...something.

A horn sounded outside, and I helped her out to the taxi, carrying the heaviest of the bags. I closed the cab door and she rolled down the window.

'You can keep the *Megane* for now,' she said. 'And you might as well give away any of my old stuff you don't want. I haven't got anywhere to put it all, anyway.'

By the time I had said, 'thank you,' she was gone.

CHAPTER EIGHTEEN

The next few days are something of a blur, the detail all but lost to me now. A compulsion to shut everything and everyone out, I recall. Not a complete corrosion of sanity – forget teetering stacks of foil-cartons or endless wine bottles unburdened. If anything, my drinking was more moderate and I became more meticulous with respect to my personal and environmental hygiene. It was, instead, a period of eerie calm. I paced and filed and searched and cleaned. I began to rein things in and pare things down. Objectives were defined and the order of their execution determined. The milk ran out, so I drank water. I progressed from fresh food to tinned. Not because I was afraid to go outside, but because mere issues of consumption were not important enough to distract me from the tasks at hand. Facing the world again would have to happen sometime, but it would be on my insistence, my terms.

Lamarck's later life had been a struggle against poverty. Bereft of his sight, he died in the care of his daughters and received a poor man's funeral. Ignominy is too often the resting place of our greatest minds, and though I didn't suffer under any such vain illusions, had I perhaps inherited something of his troubled legacy? To share his vision might also be to share his curse: to gaze deep into the storm and witness not a subdued eye but a supreme chaos. I could have forgiven myself for wishing I had never heard of the man, or that my mother had never handed me that box of family detritus.

This may all sound terribly self-pitying, but it really did feel more epiphanic at the time, some semblance of order, at last, drawn from the grey corners of that empty house. I came to believe in the responsibility I bore. That I should feel grateful – privileged even – for the chance to take his theories that one final step towards their proof. Even the music in my head seemed, finally, to have reached its coda. And the weather, which I'd started to take notice of again, was unusually clement for the season. It certainly managed to fool a few bulbs into bloom.

When I eventually left the house it was a Thursday. The students were only just back from the Christmas holidays, but already the summer exams loomed like the distant thunder of battle. The excesses of the first term had given way to a more studious air inside the Union. What few patrons there were, were of the quiet and fretful variety. More fruit-juice passed over the pale-ringed bar that evening than beer. I seemed to be the only one doing any real drinking and even I was only playing at it. I appeared to have lost the knack during my self-enforced detention at the house, the sheer effort of contemplation enough to weaken my thirst.

The discussions I could hear around me were of hopeless degree prospects and the slow turning of the academic screws. I've never heard so much whinging in all my life. Worse, a few of the students were actually attempting to revise in small, anxious knots. I was glad I had so little to do with the undergraduate curriculum. Exposed to them for too long, I might have been tempted to break into their Halls and poison the water supply.

I had no reason to expect Adam would be there. It was difficult to know quite what his attitude towards me might be. Perhaps after his mother's death, the rekindling of our friendship would have provided a welcome return to the past, to normality. Then again, I might have been the last person he wanted to see given I was pretty sure it was into his arms that Jane was running. He was probably feeling lousy about it, but I just thought it was a shame we'd lost contact, and not entirely a bad thing that he might have finally ditched Clare.

Erin's face.

I could have sworn I'd just seen Erin's face coming towards me through a crowd of Finalists. Her presence there was so absurd, so incongruous that, at first, I wouldn't let myself believe it was her. Then she was standing in front of me looking extremely nervous, reminding me of Sheila and the generic fear I seemed apt to produce in women of late. She couldn't still be thinking of New Years Eve? Surely we had managed to laugh that one off? I blanched at the thought she might know anything about Chicago.

I threw a glance into the space behind her. 'Are you on your own?'

She followed my eye towards the exit as if she was hoping to find someone there herself. Perhaps so she wouldn't have to do alone whatever it was she was there to do.

'No,' she shook her head, 'just me.'

'In that case, have you come to see me or to listen to the sound of students whining?'

She tried to smile but there appeared to be more serious matters on her mind, the kind that preclude humour.

'The guys in the lab said you come here on Thursdays.'

'Every other Thursday. Do you want a drink?'

'A beer, thanks.'

I mouthed the order towards the bar. The Union didn't usually offer table service but I knew the student on that night. I didn't want to leave Erin alone, just in case she lost her nerve for seeing the mission she was on through to its completion.

'How are you?' I said.

'Oh, I'm OK. But how are you, more importantly? You don't look great. Is everything OK? We haven't seen you around much.'

'Everything's fine, just had a lot of work to do. Trying to get a book chapter finished and sometimes it's easier working from home without you lot knocking on my door every five minutes.'

'The lab can be a bit of a zoo sometimes.'

She sat next to me, unable to hide the tentativeness in her movement, and I realised her unexpected arrival was to be my first test. I told myself that if I could keep it together with her, I could keep it together with anyone.

In practice, I lasted thirty seconds.

'Not that it isn't good to see you Erin, but did you want to speak to me about anything in particular?'

'I tried phoning,' she said. 'I was a bit worried, you know, after the business with the party, and Brian, and those bloody results...'

I felt the overwhelming urge to tell her everything. To go back to the science, to our common ground. And to impress her. To feel the radiance of her approval.

Then I told her everything.

In the end, it was almost a lecture, a mission statement. My hypothesis, the existing evidence (mostly a potted version of Lamarckian theory), our new findings, and how both of us now jointly shouldered the responsibility for seeing the proof of his theory made good. At the very least, it was a dry run for the endless explanations I might have to give in the future. Eventually, I would be obliged to tell the world of my discovery, and I would be obliged to tell it quietly and soberly, the science would be all the more acceptable for that.

I didn't stop with Lamarck either. Once I'd got going, I found myself telling her about my father, Sheila, Chicago, the whole bloody mess, I couldn't seem to stop myself. Erin listened contentedly enough, nodding occasionally with soft noises of consideration. In fact, the more I talked, the quieter she became. I assumed she was taking the time to judge the evidence for herself. I even felt proud of her. Quite right, I remember thinking, don't jump to any conclusions, take all the time in the world. We've already made our mistakes, no need to compound them with more rash speculation.

'It's terrible.' she said. 'But isn't Sheila's story the only real evidence against your father?'

'You mean, apart from my own instincts?'

'Don't you think it was a bit strange you didn't remember any of it before and yet you just happened to make contact with her?'

'Not particularly. Just because we have to start believing in Lamarck doesn't mean we have to stop believing in Freud.'

'But couldn't she...' her voice trailed.

'What?'

'Couldn't she still be making it up? She hasn't asked you for any money or anything has she?'

'Blackmail?'

'She did it before.'

'Her mother, perhaps, but even then I'm not sure you could call it blackmail. It was in my father's interests too, remember? You could just as easily say it was a bribe.'

'Sorry,' she said, 'I just think it's worth trying to corroborate her story.' (I knew where this was going.) 'But I guess your mother's the only person who can really confirm it one way or the other?'

'You're forgetting the newspaper report.'

'It only says someone claimed to have been molested; it doesn't say it was true. Why aren't there more articles? A follow up story, at the very least?'

'Because my father couldn't afford a scandal. He buried it the quickest way he could, by buying their silence. If no one talks to reporters there's no story.'

'Which makes you wonder how they got the story in the first place?'

'Don't you believe me?'

Erin pulled back a little. 'Of course I do. I'm just trying to help you work it out.'

It was me who didn't believe her, the way she was trying to talk me down like coaxing a 'jumper' from a window ledge. And why was she only interested in Sheila and my father? She'd been quick enough to challenge the validity of Sheila's story, but she had said nothing about the science, about Lamarck. I'd expected more enthusiasm, *some* enthusiasm at least, for the less salacious aspects of my predicament. Didn't she realise we were partners in all this? That my discovery was just as much hers as it was mine?

I had to remind myself that this was Erin I was being suspicious off, and try to locate some of that calm I'd been working so hard to cultivate again. What was wrong with me? She was the only person left I could even come close to calling a friend. I had to trust her to reach the right conclusions. I had to have faith in her.

She was watching me a little strangely, and I wondered if it was pity or understanding shimmering there within the small dab of light at the fringe of her iris? Her eyes widened with the briefest flicker of courage, but all she said was: 'Are you going to be alright?'

'I'm fine,' I said. 'More than fine.'

Then she moved forward on her chair, sliding her hands under her knees. 'There's going to be a meeting,' she said, 'at the institute.'

'Baxter?'

'And others. They're going to call you.'

I lifted my glass. 'A jury!'

'It's not like that. A hearing, they said. I did try to explain it to them.'

'Well, thank you for trying, but even I've been having trouble keeping up with it all. I can't expect anything more of you, Erin, you've been incredible. And my day in court's been coming. I falsified the results I showed Baxter and *Quintex*. But I did it for good reason. To buy some time. To find an explanation for the data. And I was right, wasn't I?'

Erin looked caught between what she wanted to say and what she thought I wanted to hear. She tried to convince me that the meeting Baxter was organising wasn't a witch-hunt, but since when did scientific institutions have 'hearings', and if it wasn't a witch-hunt, why all the subterfuge? We could have met over coffee and discussed it like grownups. I really had seen it all coming, part of the preparations I'd been making back at the house – planning my defence. I'd even imagined myself sitting in that cramped space outside Baxter's office, the smell of photocopy fluid thickening the air and the rattle of fingernails harrying keyboards.

The call came that evening just as Erin had warned. The voice on the line was remote and concise, and I think a little disappointed at how calmly its invitation was accepted, and that there weren't more signs of indignation from me. I refused to give it the pleasure. The next morning I dressed carefully – deliberately. I paid uncommon attention to the morning headlines coming from the *Roberts* by the toaster whilst constructing a simple breakfast I ate hardly any of. I chose to walk to the institute rather than defer to public transport, self-sufficiency being one of my few weapons against the bureaucrats – or so I imagined.

Most of the line-up Baxter had assembled was entirely predictable. Any hint of success or scandal and he could be relied upon to lick or kick the appropriate arses. And there they were, stretching away to either side of him: a grim Professorial phalanx, a thin grey line of degrees. One after the other, as my gaze slid across their blank faces, they drew their eyes up to meet mine. They did not look away. They were professionals. They had the courage, if not the taste, for battle. Some of them looked a little agitated, too, and who could blame them? After all, it can't have been a pleasant experience having to sit there in judgment over one of their own with that dry, metallic sensation creeping into their mouths like the blood of savaged prey.

Seeing Brian only infuriated me further, even though I had no fundamental basis for disliking him. He'd just always been in the wrong place at the wrong time, and an all too easy target for my frustration. I should have felt sorry for him. He wasn't going to cut it. Devious enough, perhaps, but not nearly clever enough.

It was Erin's presence, however, that disturbed me most of all. A slight, shadowy figure I had hardly noticed at first, I could sense the rise and fall of her chest, and the pulse hammering in her neck, as profoundly as if our anxieties were connected. Suddenly all my theorising appeared naïve and ill conceived. Every possible omission or inconsistency rose to the surface of my mind like a poorly ballasted corpse, the chambers of my heart paused by a hollow, hidden seizure.

I needed to sit down. I lowered myself carefully onto a fragile wooden chair that looked handpicked to belittle its incumbent or collapse beneath them like a circus prop. This wasn't the entrance I'd hoped for. I took a few deep breaths, trying to compose myself. Otherwise, I knew this trial would be over before it had begun.

From my new vantage point, I could see that the panel had been arranged not in a straight line but in a gentle curve, and I had to turn my head to see the faces at each end of the row. Directly in front of me, Baxter – sombrely dressed for once in a charcoal suit and grey tie – sat brooding in a long shadow cast by the light from a window behind. On the cluttered walls of his office hung portraits of withered alumni and bookshelves bowed by thick scientific journals like tombstones marking the death of knowledge. He lifted his head and sank back into creaking, whining upholstery, empowered by the ink blotters and the smooth expanse of mahogany that lay between us.

I smiled, while around me those gathered now wore the same look of stern bewilderment. I recalled the *Quintex* executives and thought what a poor imitation of them these fools were.

'Good morning Daniel,' said Baxter.

'Something like that,' I replied.

'I hope you don't mind, but I've asked Brian and Erin to sit in with us. We've had some illuminating discussions over the past few days.'

Baxter made a poor show of rearranging some papers in front of him, but we both knew there was nothing there he needed. He would have the speech for this one off pat.

'It's concerning the SNF project, Daniel.'

Concerning. It was the language of accusation.

'I have been made aware of a disturbing event that took place shortly before Christmas.' He glanced at the blank papers again. 'The night of your departmental Christmas party or rather the morning afterwards – Christmas Eve, in fact.'

So, Erin had told them about me following her home. All that suppressed anxiety in the Union suddenly made sense. She'd been preparing to betray me, taking her guilt out for a dry run, getting used to the idea, getting ready for the moment – for this moment – when she'd have to look me in the eye as I faced-down the indictment poised pre-orgasmically on Baxter's newly moistened lips.

I leant forward and filled a glass with water. My hand was shaking and I took my time replacing the jug again. The water passed over the cold, smooth lip of the glass and onto my own, and as the shock of Erin's treachery subsided, I found the nerve, or the stomach, to look at her again. To my surprise, I found her face inexplicably gripped by an anguished, pleading expression that instantly reignited my own worst fears. Why was she doing this? Why wasn't she trying to help me? Then her eyes narrowed, and I noticed a slow, almost imperceptible, shaking of her head from side to side, and I realised she was trying to send me a message. She was telling me to keep quiet, to say nothing.

I turned to Baxter, trying to suppress the panic tensing every fibre of every muscle that was mine to control. Baxter, too, appeared to be on the brink of a more feral exchange. Hairs were erecting beneath his crisp white shirt. I could almost hear his cuff links jangling.

'Please, Charles,' I managed to say, 'put me out of my misery.'

'I'm referring, of course, to the incident in the animal house.'

I didn't have to manufacture the staggered look of disbelief I gave him. What the hell was this?

He continued. 'In the small hours of Christmas Day, someone...' (The word stressed as if there was still an element of uncertainty in his mind as to who that someone might be). 'Someone entered the animal facility and sacrificed a colony of mice that we understand had been used as part of your aggression protocol. Would you care to comment?'

My eyes stuck to Baxter but my mind was with the signal Erin had just given me. I had to be more certain of how this was going to play out before committing myself to any kind of response.

'I'm not sure what you mean,' I said, stalling.

A new layer of smugness seemed to sweep over him. 'Daniel, we have the electronic entry-card records, which show that you entered the building at three-thirty in the morning and left approximately two hours later. The dead animals were found the next day. No one else had been in or out. You didn't exactly make it difficult for us.'

Someone had had a busy night.

I decided to play along. 'Those animals were part of my experimental programme,' I said. 'It's up to me as the PI on that project to decide what's done with them, and that includes when they should be sacrificed.'

'That's as maybe but, not withstanding the ethical implications and what the Home Office will have to say, the university has its own rules regarding this sort of thing, as you well know. What did you do it for? And why in the middle of the night? It hardly supports the legitimacy of the act.'

'They were simply no longer required. Our experiments were complete.'

'From what I gather, that's rather debatable.' Baxter glanced at Brian. 'I've seen the results of those experiments. Contradictory isn't the word.'

I smiled 'I'm sure you have, and I'm also sure you wouldn't have the faintest idea how to interpret them.'

Baxter's sighed impatiently. 'I think it's pretty obvious what they mean, Daniel. Some idiot mixed up your breeding cages.'

I placed my hands palm down onto the desk. 'I'm comfortable that possibility has been excluded. You still haven't even bothered to ask for my side of the story. You've never been even a half-arsed excuse for a scientist, Baxter. You're an egomaniac and a fucking bureaucrat and should have no part to play in the execution or interpretation of experimental biology. Frankly, I'm not even sure why I'm here wasting my breath.'

'Yes, Erin's told us about your interpretations, Daniel. Risible would be the best way to describe what we heard. You rather seem to have missed the obvious.'

A long pause followed. Everyone took the opportunity to rearrange themselves in their suddenly uncomfortable seats, or clear their suddenly irritable throats, or moisten their suddenly dry mouths with a fresh sip of water. I couldn't look at Erin. I didn't want to risk betraying her part in this. I was sure she had killed the mice, but what had she imagined she was covering up for on my behalf? Obviously, she hadn't believed a bloody word I'd told her.

Baxter spoke again. 'Your father's death must have been hard on you. We're not inhuman, Daniel. But you must also realise that there's more than your own reputation at stake here?'

'Do you think I'm not prepared for your ridicule or anyone else's?'

'Isn't the obvious explanation for what you think you saw was that the younger mice simply mimicked their parents? They learned the behaviour from them, reinforced by the usual pheremonal signals. You know the mechanisms better than anyone. And Brian shouldn't have used the mice from your old experiments to breed a new batch. I'm surprised it takes a half-arsed scientist like me to point it out.'

I managed a smile. 'Your modesty is touching, but how can their behaviour have been learnt when they were separated from their parents shortly after birth?'

'They weren't separated from their parents immediately, where they? Not until they were weaned. They had ample time to pick up the behaviour patterns you observed. The parents were conditioned according to your protocol and the pups copied them. And even if that wasn't the case, how, in God's name, did you imagine they had inherited the behaviour? Where's the mechanism, man?'

'It's Lamarckian.'

A titter rippled along the line.

'Lamarck?'

'Or a version of it. It's a potential explanation, if the selection pressure is strong enough. The offspring acquire the conditioning of their parents directly – genetically.'

An outbreak of frank laughter now. Baxter, making a particular demonstration of his of amusement, rocked back in his chair. 'You mean Giraffes lengthening their necks reaching for the higher branches, that sort of thing?'

'Not quite, Charles. You should leave the original thinking to those more capable of it. I have evidence that a similar sort of mechanism exists. I certainly do not believe the behaviour patterns we observed were simply picked up by our mice as learned experience. We can run more experiments, if needs be…'

'More experiments? What with? You slaughtered all the mice, Daniel, thousands of pounds worth. I don't think you understand the trouble this has caused.'

It was the perennial problem with peer review: one's best work is doomed to be judged by those hopelessly ill-placed to determine its merit. Who else could have understood my theory as thoroughly as I did?

I rose from my chair. 'If the university doesn't want a part of my research, all the better. I'm sure *Quintex* will be interested.'

Baxter adjusted his imaginary paperwork a final time. The smiles of The Panel vanished.

'Well, now you mention *Quintex*, there is another matter.' He gestured towards the chair and I sat down again. 'That data you presented in Chicago, I'd like to know where it came from? It certainly wasn't Erin's. I've seen her lab books. She had the same results with the antisense Brian had shown us at the Monday seminar, and yet you deliberately withheld them from *Quintex*. I've already had a conference call with Frank and his team and they want answers, as do we.'

A few of the heads lowered along the line. None of them said anything. This was a one-man show.

I brought my fist down onto the table, jerking water from the jug. 'I'll tell you one thing Charles, if you've fucked this up for me...'

'Hardly necessary when you've been doing such a good job is it Daniel?'

'I couldn't show *Quintex* the data until I was sure what it meant.'

'On the basis of one botched experiment? What on earth were you thinking, *are* you thinking? I'm sorry, but it's rather a leap from a band on a northern blot to the possibility genes are being specifically mutated within a living cell during the life of an organism as part of some adaptive process. It would have to be occurring in the gametes, for goodness sake, in the sperm and ova for it to be inheritable. You can't inherit something from a brain cell. Where's the feedback mechanism to the ovaries, the testes? It just doesn't stand up to scrutiny, Daniel. Surely you can see that?'

'Great theories never do, at first. This could be worth a stream of *Science* and *Nature* papers, and you know it. The institute could be funded for decades on the proceeds. What have we got to lose by at least considering the prospect?'

Slowly, and with visible relish, Baxter removed his glasses and leant towards me as if in confidence. Then his face seemed to ice over as he whispered, 'Our minds?'

PART TWO

CHAPTER NINETEEN

I see the window again.

There is a small crack in one corner, hastily and ineffectively repaired with what I can only assume to be a technologically enhanced form of *Sellotape*, a series of opaque strips that cross each other like a child's star. The construction is strange to me – funny even – and I think how readily dreams plunder our lives for their material; experiences selected without care, it seems, and then thrown together into badly repaired unconsciousness.

But this is not a dream. And this is not my parent's house. This is a different place altogether.

Outside, the shadows of leaves sway along a pale wall. Sunlight draws towards me across a wooden floor, set free by the parting of a cloud. I am in a low leather chair. The hide beneath my palms is smooth and cool. Next to me on a small round table is a glass of water. The water is exceptionally still. Solid. There are human sounds in the distance, the clog of steps on boards, voices I do not recognise.

Time passes. The light outside has dimmed, replaced by a brash, more unpleasant illumination that strikes out at me from the centre of a high, grey ceiling. The shadows on the wall, too, have faded. Now black tentacles of ivy slap the windowpane. A sensation of cold seeps through me, flowing from somewhere deep in the marrow. There is a blanket around my legs that I hoist up to my chest.

I sleep strangely. The night is a single dream long. Then it's light outside again. A wind gathers. It teases the wayward growth of the garden. The grass bristles and shines to it. My pulse leaps. A burst of heat to my face. Where is this place? Suddenly all I can imagine is that I might be very ill, or that I might be dying, or that I might already have died, in which case I am in a state indistinguishable from being alive. Then I remember, and settle again, and imagine how all of this would be such a disappointment to Dr Ridgeway, who has done his best to reassure me that I am very much alive, the function of my various organs having undergone intense scrutiny of late under his careful direction. He would also be less than pleased to learn that, despite his best medicative efforts, I am still prone to such fits of anxiety.

Someone else is in the room.

'How are you feeling?'

Erin is leaning against the doorframe, her palms pressed tightly into the pockets of her skinny-jeans. Her hair is much shorter and she looks older for it. I try to remember how long I've been here, but find it surprisingly difficult to do so with any degree of accuracy.

It's my voice's turn to test the room. 'I'm fine. Thanks,' I say, the early reflections returning from the walls and the floor, followed by a more complex tail of reverberation that, if analysed, would reveal the precise dimensions and construction of the chamber I find myself in (although I don't appear to be in any fit state to make such a calculation).

'And how are you?' I ask, with the feeling I have found my voice for the first time, the very concept of speech suddenly enthralling. My mouth plays with the words like boiled sweets. It is what being here has been like, a re-discovery of things.

'Never mind me,' she says. 'You look like you've just seen a ghost.'

'I keep playing the last few months over in my head.'

'That's understandable. But you're settling in OK?'

'When I woke up I thought I was still in hospital.'

Erin laughs. 'Well that's not a ridiculous idea either. I'm afraid my father's responsible for the decorating – or lack of it. These walls could do with a bit of livening up.'

'You can't expect too much from a rig-diver.'

'Very good!' She looks impressed. 'The tablets can't be making you all that muzzy then?'

'Well the size of him for a start, and those tattoos, and that general caber-tossing thing he's got going. Plus all that equipment he has in the back of his car. It wasn't hard to guess.'

Erin smiles again and looks beautiful. 'Doctor Ridgeway did say the change might make you a bit confused for a while, but you seem to being doing alright.'

'Really? Christ, my neuro-chemicals don't know whether they're coming or going. None of those quacks have a bloody clue what they're doing tinkering around up there. It's all trial and error; there's sod-all science involved.' I pause, then add, 'I think I might be a little disinhibited.'

'Yes,' she smiles again, 'I think you might be.'

Sitting here, day after day, it has sometimes been difficult not to conclude that I have been closeted in some small, long-neglected part of my mind from which there is no obvious chance of release, entombed with thoughts that cannot escape me, nor I them. I have been able to recall some of the events that have brought me here, and even something of the sensation of living them, but their connection to this moment – to every moment now – remains unclear.

Erin leaves to prepare lunch and I am on my own again. Though I have grown more accustomed to these surroundings, I still find myself questioning the possible reasons for her hospitality, and ponder the origins of that word, and how readily it applies to me because I do feel so utterly...hospitalised. Certainly, I don't imagine I have done much to warrant even the slightest gesture of affection from her and yet here I am, and here she is. She is always here. We have talked much, but not about much in particular. I am more conscious of what she omits to say as she tiptoes her way across the verbal minefields. It's as if she thinks I might become unhinged if I am exposed to whatever truths she believes it is in my best interests to keep from me. I don't press her. I content myself with the fact I'm getting to know her better. From that first embarrassed moment in the seminar room she has surprised me. Being with her feels like my only original experience, and if such wistfulness is an effect of the medication I don't want it to wear off.

Ultimately, however, the drugs are being modified in preparation for what appears to be some sort of controlled liberation. Dr Ridgeway and the numerous trainees he brings to interview me in his clinic each Wednesday (perhaps encouraged by my own professional origins) have dressed my condition up in all manner of meaningless jargon. My father's death, they propose, has precipitated an acute form of 'schizo-affective disorder' characterised by 'grandiose and mildly paranoid ideation' and a hefty dose of bipolarity thrown in for good measure. It sounds more like an excuse than a diagnosis, but if it helps them get through their day and minimises the time we have to spend together then I'm happy to let the labels stick. I can't help but laugh out loud at some of their absurd theories, though I soon learn to curb such outbursts, as they only seem to prompt an escalation in my dosage. I'm also careful not to mention my own theories on Lamarck. Raking that up again would only risk disturbing the state of mutual deception Dr Ridgeway and I have attained. It would only prolong the agony.

In the course of our sessions together, he inevitably steers me round to the subject of the codeine. Apparently, I had taken so many an antidote infusion had been required to reverse the effects, and I was to be grateful for the continued functioning of my kidneys. Dr Ridgeway speculates with an habitual lack of invention that I didn't really want to kill myself, an effort he politely terms *para-suicide*. It is a strange notion to conjure with. A *cri de coeur*, perhaps, or just another failure in a long line of failures? He asks why me why I took so many of the tablets and I tell him that I can't remember.

The receptionist at the Abbeyford had remembered me though ('Welcome back Dr Hayden'). She had even offered me my old room. It's one of the few consoling aspects of those places – their persistence. Everything was precisely as I had left it: the drinking glass on its mat next to the mirror, the beige toiletries, the towels stacked like Russian dolls on a shelf above the bath.

After my humiliating ordeal at the hands of Baxter there didn't seem any point in hanging around the institute. I didn't have the stomach to face Erin either. She'd sacrificed a whole colony of mice trying to protect me, poor thing. Apparently she had tried to tell me what she really thought about all my ideas, but clearly I wasn't listening to anyone else's opinions at the time. Even Ulrich was probably just boozed up after the *Quintex* meeting and having a great time pulling my leg. So it seemed like my only option in the face of such overwhelming ridicule was to run away to the anonymity of that hotel room.

I began by rummaging through a collection of papers I'd brought with me, an extensive search of the scientific literature I'd made during my final hours in the institute. I had every abstract and paper on the subject of Lamarckian inheritance within the last 30 years stuffed into my briefcase, anything that might support my theories. The fact it didn't amount to more than a few dozen manuscripts was something of a mixed blessing. Too many references on a given subject suggested derivation, too few a thesis without precedent. Familiarity is the basis for comfort, even in science, whereas I believed I was on to something more radical and would have been disappointed to find more.

I did speak to one person. It was a last desperate attempt to recover my self-respect, but I should have known better than to trust my self-respect to a man I hardly knew four thousand miles away. From the first hesitant words to leave his mouth it was obvious Frank had already been primed to disregard me. Baxter's handiwork, I assumed. I tried telling him how valuable my discoveries could be to *Quintex*, but I could feel the pauses growing longer and his breathing heavier until there was just a fuzz on the line, the random chatter of satellites. Even towards the end when he suggested, tentatively, that we meet, it was at an all too obviously vague point in the future and I promptly declined to save us both the embarrassment. 'I really do have to go now, Daniel,' he kept saying until I finally lost my patience and threw the phone across the room. It rebounded against the desk and came to rest at my feet. My follow-up kick lacked enthusiasm and it didn't travel any distance at all.

I went into the bathroom for a glass of water. Perhaps that was when I took the pills. I meant what I said to Ridgeway, I don't remember. All I know is that I went back into the bedroom, lay down on the bed, and started pulling the bedding over me, sheet after sheet like the endless layers of a petticoat. An immense tiredness pressed down onto my eyes, my face falling inward under the sheer weight of exhaustion.

Abiding scrupulously to the instructions on the 'Do Not Disturb' sign I had absent-mindedly left slung around the door handle, the hotel staff let me drown in my own vomit for almost twenty-four hours. I was found face down on the floor laced with my stomach's contents, apparently a not uncommon consequence of opiate ingestion. Codeine is a depressant like alcohol. My breathing was so shallow that, for a time, it was difficult for the paramedics to know if they were going to need a stretcher or a box to carry me out of there. An oxygen monitor was the only thing that convinced them they could still take me through the front entrance of the hospital and not around the back where the rubber doors and the gullied, steel gurneys await the 'DOAs'. A few more hours and I might really have been dead, instead of just feeling like it.

So far, I haven't figured out how they managed to get hold of Erin, but she was there when I woke up. I presumed she'd been contacted via the lab, but that didn't explain the fact she had actually bothered to turn up. She had no obligation to keep vigil for her possibly deranged boss of only three months. Was she the only one in the lab whose conscience had been pricked, or was she just the one unlucky enough to have answered the phone? There would have been no answer at my house, of course. Erin says she did make contact with Jane shortly after my admission, but that my ex had asked only to be kept 'up to date'. No message.

I was allowed home from the hospital four days after I went in; when the codeine had been flushed from my system and when I was no longer considered 'at risk'. This judgment appears to have been based on a faltering encounter with a young psychiatrist the day before my departure, who ran through a list of pre-prepared questions like a pollster and nodded vacantly at my answers before recording a verdict of 'No Serious Intent' in my notes. Which seemed a little harsh.

The days that immediately followed my transfer to Erin's house will likely always remain a blank, probably for the best, and probably one of few merits of the tablets the men at the hospital (they are all men, I notice) had started me on. Ironic to think that within a week of my misguided attempts at self-medication, I was rattling with prescribed psychotropics, which promote a blend of alternating clarity and fog I have had to work constantly against to piece together the events of the past year. Although, under their burgeoning influence, my memory has finally run aground on the present. They have successfully delivered me back to now.

...

I have been staying in Erin's house for almost a fortnight, and like a disfigured man confronting the horrors of his reconstruction I caught a glimpse of myself in a mirror for the first time yesterday. I've shed weight like a prize-fighter, my face has sprouted a grey beard that ages me a generation or two, and my eyes sit in dark pits on my face as if they have burrowed away from a cruel and unforgiving light.

'You don't have to tell me what happened if you don't want to.'

Erin and I are talking quietly in the front room of her father's house beneath a high ceiling like a winter sky. Erin was right; the walls are *White With a Hint of Institution*. She is curled up like a child on the window ledge, watching me closely.

'At the hotel?' I reply. 'There isn't much to tell. It was just a stupid mistake.'

'You weren't very well, that's for sure. I wish I could have done more to help.'

'I don't think I was listening to anyone much.'

She pauses. 'Did you really believe what you said in the bar, about Lamarck?'

'You can think what you like about the theory, but I still say what we stumbled across could make your career, if you have the nerve for it. Mine's buggered, but there's a genuine chance you could make a name for yourself.'

'I'm not sure what you mean?'

'The antisense. Regardless of whether it has anything to do with a Lamarckian system of inheritance or not, I really do believe we found evidence for a natural form of antisense. And there's plenty to do to try and understand its function.'

Erin just stares at me. Words seem to arrive at her lips, but they must cancel each other out because none emerge. The truth is, I don't imagine I will ever be able to divulge the full extent of my theorising to anyone, least of all her. That I might be the living proof of my own hypothesis, damned by my father's Lamarckian legacy to suffer his wretched life all over again. And that I can hardly look at Erin – at any woman – so horrified am I by how close I might have already come to fulfilling that destiny.

'You don't believe me,' I tell her.

'It's not that...'

'It's alright. I don't mind. You don't have to 'believe'. This is science. You don't have to have faith. In fact, it should be actively discouraged. You just have to want to know the truth. Look at it this way, by at least following up on the antisense you'll have the perfect chance to prove I'm wrong. If I'm insane, you'll generate the evidence to convince us both. Then you can send me back to the nuthouse.'

'Don't joke about it. We were bloody worried about you.'

Who is "we", I wonder? No one else that I know of has shown even the slightest interest in what has happened to me.

'Just think about it,' I tell her.

Erin looks unconvinced. 'I suppose there are a few additional experiments we could run,' she says. 'Except, I won't have access to the probes once I'm in the Mendes lab. And I'd need some new antibodies made, which I doubt he'll want to pay for. And I'd need you! And you're not in any state to go back to the lab, even if Baxter lets you.'

'Don't worry, I don't intend ever setting foot in the place again. Not after the way those bastards treated me.'

Erin hesitates. The words that must follow – the speech I know she's been preparing to give – do not come as easily as mere platitudes of sympathy.

'You might not see it just now,' she says, 'but your father's death and Jane leaving are pretty major life-events. If you moved house you'd have the full set! It's understandable that you might...you might lose it a little.'

I wish there was more truth to what she says. That my particular brand of nervous breakdown might have been triggered by such a commonplace emotional spasm as grief. And like a record needle skipping across the surface of my heart, the panic returns, reminding me that my sedatives are being weaned and that, at the same time, I'm becoming more tolerant of the anti-depressants Dr Ridgeway is cranking up to take their place. Certainly one of the recent adjustments to my medication has to be responsible for setting the instruments of fear to work so avidly upon me again. It actually crosses my mind that I'm being kept here in this house so that Erin can keep an eye on me, a spy for the institute or Ridgeway. I expect I will have to face many more moments like these. Paranoid breakthroughs, the Doctor calls them.

'Are you OK?' she says, visibly concerned.

'I'm just so glad that everyone's suddenly such a bloody expert on what happened to me,' I snap, 'because I'm keen to try and understand some of it myself. Like why you were there at the hospital, and why you've taken me in here, and how you got hold of my entry card? Tell me that and I'll try and figure out if I tried to top myself or not.'

She looks a little shocked, at first, and struggles to respond. But when she does it is with typical steel. 'I just don't imagine it's something that would pass you by,' she says. 'I mean, if you were really trying to kill yourself.'

'You would think not, no. But nothing seems particularly clear-cut anymore. I was probably half-pissed at the time.'

Erin's look softens again. Her face is caught in a slot of sunlight with that same expression of empathy she used on me in the Union. 'Actually, they said your blood alcohol wasn't that high.'

She slips self-consciously from the window ledge onto her stockinged feet and begins to half-skate, half-walk around the room with her head bent towards the floor. 'Anyway, you were saying something about my glittering career?'

I admire her for trying to change the subject. And yet, I do find myself contemplating her future successes and whether I'll have any part to play in them. There is some comfort in the thought that people like Erin will fare well in the world. But I wonder if she is too good for academic science, that she might be corrupted by it, somehow?

'Glittering isn't quite the term I'd use,' I say, 'But you might at least end up in a tenured position with the university instead of scrounging for money from the charities if you can get a big publication under your belt.'

'Jesus, don't try and give me the hard sell or anything. I might get star-struck!'

'You certainly won't get far if you try and pull a bloody stunt like that one in the animal house again.'

'Sorry, I just thought if I got rid of the mice maybe everyone could move on and forget about the "bloody" data.'

'No mice, no theory?'

'Naïve, but at least my heart was in the right place, even if my brain wasn't. Anyway, keeping them any longer would have broken Home Office rules. You could have used that in your defence.'

'Possibly, but it wouldn't have explained why I was so keen to adhere to Home Office policy at three o'clock in the morning, would it? And how did you get my entry card, by the way? I didn't even notice it was gone.'

Head still lowered, her eyes flash at me through swaying strands of hair. 'Hardly surprising. Have you seen the state of your office?'

Our smiles rip open into laughter. I can feel the raw sting of tears, too, and I'm glad to see Erin is distracted by the humour because I don't think it would help either of us for her to see me cry. Then I think she may already have noticed because she spins around to face the window as if alerted to something outside and I have time to lift the arm of my dressing gown and wipe the dampness away.

...

A week later and it's time for me to leave. Erin has offered to help me 'settle back in', but I decline. It will only make me feel even more like a prisoner readjusting to life on the outside. Saying goodbye on the doorstep, I realise how little I have seen of her father. A distant, gravely voice, wordless and remote, yet able to find me wherever I am in the house, is all he has been to me. Has he been avoiding me, I wonder, or me him?

On the way home the taxi stops for me to buy milk and a *Guardian*, and I try to suppose I'm just a holidaymaker heading back from the airport with my luggage stuffed into the boot and my memories screened from daylight like a roll of unprocessed film.

The *Megane* is missing from outside the house, I hope reclaimed by Jane and not by the local car-thief franchise. I pause on a broken paving stone examining the brickwork and the roofing for any signs of age that may have surfaced in my absence. But the split pointing and splintered wooden frames are just as I remember them.

Lock and key rotate in arthritic unison. The door, too, resists me, grinding slowly on the hinge, though I won't be deterred and I push on inside. Fresh shadows breach the quiet symmetry of the house. Sounds dart into the gloom like hounds unleashed. I drop my case to the floor. A shiver skewers my spine. There has been no heat in this house for sometime, and the cold – unfettered – has evolved and thickened like a mould. It is the new tenant here.

I walk to the back of the house and stare out through my reflection at the small neglected garden. It is not quite February but a surprisingly mild weekend is predicted by the newspaper. I find the whole idea of a weather report oddly reassuring.

The phone rings but I let it cry itself to sleep again. The medication has its advantages, like sleep, which I do frequently, except it's not of a satisfying kind. It is superficial. Cloned. I skim the surface of sleep. Awake is not completely awake either, just a more tactile form of dream. And in the many hours I spend drifting between these hypnotic poles, I pace the house trying to find my bearings again. I can't remember ever having had so much time to take in these surroundings before, and in so much detail. Living with Jane was always too much of a distraction, avoiding her or finding her, engineering silence or disagreement. The house is humming with our history and I almost feel sorry for having abandoned it for so long.

Inevitably I am drawn to the study. Tipping the contents of the shoebox on to the desk, I search for the cutting from *The*

Gazette but, of course, it isn't there. The only tangible evidence of my father's crime has been lost somewhere along the way, and now there are only these dumb photographs left to shuffle through. Without the article there to distract me, my concentration focuses more readily on them than it has before. Might there be more here to discover? Or had my mother put them there merely to provide some sort of 'cover' for the thing that really mattered? To make sure I was far enough away from the house before I found the article, when it would be too late to go back and question her?

In the photographs my face has been captured at an age before I had learnt to avoid the lens. There is a picture of my father, his sister and Aunt Beatrice on a seafront. My mother is there, too, and Uncle George, and me, a small pale bundle cradled in matchstick arms, all of us frozen on a promenade somewhere in some other time. Everyone's hair has been *Brylcreemed* or lacquered into frightening rigidity, and it is only my wayward curls that belie the prospect we have been embalmed and preserved for posterity. The pictures slide one over the next, faces at tables, group-shots at weddings, tatty churches, and tatty front doors. Someone else's past, it seems to me. Someone else's jumble.

My sifting pauses at a photograph from a cousin's birthday party, and not one I have taken any notice of before. Something about the scene jars. The subjects are familiar enough – Beatrice, Mother, Father and Uncle George in a crowd, all beaming and glasses raised – but my stomach tightens at the sight of something missing, or perhaps something that shouldn't be there.

Downstairs, the phone is calling again. Erin's voice follows on the answering machine offering to meet me for a drink. She doesn't think I can be left alone. The hint of social worker in her voice riles me, even though I know it shouldn't, so I just listen, ear cocked, from the landing as the echoes of her voice implore me to save her from a tedious day running assays in the lab.

The tape-spool locks then rewinds itself. The photograph stares up at me. It won't leave me alone. And suddenly I realise why those young, blanched faces are bothering me so much. It's because they make it possible that everything I have come to believe about my father is wrong.

CHAPTER TWENTY

Erin leaves her father's *Range Rover* out in the laneway, aware of the narrow drive she'd have to navigate, and that she is no more used to driving than I am, let alone driving this monstrosity of an environmental hazard her father calls a car.

We spend an age shivering outside the door to my mother's house, wondering if anyone inside has heard the knock or, indeed, if there is anyone in there at all. But then the door peels open and there she is, peering out into the daylight like a stowaway, so slight and pale her features are like watermarks on the canvas of her face. As I introduce her to Erin, her eyes sweep us up and down. She has every reason to be curious, though her look might be more one of resignation, as if she already knows why we are here. Her gaze rises to meet mine and I sense the knowledge that all the things she might have wanted for me, all the things any mother would want for their sons and daughters, have always been beyond her reach. History has been against us.

The three of us move quietly into the darkness of the living room. No fire has been lit and it is no warmer here than on the doorstep. Erin and I keep our coats on and yet my mother, despite her obvious vulnerability, shows no sign of feeling the cold the way a ghost mightn't. Everything in here is just as it ever was, a tribute to my mother's diligent housekeeping and the stifling quiescence she works so hard to preserve. Even as we enter, she is placing the china figurine of a milkmaid back into some predetermined position, and

I try to imagine what, amidst the intense stillness of the house, could possibly have disturbed it.

I offer Erin a place next to me on the sofa, while my mother – order restored – stands by the window and stares outside as if she barely knows we are here.

'You've spoken to Sheila.' she says without turning.

'How did you know?' I reply. A stupid question, and one to which I immediately know the answer.

'Her mother called me,' she confirms. 'Wanted to come round here, though I managed to talk her out of it. Good God, the woman has a filthy mouth! She wanted to know what you were up to knocking at her door in the small hours and following her daughter to work.'

I have no intention of defending myself to my mother, nor to Sheila's.

'Sheila told me about the business with father,' I tell her and instantly regret the phrasing. It was more than 'business'.

My mother's eyes move purposefully to find me. But they do not defend, they acknowledge. 'And what exactly did she tell you?'

'That he molested her.'

'That is what she believes.'

'Is there any reason to doubt her story?'

Erin shifts on the sofa and mouths something about waiting outside.

'It's OK,' I whisper. 'It's fine.'

My mother has heard. 'Oh, if Daniel says it's fine with him, then it's fine with me, dear.' She pauses to catch a tear with a fingertip. 'Your father made me promise, Daniel. He made me swear to it.'

'And now he's dead,' I reply. 'And I assume – if that shoebox is anything to go by – you're as keen as I am this doesn't screw up our lives any more than it already has? So why don't we finish it here and now?'

My mother sniffs and twists away towards the fireplace, fumbling idly with her sleeve in search of a handkerchief like a hapless magician. Eventually, she sweeps the tears away with the back of her hand as if they are an every-day nuisance she has become inured to. There is a part of me that wants to apologise for the way I've treated her in the past, even though I couldn't have known what she was going through. But if she helped to cover up Sheila's abuse then she is as guilty as the rest of them. And if she had faced up to the truth at the time she might have saved us the prolonged agony of the past twenty-odd years.

She settles into an armchair like an autumn leaf. 'I wish I hadn't given you that bloody box,' she says, tugging the hem of her skirt down over her knee. 'I've already broken my promise. But I wanted you to know what it's been like for me all these years.'

'It was the right thing to do,' I say.

'I'm human, Daniel, that's all. I was tired of defending them, tired of trying to do the right thing for other people. You can't expect someone to give up their whole life for something like that. Because of one thing that happened so long ago. Let it be someone else's problem for a change.'

My mother doesn't try to hold back the tears any longer. Her arms fall loosely back from her shoulders, and her face lifts up to the ceiling as if offering herself to unseen Gods. Then her body begins to jerk and buckle with violent sobs as if suddenly possessed by those same avenging spirits.

Erin rests a consoling arm across my mother's shoulders and shoots me a stern look. 'Maybe we should leave it for now?' she says.

'You don't understand, she said "them", didn't you mother, "defending *them*"? Because we're not just talking about my father anymore, are we?'

My mother's eyes, swollen and red, blink falteringly open. Her crying relents, the heaves declining into a series of small gasps for air.

'We were just trying to do what was best,' she manages.

'But who are you really protecting, and, more importantly, why after what happened?'

'I loved your father, Daniel. And I believed him, of course I did. Why should I have had any reason to doubt him? Paying the mother off was something he and George cooked up together. We certainly didn't have the money, that's for sure. And having it drag on any longer wasn't going to do anyone any good. Even I could see that.'

'Have you even spoken to Sheila? Because if you had you would have known she was telling the truth. She was raped, for God's sake! And that makes you as guilty as they are. She was a bright girl at school, and now she's a shop assistant living next to that witch of a mother. It's almost the worst thing that could have happened to her, being trapped there like that.'

My mother shakes her head. 'I just don't know anymore, Daniel. I honestly don't know. George and your father were convinced it was all a pack of lies. And I could just imagine the mother putting Sheila up to it, the way they lived. And I did it for you too, you know? We'd never have survived the scandal.'

She reaches out to me with a tenuous, white hand. The gesture seems odd, out of character, and instinctively I draw back from it, forcing her to lean further forward until she stumbles onto her knees in front of me, knocking an antique table over in the process. Something skitters onto the carpet. My mother lunges for it, but my hand is quicker, and I snatch a small blue address book from the floor. Leafing through the pages, I recognise at once the tiny loops and curls of my mother's grammar school handwriting, every line a subtly different colour of ink like so many moods or states of mind.

Erin is helping her back up onto the chair. I wave the book in my mother's face. 'Is it in here?'

Her features are now cast in stone, though this outward show of defiance belies an inner satisfaction I can see thickening the creases around her eyes, her conscience appeased by these sleights of hand, these contrivances she uses to convince herself she has kept her misguided promises to the past.

...

Sheila is clearing pale crockery smeared with ketchup from a table close to the checkout. She startles as I approach and, without looking up, lets the plates clank down on to the melamine, and makes a beeline for the kitchens. Erin is still somewhere on the stairwell behind me, and I am alone when I catch hold of Sheila's apron and pull her back through the swing doors, inches shy of sanctuary.

She takes a sharp breath as if preparing to shout, and I have to talk quickly. 'Just one question, I promise.'

'Until the next time, you mean.'

'No. I promise. One question, and then you can tell me to bugger off.'

'Why are you torturing me? I told you everything you wanted to know. How long is this going to go on, Daniel?'

She tugs the uniform free of my hand, or, rather, I allow it to slip because she knows I won't leaver her alone until this is done. Behind us, there are unwelcome looks coming from the staff and the diners.

'Is there somewhere else we can talk?' I ask her.

'For fuck's sake,' she sighs, pushing the door open with obvious reluctance.

Erin is now standing by the tills, and I raise a hand telling her to stay where she is as I follow Sheila into the Kitchens. We weave through a maze of sinks and stoves and precariously stacked pots. Around us, tall white hats tilt and sweaty faces gawp. We reach a door that is half-glass, half-wood. Inside are changing rooms, the floor littered with discarded uniforms and hairnets. Home territory.

Sheila closes the door behind us and starts to scream where she left off. 'What the hell is it with you? You're going to drive me nuts!'

'Where did my father rape you?'

'What has that got to do with anything?'

'Just believe that it has. It wasn't at The Surgery was it?'

Her hand moves quickly to her mouth where she starts to chew at the edge of a ragged nail on which only patches of a dark polish remain. Caught in the final throes of resistance, she kicks a pile of clothes around the floor then puts a dent in one of the metal lockers with the toe of her shoe.

'It was a house-call,' she says.

I had always assumed it was at The Surgery, but he had been there in the house, right under her mother's nose.

'And who telephoned the surgery?' I asked her, 'Was it you or your mother?'

Sheila looks perplexed. By all her instincts, it must seem like there's no obvious reason not to divulge any of the apparently trivial details I'm pressing her for. Yet, it must also feel rather too easy just to hand over the information without knowing what I'm going to do with it.

'*I* did,' she says, defiantly. 'I phoned the Doctor's, so bloody what?'

The next question is already waiting, primed, on my breath. 'And was the visit during surgery hours?'

Sheila sits down on a slatted wooden bench and, without any further prompting from me, allows the memories of that day to return again.

Her mother had been very ill with vomiting and diarrhoea. Confined to her bed, she had kept very little down for the past three days. It was Sheila who had made the call to the surgery. My father was already out on his afternoon rounds, but knowing he lived only moments from Sheila's house, the Receptionist logically suggested that he made the house call in the evening. Sheila then recounts the one small deviation from practice procedure that supports my new theory. The over-burdened Receptionist, perhaps unaware of the age of the caller, gave Sheila our home phone number. There were no mobile phones, of course, so Sheila had to phone and leave a message with my mother asking my father to come round when he got in. Sheila did as she was told and called the house immediately, but was surprised to find herself arranging a time for the house-call with a man, and could only assume that my father had returned home early from his calls.

Only I am certain that man was not my father.

It was also Sheila who let him into the house. He took his time, she remembers, as he made his way along the hallway, taking everything in, getting familiar with the place, which struck me as strange because surely my father must have visited the house before? Another oddity: Sheila is to be examined first before her mother. The Doctor must understand how the virus (for it is almost certainly a virus that has her mother lurching from bedclothes to bathroom) has been transmitted. Sheila tells him how well she feels, but it seems to make no difference. You can carry the bug without the sickness, he says, and most infections come from children. (Sheila has heard her mother blame a take-away with no mention that it might be her fault.) There are signs, too, he goes on, signs that must be looked for, clues to the diagnosis that can only be detected upon close examination.

The rules of childhood could offer her nothing. It's what adults did. They made you do things you didn't want to do, his request no more unusual than any of the other pointless curtailments of freedom they imposed upon her. And Sheila was already old enough to know, from experience, that a Doctor's administrations were often accompanied by pain. So wasn't it perfectly reasonable that she should be checked for signs of her mother's condition in all those same places? The places that troubled her mother so much?

His voice was quiet and calm – like a vicar, she says – just as she, too, had to be quiet and not disturb her mother snoring away in the bedroom upstairs. It wasn't going to hurt. And it would make everything better. What Sheila had done to make her mother so unwell would now be undone. She would be forgiven.

No one could listen to what Sheila now tells me – in tones so cold and dead they stop my heart – and not experience the full horror of what was done to her, nor be in full knowledge of the unspeakable theft that took place that night. Countless times I try to tell her that she doesn't have to go on, but she will not relent. She has to finish. Her hands won't keep still, but her eyes stare purposefully ahead as she relives those desperate minutes in such appalling detail it is my own gaze, and not Sheila's, that is forced to fall in shame.

And when it is over, and we have sat quietly together listening to her colleagues shouting and joking in the kitchens beyond the locker room door, it is time for me to tell Sheila what I know of that night. That the man who abused her was not my father. That she has been wrong about him – we both have.

She doesn't respond immediately, but just shakes her head slowly from side to side. Then she turns to me suddenly, heaving the back of her hand into the side of my face. My nose stings and bloodies, my left eye is blinded, and a new watery vision of the locker room emerges in which Sheila is standing above me, screaming hoarsely and threatening me with her fist.

'You bastard! You put me through all this just so you could get your dad off the hook? It was your father, Daniel. Your dirty, child molesting bloody father who raped me. He ruined my life. He ruined my mother's life. He ruined all of our lives. Now it makes sense, all this digging around trying to find some way to convince yourself it wasn't him who did it. Well, it was him. I'd know him a fucking mile off. Pervert. I'd seen him before, looking at me funny, eyeing me up. You think I'd get something like that wrong? You think I'd make it up?'

She slaps me again, harder. Anger wrings the tears from her, the full force of her shameful rage at last unleashed. 'Look at me, for fuck's sake! Look at me!'

I've had this coming. Rising from the bench, I start to back away from her.

'I'm a wreck!' she shrieks. 'I haven't ever been with a man. Did you know that? Good fucking job he's dead and buried or, you're right, I'd have killed him myself.'

Sheila drops down on to the bench and covers her face with her hands.

I reach into my pocket and hold the photograph out in front of her. 'You need to look at this.'

For a long time she doesn't move but goes on crying between her fingers. Then, slowly, her hands fall away and I watch as her face gathers and twists like paper burning in a fire. 'What the fuck is this? What are you trying to do to me? I swear I'll call the bloody police if you don't leave me alone right now!'

'Please, Sheila, look at the faces. Look at them carefully. Do you see the man who raped you?'

She snatches the photograph from my hand and in a few brisk strokes reduces it to a flurry of white flakes that flutter down onto the linoleum.

'There's nothing you can do about it, Daniel. You can't argue your way out of it. The only reason we stay around here is to make your family sick at the sight of us. To remind them, just like we get reminded every time we look at each other. Can you imagine how that feels? If my mother hadn't been ill. If she'd made the phone call to the surgery. If she'd come to the door instead of me?'

They still lived in those dreadful houses. They had taken my father's money and punished him with it, the Lane a scar on the landscape, a reminder of the damage done.

'Sheila, if you'd just listen. I promise you we've both been wrong.'

A warm gob of saliva lands on my face, an acid burn that stings far more than any fist. And by the time I have wiped the back of my hand across my cheek the bench has been kicked aside and the door has been slammed shut behind me.

CHAPTER TWENTY-ONE

There is a number and four letters by his name. But numbers and letters are of no use to me; it's the man himself I need. I don't wait to get home either. In a garish Internet café full of purple computers and steel furniture I shrug off the disapproving looks from the cyber-waiters, pay my fee and install myself at a terminal. Keying the four letters from my mother's address book into a search engine produces a ludicrous number of hits, but it's only a couple of false trails before I find what I'm looking for.

CPLS. I might have guessed.

Then I dial the number.

'Psychiatric Liaison, how can I help?'

The voice is inane and breezy, as if its optimistic tones are an auger to the therapy Camden Psychiatric Liaison Services might offer their prospective clients. I give the woman my uncle's name and it is explained to me in a series of well-rehearsed phrases that no personal information can be given out over the telephone without prior written consent from the 'client'. The suggestion I then offer (that my purpose in calling might constitute a genuine emergency concerning a death in the family) only draws the reply that there are no exceptions to the 'no details over the phone' rule, but that, in such circumstances, my contact details might be forwarded to the client for him or her to get in touch with me at their convenience. I consider there is little to lose in declaring my interest in Uncle George. It might even help to flush him out. 'Some fat bloke standing in front of the driveway,' Sheila had said, and her words are with me as my name and telephone number return in bored echoes from the other end of the line.

Camden is dingy and littered with strays and Goths. The old, the young and the vagrant are united in streets I once found so exciting as a student, but which now seem threatening and claustrophobic. It is perfectly disorganised. Stalls of cheap black clothes and Doctor Marten's boots, record shops that still sell records and shabby brown pubs jammed with generationless oddities bound by a love of stale smoke and facial hair. That my uncle should exist here is entirely conceivable. My head is constantly turning, seeing him over and over again, those dropped shoulders and the loping walk. But they are all ghosts. And like a tightrope walker suddenly aware of the height below, the seemingly irrefutable logic that has brought me here evaporates. The crowd closes in. Cars rear up at me. The sounds and screams of the market merge cacophonously. Tremulous and faint, I plough into an Italian coffee house, anything to get off the street. I need to focus, literally. My eyes have fogged. I widen them and force my lids to pat the moisture away. Then I stare at the mouths and faces around me, studying the people, trying to reassure myself that we are all really here and that this isn't just some figment of my imagination.

Thankfully, the sniggering tourists and snide locals perform perfectly to type. Their worn faces and shrill laughter bring me back again, and I remember that there is nowhere else I could possibly be at this moment. I am compelled to be here. This is my last chance.

My gaze slides off the residents of the café and over to the other side of the road. While I've been sitting here, men have been skulking in and out of a green doorway opposite, the door part of what looks like a shop front but without any obvious shop behind it. It's the place I've been looking for. A new plan materialises. I throw down change and head out across the street dodging stagnant traffic.

But it's only in the third of the bookmakers I go into that I finally summon the courage to speak to someone and discover (by virtue of what will become a familiar litany) that although everyone has heard of Uncle George (some even speak of him with unquestionable affection), none of them seem to know where he is with any useful degree of precision, except that he is not...here. This, the seventh of them in as many blocks (their density is a revelation), lies at the more unsavoury end of the turf accountant spectrum, with its smoky, speak-easy air.

I scan dry, saggy faces looking for the man most at home. The man least interested in the racetrack. The man most used to losing. He is slight and thin, and wearing a waistcoat and jacket, propped against the wall like a broom handle with a newspaper tucked under one arm. He pays no attention to the TV screens, all his efforts clearly focused on a dwindling cigarette he has wedged between sepia fingers. A betting slip peers from his top pocket like a fop's handkerchief. Indeed, he has the vague look of a fallen aristocrat: an angular jaw, the eyes a faded blue, his fair hair tied back into a short ponytail in a nod to modernity, perhaps, or rebelliousness. He does not stir, even as I approach. The corner of his eye must surely have caught me but it seems oblivious to anything but the nicotine-laden stub of his fag.

'I'm looking for George Hayden,' I say. 'I'm his nephew. Do you know where he is?'

The man doesn't look up but continues, vainly, to relight his cigarette.

'Are you now?' His well-spoken words tumble down into cupped hands, which then part to relinquish a thin veil of smoke.

He shakes a match vigorously, observing me through narrowed eyes. He's used to people leaving him alone. He knows my uncle; his indifference acknowledges as much. He is trying too hard not to show his annoyance. I've caught him with his guard down, forced him to give away something he was not meant to give away. And as we size each other up, I know I've already convinced him that I'm not going anywhere without answers. I lean back against the wall to watch the screens, waiting for him to tell me things, and pondering the similarities between gambling and genetics.

'Are you with Harvey's lot? You look the sort,' he says, eventually. The voice is laconic, the vowels rounded, all part of the air of disinterest he is trying to convey.

'I don't know who Harvey is,' I reply. 'I really am his nephew. I just want a word with him.'

'Doesn't everyone. But I'm afraid you telling me you're his Nephew is one thing; my believing you is another.'

When I open my wallet to show him my university ID, he recoils as if they might be police credentials I'm flashing. Then he tries to conceal his discomposure by studying my faded mugshot far too closely, before returning to his cigarette, by now no more than a puff of smoke in his hand.

'As you can see, we share the same surname.' I tell him.

'I can read. What are you, a lecturer?'

'Amongst other things.'

A smile. 'You won't find Georgey in any of these places.'

I sigh. 'I'm sure it won't surprise you to hear that you're not the first person to say that to me today. Everyone seems to know him, and I know he likes a flutter,' (I'm hoping the vernacular will surmount the man's inscrutability), 'but no one seems able tell me where he is.'

'Probably because none of them know. There are plenty of people who'd like to find Georgey. The problem is they generally find it difficult to leave him alone when they do. Ironic, considering none of these arseholes will have him back.' He scowls towards the cashier's desk and a young woman looks away. I picture some awful display of violence: another poor loser threatening her and scaring the punters.

'Bad debts?' I ask.

'Hardly!' The man coughs too long and too hard for an affectation.

'So, do you know where I can find him? It's a family matter.'

The man checks me, then his watch. 'You can come with me, if you like. I'm not sure if he'll be there, but I'm heading that way. This is a waste of fucking time, that's for sure.'

He tosses betting slips to the floor. No matter the suspicions I might have of this man and his motives, I have no choice but to do as he suggests. His *Racing Post* concealed in a rolled up copy of *The Times*, he picks his way through the expanding and increasingly intransigent crowd while I follow less adroitly.

Out on Camden Market, the business of the day has ended. Corrugated lids droop down over the glazed eyes of curious outlets. Crates sit detonated at the curbside. Plastic bags tumble in the gutter. The crowds have vanished like the balloon's gone up, and only a few persistent foreigners linger, pushing perfume and fluorescent toys. Down a more residential-looking side street we stop, sooner than I expect, at an innocuous brick building, a warehouse hemmed between two quite fashionable Edwardian semis. There is no obvious sign to indicate the activity within, though it isn't hard to guess. Beyond a shuddering iron door a large, loft-like space appears. There are blackboards nailed along one of its otherwise bare walls, while gruff men clinging to beer cans litter the concrete floor ogling two oversized televisions: one for the *Teletext*, one for the action.

'Snooty!'

'Terence!'

A stout man in a black leather jacket pulls away from a group of stout men. An even covering of white bristle leaves no distinction between his beard and the rest of his head. A T-shirt drapes his potbelly like a butcher's awning, which feels appropriate because, like everyone I've encountered today, he inspects me cautiously like I'm green meat.

'Who's your friend?'

'He's looking for Georgey.'

'Fucking hell, Snoot.'

'I'm his Nephew.' I say, and am ignored. I decide to let 'Snooty' do the talking. All I can think of is *Lord Snooty* from *The Dandy* comics.

'He's OK,' says Snooty.

'What is he, one of your lot?'

Snooty raises an eyebrow. 'God, no!'

Terry looks about him. 'We're expecting him any minute.'

'Thanks.' I say, and they both look at me as if questioning what it is I have to be thankful for.

'You can sit over there,' says Terry indicating two institutionally uncomfortable chairs. Sitting, I can appreciate why everyone else is not.

At the end of another race (emaciated dogs hopelessly pursuing a ball of fur around an oval dirt track) the men congregate next to one of the boards, groaning and laughing and exchanging fifties and twenties. It all seems unnecessarily clandestine. Men are so keen to generate the allusion of mischief where there is none. As if the world outside could give a damn about how they chose to lose their money; and this despite the fact that, for most of us, resisting such urges is just a side-effect of regular employment. Enough time on our hands and we'd all be addicts.

Transactions complete, the men return to their posts to keep watch over their on-screen investments. No one is keen to have anything to do with me, and I'm beginning to regret not having Erin here. I told her I was going back to apologise to my mother. Something I needed to do alone, I said, and a welcome ruse, apparently, because Erin looked positively relieved to be excluded from any potential run-ins at the cottage.

But I was right not to bring her along. There is a distinct element of danger here, and no way of knowing how all this is going to pan out. I've hardly considered the fact Uncle George is a man in need of psychiatric attention. Who knows what he is capable of? And yet, bizarrely, he has a following here. These men obviously hold him in high esteem, and the betting people of Camden have done their best to keep his movements a secret from me all day. And though I've no doubt what I'm about to confront him with will strike his name from a few Christmas card lists, I find it hard to reconcile his high-standing within this, albeit shady, community with the image I have of him as a bumbling tramp living in his car.

As I sit listening to the monotonous racing commentary and the vulgar words of encouragement from the floor, another vision of childhood seeps into my consciousness. My father has arrived home from work in a tentative mood, the way he places his jacket carefully over the banister and sets his car keys delicately down onto the hallway table. Uncharacteristically soft cries carry into the kitchen and up the stairs, seeking out my mother. She is hiding in her bedroom. I'm not long home from school myself and she's been up there since my return. From my listening-post in the dining room, poring over the grids and arcs of my geometry homework I hope my father will come home to catch me doing, I have heard her rearranging things up there. I think at one point she has been crying, but it may just have been a bed creaking or a tap turning and I don't feel the need to check in on her, as I sometimes do.

As my father climbs the stairs, his voice changes from a searching to a more insistent tone. His footsteps deaden and slow until I sense he is hovering outside my bedroom door just a short distance above where I am sitting frozen to my chair. He continues to repeat my mother's name over and over again as if the echoes will sound out her location. He edges across the landing, each floorboard with its own distinctive voice I have studied and committed to memory. Their unique whines and creaks mark his progress towards my parent's bedroom as precisely as if I were there walking beside him.

A handle turns. A loud crack as the door and the frame move apart. A mattress groans, relinquishing my mother, and she rises to him with words I cannot make out except for their unmistakably vicious tone.

Silence follows. It hurts my ears to listen. Then voices re-emerge, bickering breathlessly, and now I don't want to listen.

The next day my father is gone before I wake. I dash about the house ill-prepared for a school trip to the Lake District, partly because I am late rising and partly because my mother hasn't kept up with the Laundry. I have to pack unwashed and un-ironed clothes, but I don't mention it because she seems in such a fragile mood I think she might break like a dropped ornament if any criticism is levelled against her.

It is a trip Sheila was meant to be on. Absent through illness, we are told, though the gossip, I recall now, was of something more intriguing. We shiver on mountains, half-drown in lakes, and by the time I return home, my parents have transformed themselves into the remotest of strangers. There must have been other conversations – conversations they have successfully shielded me from – reserved for the dead of night, perhaps (they never seemed to go anywhere) or conducted via their ever-hardening stares, but nothing I was ever privy too.

The door of the warehouse rattles and screeches. I turn towards the sound and am so shocked by what I see that I'm suddenly grateful for the support of a chair. My father is standing in front of me, a figure etched in sunlight, a long shadow cast in front of him that stretches to my feet. This proof, this final revelation, is so disturbing, so confounds all my senses, that my bones feel prone to shatter.

But my heart is a beat ahead of my brain. As the outline of my father steps forward, the bare white lights that swing from the rafters draw new dimensions from the angles of his face. This George is a very different George from the one of my childhood or my father's funeral. The ungainly beard has gone and that suit looks brand new – a crisp, grey pinstripe no-less, white shirt and red bowtie. A raincoat, drab olive with blackened edges clawed by London-soiled fingers, exaggerates the size of him. His eyes challenge me behind sleek spectacles. And at his side – in strange contrast, and in faint testimony to his former-self – a moth-eaten Labrador nudges his leg constantly as if to reassure itself of its master's abiding presence.

'Daniel, my boy!'

Even his voice has changed, deeper, more resonant. Operatic. It cleaves the bricks and mortar. Striding in my direction, he is unrecognisable in both purpose and energy. Who is this man?

Snooty withdraws into the shadows at the sight of them, more wary of my uncle, I suspect, than the dog, even though the latter carries with it the distinct smell of stale laundry. Snooty looks the type to scare easily. While I, on the other hand, have no trouble girding myself.

'How are you?' he bellows. 'And how's your mother?'

'We're both fine,' I reply coldly.

'Thank God,' he says and makes a show of relief, yet he must sense the strain in my every syllable. 'I did wonder if she'd be OK, you know, after the funeral.'

'I'd like to talk to you,' I say. 'Alone.'

It's more a threat than a request, but my uncle seems oblivious. In the shadow of his eyes I search for any hint of discomfort, of culpability, but sense only a terrible excitement barely restrained. He does not appear in the least concerned by my presence here.

'So what brings you this way?' he says with what now seems offensive good humour.

'We need to go somewhere private,' I insist.

My uncle checks himself. 'Course we can, Daniel. Course we can. I just need to sort a couple of things out with these lot first, if that's alright?'

He signals to the men and they gather round him, hanging on to his every whispered word, and nodding gratefully as he pulls tenners from a roll the size of a sleeping bag. These are the 'Runners', placing the bets he is unable to place because he is too successful, because he is a winner. And like all those who win too often or too easily, he has quickly made his way onto the bookies' blacklists. But with the bets divided into more modest sums, placed by this team of anonymous punters, they will be accepted without suspicion. And if they win (and by the way the men crowd round him like chicks snatching food from a hen's beak, they do so with frequency) they will take their, no doubt, sizeable cut of the proceeds.

Snooty glances over at me. 'You have to hand it to him. When he's up, he really is up there. There's no stopping him when he's like this.'

I can't take my eyes off my uncle, who now looks more like he did in the photograph: slimmer, kempt, beardless. The likeness to my father is demonic. How could a ten-year-old girl have known the difference? Sheila had called for a Doctor, and a Doctor had come, with his stethoscope and his reassuring patter. Why wouldn't she have believed it was my father, even if she had seen him before, they were so alike? I watch as he doles out the cash thinking he should enjoy this last moment smiling and surrounded by friends while he is still ignorant of the indictments I harbor.

The huddle breaks. George gestures to the doorway then sets about untangling a fraying leash from around his legs. There is a short whimper from the Dog (Rufus, I assume) as the lead is handed over to a reluctant looking accomplice.

Outside, the sun has fallen behind the rooftops. The Camden night shift is about to clock on and already a few early drinkers amble down tributaries to what will soon become a river of humanity that will flood the High Street and swell the drinking-dens and doorways.

Keen to walk at a faster pace than George's shuffling gait will allow, I have to hang back for him to catch up.

'Good bit of detective work you did tracking me down,' he says, moving breathlessly alongside.

'I found the number at my mother's.'

He looks at me quizzically.

'CPLS?' I say.

'Ah! I was going to say you would have had a tough time getting me on the phone, seeing as I haven't got one,' he chuckles.

'Too many people trying to track you down?'

'Something like that. Popular man!' He pauses to brush something from the lapel of his raincoat. 'You're looking well.'

'And you seem to be doing better than when we last met.'

'Me? Yes, fantastic, couldn't be better. They're a great bunch of lads, you know. Do anything for you.'

'And for a buck, I presume?'

'Well, they're not doing it for charity! Hearts of gold though. They all like the money, fair enough, but it's more than that. There's this sort of bond between us.'

'Especially when your luck's in.'

'Don't misjudge them, Daniel. You couldn't wish for better friends. Always help you out in a fix. And I should know; I've been in a fair few.'

For a moment his eyes are drawn to the vanishing point like an Admiral scouring the horizon for land. 'So where are you taking me?' he asks.

'An old haunt.'

'None of your fancy nonsense,' he grins. 'I need a proper pint.'

It feels good to be leading for once. I wouldn't say I was in control, not yet. This clown – this showman – George has turned into is still capable of wrong footing me at any moment, and I know I'll have to be on my guard. I hope the place I'm taking us to is still standing; it's been a while. We turn onto Chalk Farm Road and then under the bridge into Castlehaven Road, and on the next corner is the foreboding structure I remember from my youth with its striking black-stoned turret. Bands used to gig here on a makeshift stage, the drum-kit and the amplifiers crammed on top of each other, and the players banging their heads on the ceiling. Old photographs from those performances adorn the walls – outraged young men flailing *Fenders* and *Gibsons* – but they are no one you would have heard of. There is a pervasive smell of wood and hops. A chalked-board of selected real ales recalls a student fetish I went along with for a while before coming out of the closet in my final year to confess I was more partial to a glass of chilled white than I was to a tankard of frothy brown.

Beneath the gothic beams is scattered a multi-coloured clientele, a zoo of studded, painted creatures that make Uncle George look like a Seventh Day Adventist and me a village librarian. But there is no inverted snobbery here. It's a live and let live establishment, a truly Free House, and I am able to move unnoticed and unhindered to an empty table at the back of the pub while George pays for our drinks with notes pried from the same thick bundle I've seen him draw from in the bookmakers. I can only guess, but the bets he was preparing to place must have run into the thousands.

Compared to recent confrontations with Sheila and my mother, these dealings with George have, so far, been couched in civility, the criminal afforded more courtesy than the victim, it would seem. Really, I should put him up against the wall but, since seeing him again, a slight despondency has begun to settle over me, a sign of resignation perhaps, because I already know so much of what will transpire between us; some details yet to be added but, on the whole, I'm sure most of what I learn today will be confirmatory. By rights, the conversation we're about to have should be the beginning of a punishment he is long overdue, and yet, suddenly, there seems little solace in the prospect of it, and I wonder if this apparent waning of my retributive appetite isn't also because the more I look at him the more I fear my own distorted image is there staring back at me like a reflection in disturbed water.

He returns juggling two muddy pints, still able to turn a smile even with a packet of crisps clenched between his teeth, and I anger again at the thought that his madness – in whatever form it takes with him – will somehow excuse his crimes, his plea not so much temporary insanity, but one of a more permanent kind. More alarming is the possibility he might lack insight into the suffering he has wreaked upon Sheila and our families, that he might never experience the sickening, gnawing guilt his crimes, in all reason, should foment. Perhaps Erin and Sheila are right? Perhaps there is no hope of a satisfactory conclusion to the manuscript of our lives that I've been drafting in my head all this time? Perhaps my only achievement will be to expose the ever more duplicitous layers of my family's sad history.

He takes a long and lasting sample of his beer, it would appear, in search of fortitude, and the first suggestion he might be mindful of what is to follow. The first few mouthfuls of my own drink allow a faint clouding of consciousness to temper my mood, which should help me to keep my cool, at least until I have it out of him. This is more than I can say for my uncle, whose visible and mounting agitation I am increasingly aware of. He can't keep still. Stacking beer mats and un-stacking them again, winding his bowtie like the propeller on a model airplane, constantly interrogating the hands of his watch, not at all the man who just a short while ago was throwing ten pound notes around like language school flyers, and in such high-spirits they verged on the euphoric. Is this the beginning of the long fall from those heights Snooty mentioned?

His voice flattens. 'So what brings you here, Daniel? It was quite a surprise seeing you back there.'

'You seemed to take it well enough.'

'Your mother *is* alright, isn't she?'

'My mother will be fine, considering everything that's happened. I know about Sheila, George. She told me.'

'The girl?' he asked.

I stare blankly at him. 'Yes, George, the girl. Who the hell do you think I mean?'

More tinkering with his tie. His fingers search for a lost beard.

'Do you want to tell me what happened?'

'Not sure what you mean?'

'George,' I sigh, with a tired legal tone. 'I've already spoken with Sheila myself. My mother hid a cutting from *The Gazette* in a box of old photographs. It took me a while, but I eventually worked it out. I can't quite believe she's protected you all these years. She's so sick with guilt it's nearly driven her insane, while you've been gambling your life away with those parasites you call friends.'

His eyes glisten. For a change, he has nothing to say.

'I actually thought it was my father to begin with, but seeing those photographs of you two together I realised how easy it would have been for you to pass yourself off as him. You were like twins back then, before the beard. I guess they figured you'd end up in the nut house and my father's reputation would be buggered either way. But even at the end, when you knew he was dying, you had a chance to make some sort of amends, if only to stop my mother having to go on covering up for you. Just what kind of an animal are you, George?'

George looks an increasingly unwell animal. His various tics and movements have now fused into a more generalised convulsion that seems to have stolen the air from his chest. I wouldn't have imagined a person could have such an acute physical reaction to stress, despite the nature of the accusations I'm making, and it's my guess some form of medication is making a major contribution to this dyskinetic display of his. If it's anything like the chemistry they've loaded me with, it will have more side effects than this pub has real ales. Medical assistance may be required if he carries on like this, and I'm acutely aware my PhD in neurobiology will be of little practical use. Though, if anything, the thought only spurs me on.

Gradually, he manages to bring his twitching under control. What was a thin film of sweat over his blood-engorged face is now a series of beads that abseil his cheeks and lips. His white shirt darkens to the colour of chest hair. He reaches into his overcoat and pulls out a small canister. With the thumb of the same hand he casts off the top and pumps two short sprays under his tongue – a nitrate to relieve angina, I'm guessing. But I don't wait for him to recover. I press on before he get's any worse, before he loses what little capacity he might have for confession.

I remind him of the facts. 'I know what you did, George, pretending to be my father to get to that poor girl.' I grab his arm. 'I'm right, aren't I?'

He doesn't try to resist. He just stares beyond me at the treacly floor, his mind groping for something.

'What's wrong with you?' I ask him. 'Is it your heart, your head, what?'

The effort it takes for my uncle to raise his eyes is almost painful to watch. 'Probably a bit of both,' he says. 'But I still know when I'm in love.'

I stare at him aghast. What kind of a lunatic is he?

'What are you talking about?'

'Your mother. I was in love with her, Daniel. I still am.'

I can't make any sense of this. I refuse to. I need to stick to my objective and not be sidetracked by his idiotic meanderings.

'Christ George, even if this new fantasy of yours was true, I'm not sure why you think it makes a difference? Didn't you hear what I said? I spoke to Sheila. I still don't quite know how you did it (I don't really give a shit to be frank) but it's time you joined in the suffering along with the rest of us.'

George winces, lifting his arm awkwardly onto the table as if it is someone else's. 'She begged me. Daniel. Your mother, she begged me. And he was my brother, a Doctor. What else were we supposed to do? We just tried to make it all go away. I can't understand why she's dragged it all up again. Can't see the point after all this time.'

'Perhaps because she couldn't live with herself anymore, George, because she has a conscience. Did you think of that?'

'She can't be blaming herself for being loyal. And even if the girl was telling the truth, plenty of wives have forgiven their husbands for less.'

Even if I hadn't seen the terror in Sheila's eyes for myself, I wasn't going to be persuaded by this bullshit for a second. There is no mistaking the cruelty of what happened to her at the hands of my uncle, and the more I hear from him, the more I am sickened by the near-delusional state of his mind. Yet, whether a product of this illness of his or just a trick of the subconscious, I still cannot be entirely certain of what took place that day. It is with him, just as it is with Sheila and my mother – and even by my own fragmented memories of the time – a nightmare riddled with inconsistency. There are no facts, only circumstances. Nothing tangible has survived, just a knot of deception and contradiction from which I must try and unravel the past.

'I can't believe you're even attempting to deny what happened. And then 'nice old Uncle George' came along with his big pot of money and helped everybody out, is that really the story you're sticking to?'

His voice is suddenly low and tremulous. 'It was the girl's mother started making accusations. And your mother was always going to stand by your father, whatever, I knew that. I could see how much she still loved him. She couldn't believe it was possible, that he had it in him. Neither could I. And none of us really trusted that girl and her mother much, bunch of scallywags. It was only ever going to be his word against theirs, and if we didn't do something your father's career would be ruined and your mother's heart was going to get broken every day for the rest of her life.' He pauses to collect sweat from his forehead, his face corrugating. 'It was the mother went to the police. A sort of threat to your father, I reckon, because she was very keen to let him know about it. And then somebody leaked it to the papers (and you can probably guess who), but once she saw the money, your father soon talked her out of taking it any further.'

'The *Lloyds* account?'

'Hard to believe the irony, but I was on a winning streak at the time.'

'Like now?'

He tries to smile but it distorts into something more resembling pain. 'You've always been a bright lad. Manic-depression, except they call it bipolar now, sounds a lot more fancy. Had it since I was a teenager. Has its benefits, I suppose. I was probably trying to impress your mother too. I never know what to do with the winnings. It's never been about the money. I even put few bob more than they needed in there just in case Sheila's mother got greedy again. The cash was always going to be better off with them. I'd have only have lost it all, eventually.'

His were not the actions of a manic-depressive. Psychiatry is no excuse for what he has done. More depraved impulses, stirred from the dark, fathomless pools I fear lie shadowed within the minds of all men urged him on; impulses I am only too mindful of, and wonder I have ever consciously managed to resist. But I am not like him. I have to believe that. My foolishness with Erin, the night I spent with Kim or whatever the fuck her name was – though I'm far from proud of them – were drunken follies, surely? And that poor girl in Chicago, a misunderstanding, a misreading of my mood, my intentions? And yet precisely what separates me from my uncle I cannot begin to comprehend.

George is waiting for me to say something. In his eyes I see the hands of a drowning man that claw the surface of those same bleak waters, empty and pitiful. Though I do not believe his condition excuses his actions, it might at least account for the absence of any obvious sign of remorse, and this delusion about my father he seems to cling on to. And how much I can believe of the love he claims to have had for my mother is anybody's guess. Was it her who persuaded my father to go along with George's plan? Had she been in love with him too? Sheila's mother, on the other hand, was cold enough and vengeful enough to have taken the money and buried the knowledge of her daughter's abuse, knowing there would be so many other ways to make them all suffer. Ways far from the prosaic.

Ways that would last. And yet burying the truth has made hers a punishment we have all had to endure. A slow-killing. And each of us slow-killed.

'Tell me, George, if Sheila and her mother have been making this up, why did my mother give me those things? Why, would she want me to put the pieces together? What would be the point if it was all a pack of lies?'

An unmistakable spark of hope flickers across his face. A last card to be played. A last chance at redemption.

'But did she even know the cutting was in there, Daniel? Other than that it was just a bunch of old photos, a few memories for her to pass on to her son. Maybe there was no "message", but you being so bloody clever managed to figure out something had gone on? You've just taken it a bit too far, that's all.'

Was this the way he had been with Sheila, I wonder, this imploring, despicable logic?

'Think about it,' he continues. 'It was your father they would have called to the house. How could I have known when to be there? And do you really think the girl wouldn't have told us apart? There was a likeness back then, I'll admit, but when you think about it, it's all a bit far-fetched.'

'I have thought about it George, don't worry. You were there. Maybe you were with my mother when the call came through and covered up by pretending to be him, that would do it. Or you could have found out her mother was ill and gone over there hoping Sheila would be alone. All I know is that my parents covered up for you through some foolish sense of loyalty or because they took pity on you and your "sickness". Maybe back then you could convince them nothing happened, but my mother knows that girl was raped, and my father never forgot what he did for you. He just buried the truth with numbers. It's one of the few things you seem to have in common.'

George rests a hand on my arm, and I am incensed by his audacity in trying to intimate tenderness. 'I understand how you must feel,' he is saying. 'It must be a shock and everything, but you've been adding things up the wrong way, Daniel. I swear I was only trying to help.'

They are words I have heard once too often, of late, in those familiarly polite yet condescending tones. And with them comes a terrible pall of confusion, a pang of sickening doubt that swells inside me, expanding into frustration and then to outright rage. Rage at my uncle's simpering, inelaborate refutation of everything I am accusing him off. But rage, too, at the prospect that he could be telling the truth, and that I have become lost inside my own head again, chasing shadows.

From nowhere my hand lashes out. Just a girlish slap across his face, but its strength surprises even me as I watch the exaggerated jerk of George's head backwards against the wall, almost tipping him over in the chair. Violence has never had any place in my life – never the necessity with all my anger so inwardly reflected – but it is here with me now, and my hand stings to the warmth of it, symbolically raw and crimson.

Apparently ignoring any new pains I might have inflicted, George struggles desperately with his spray again, frantically firing off another volley of poorly directed jets into his mouth. I could delay questioning him further, of course, until I am less agitated, and when he is at less of a disadvantage, but if he can lie so convincingly now in such a perilous state, he is hardly more likely to open up when he's well. And I'll have trouble convincing the police to listen to me, being such an old case and with Sheila and her mother unwilling to bring charges. I can just see myself sympathising apologetically with the short shrift given to me by some slack-faced detective. Perhaps my only hope now is that George's punishment will lie in his progressive mental deterioration, and that I might already have received punishment enough to forestall my own.

He takes one final burst of medication. But there is hardly time for the drug to reach its target before his head lolls to one side then topples forward. It catches the sharp edge of the table, a small patch of blood left to mark its descent as the weight of it drags him downward onto the floor like a plumb line. Lying on the floor, his face, which has for so much of the time been twisted in pain, is now serene – the eyes half-closed, the mouth barely parted – as if he has drifted off into a deep and luxurious dream.

Fearful instincts continue to rise in me, instincts that would have me finish him off here and now, although I'm shaking so much I may hardly be capable. Around us, people are staring. One or two even start to scrape their chairs back in a show of willingness to provide assistance, but I wave a reassuring hand and stoop down to take a closer look at George. He is still breathing – just – his face mottled and lifeless. I look up and smile at the assorted spectators again, then gaze to the heavens in mock despair.

Gradually, George begins to show more obvious signs of being alive. Within a few minutes I have him onto his feet and in a vaguely stable position. Now we're up I think it's better to keep going, and we shuffle slowly towards the door with his arm draped across my shoulder and my arm curled around as much of his waist as I can get hold of. By now, the rest of the bar has obviously grown more comfortable with the familiarity of the scene and their burble rises again to drown out the coarse sound of George's shallow breathing in my ear. I wonder if there is a slight blue discolouration to his lips, though it's hard to tell in the light.

Outside, the blade of a chill wind has taken Camden by the throat. I am also trembling, I realize, under the weight of my uncle who with every gasp is less able to support his own mass. I try asking him which way to go, but there isn't the time between breaths for anything sensible to return. I manage a glance back the way we have come earlier, just long enough to appreciate a further sharpening of the wind as it is driven under the arches of the railway bridge. In the other direction, along the grey and greasy street, a man and a woman bound together in defence against the elements hurry away from us into the darkening distance. My uncle and I, too, are bound, and we head under the bridge towards the canal, stumbling past the shuttered blinds and pulled curtains, one hesitant footstep after another.

CHAPTER TWENTY-TWO

Dr Ridgeway is making small circular movements with his pen. The imperfect rings he leaves on the paper in front of him cross each other and back again, but none of them will ever completely overlap another the way he would like them to, no matter how many he draws. Something random in the pulleys and levers – the microscopic contractions – of his hand seems certain to prevent that possibility from ever being so. A few of the circles are close to being round, but for most he can manage only an ellipse, and in the dense blue spirals that form I sense the same unerring progression towards entropy that has been shadowing me all this time.

This is the way it has been with us. I think much and say little while he scribbles and waits for the answers to leach from me. Answers, I'm sure, he hopes will allow him to fit me into another one of his neat little diagnostic categories. But it doesn't seem to be that simple for him either.

In his fifties, I'd say, balding and easily bored, the elbow of his non-circling arm is perched on the desktop, the ruffled skin of his face collecting in its hand. It is his affect, far more than mine that dominates these proceedings. We've been sitting in this draughty, flaking consultant room for almost an hour now and it's, no doubt, a relief to us both when a nurse carrying a block of notes enters to tell him the next patient is waiting outside. I wince inwardly at the mention of the word because I don't believe what has happened to me can be described as an illness. A 'state', an 'indisposition' perhaps, but how far outside the realms of normal biology even I am not qualified to say.

Of course, this is one of the many opinions I'm careful to keep from Ridgeway, who will only tell me I lack 'insight' even though this is precisely what I'd like to give him more of. The Good Doctor and I have our amiable, if laboured, conversations every month, but increasingly they have become more coffee-morning than consultation in nature. We discuss life in general more than we do mine in particular, and I don't believe he's understood a word of what little I've deigned to disclose on that subject. So it's hardly a surprise that he's just asked me whether my period of intensive treatment mightn't have come to an end? (By 'treatment', of course, he means these stilted conversations we endure together rather than the medication I endure alone, and which, though weaned, I will need to take for a while yet.) My inclination is to tell him that it's his bloody job to decide, and that if he did it would constitute one of the more meaningful contributions he has made to my recuperation. But I'm not going to miss the opportunity, so I say yes, it's been 6 months now, I've made great progress, and I feel very much ready to be released back into the wild.

I have one final lecture to suffer from him on the importance of being compliant with my medication, and I reassure him for the umpteenth time that I haven't missed my tablets for so much as a day since that time leading up to my run-in with George when I rather foolishly believed I could get by without my chemical minders standing guard. He knows something of my Uncle and what happened between us, but only because George is a "highly relevant part of my family's medical history" according to Ridgeway, the genetics of mental illness being a particular interest of his, and an irony not entirely lost on me.

More circling of pen. This time Ridgeway is ringing the box marked: Discharged. Like most of the terms he has used to describe or manage my case, the vernacular feels out of context, as if it might be missing the word 'Dishonourably'. We exchange a limp handshake and an even limper smile across his desk and I leave the hospital on what has become another cold and overcast morning. Autumn is already bronzing the trees, and in the café on the High Road it's well below the acceptable temperature for dining *al fresco*, unless you want to sit self-consciously beneath a gas-heater.

Erin is anxious to ask me something. From the moment I see her at the doorway I detect the burden of a question. She sits opposite me, spooning foam from her coffee and trying to make a meal of her bottom lip. Yet (and so typical of her) she still troubles to ask me about my appointment with Dr Ridgeway first. And when I tell her my time with the psychiatrist is at an end she appears to be genuinely happy for me, expressing a selflessness I still find hard to fathom. It was another one of the 'themes' Ridgeway kept bringing us back to: how readily I disparage the people in my life who try to show me affection. An apparent lack of perception on my part, like trying to appreciate a third dimension from within the confines of two, its existence implied only by the feint imprint it leaves on that blander, shallower world.

My feelings for Erin are those of a brother towards a sister – stolid, if that isn't a complete contradiction in terms. Beyond the odd handshake, I don't think we've so much as touched each other since our fumble on the doorstep of her house, and I'm grateful not to have risked the valuable friendship we now share with any of the more clichéd inclinations towards youth I have displayed in the past.

Forgetting that she has something to ask me, I continue to blither on about Ridgeway's circles and the inherent foolishness of reductionism. But Erin's obvious preoccupation must get the better of her because suddenly she sits forward and interrupts me as if is she hasn't been listening to a word I've said.

'Can I ask you a question?'

'Of course.'

'About your uncle. I appreciate there was no love lost between you both or anything, but you never told me why you suddenly went after him like that?'

Despite my instant apprehension, I know that, after all she's done for me, Erin deserves some explanation for what happened.

'Because I couldn't have my father being the person who did that to Sheila,' I tell her.

'But that's totally understandable...'

'No, you don't understand. It was more than shame. I was afraid of what a Lamarckian world makes possible. That I might never escape who he was.'

'So you blamed your uncle?'

'I stopped taking my medication just before I left your place. You were doing too good a job! I felt so much better; I didn't think I needed those bloody tablets anymore. And when I saw that photograph I became so utterly convinced Sheila had mistaken George for my father. And George was so full of the joys – you had to see him to believe it – as if nothing had ever happened. But, either way, he was a lying bastard, and he was still culpable. He gave my father the money to pay Sheila's mother off and still had enough left to fund his little army of leeches.'

Erin hesitates. 'Do you think one of them did it?'

'Did what?'

'He was mugged, right?'

'A heart attack, the coroner said.'

'But brought on by a mugging?'

'Or he had the heart attack first. It's almost impossible to know which came first.'

'You said he was using his nitrates alot when he was with you.'

'Exactly, he could have had it right there in front of me, according to the Doctors. Sometimes it's difficult to distinguish from regular angina, and then the heart fails later on.'

'It's a shame you weren't with him.'

An uncomfortable lull in the conversation as Erin's less than subtle fishing for information about that evening grows more obvious to us both. She is a true scientist. And she is a woman. She wants to know every last detail. But she cannot.

George looked peaceful enough laid out on that bench next to the stagnant waters of the canal. I suppose I must have known that the ridiculous amount of money he carried around with him would make him a beacon for the kind of youths I'd seen hanging about The Lock. But just like the mice Erin had culled on my behalf, I wondered if all the lies mightn't be better off buried with him? Perhaps he didn't deserve to die, but then Sheila and my mother didn't deserve their particular fates in life either. I thought it was time to let Gods rather than genes decide for once.

The noise of the café reaches a crescendo, which silences Erin and I a while longer. When she does speak again, I have to ask her to repeat herself before I realise she is trying to tell me something about Jane.

I saw her only a couple of weeks ago. She looked happy – from a distance at least – strolling across Turnham Green, a mobile pressed to her ear, her head thrown back in laughter. I could have gone over, said something, but I didn't want to spoil the moment because she looked so different, so…loved. Perhaps she was talking to Adam at that very moment, planning to meet him for a drink, perhaps, or exchanging a funny story from the day?

Apparently Erin has been nervous for weeks about telling me, but she's the one who's most surprised when the only acknowledgement she gets from me is a small lift of the shoulders. She probably thinks I've misunderstood or that Ridgeway has been too hasty in taking me off his books or not hasty enough in cutting down my sedatives.

'I've known for a quite a while,' I tell her. 'I hope they make each other happy. They deserve it.'

'That's very magnanimous of you!'

It must be difficult for Erin to appreciate that, like so much of what has happened, my feelings for Jane (what little they amounted to) are nothing more than a lingering reminiscence, like words drawn in sand the tide has only half-washed away. I also know that dealing with Adam's particular genetic legacy will require all their strength to endure the way his parents had.

For another hour or so we drink more coffee than is good for us and catch up on university intrigue and the latest gossip from the world of academic publishing I've been banished to (neither of which I know much nor care about, and it's Erin who turns out to be the expert on both). But I never get around to telling her my other news. That a paper in this week's edition of *Nature* appears to vindicate my Lamarckian theory. It seems that modifications to the numerous proteins that bind and surround DNA, rather than to genes themselves, are able to adapt to the environment. And some of them, at least, can be passed from one generation to the next. There was nothing wrong with the northern blots Barry and Erin ran. The natural form of anti-sense we detected was real enough – a number have been described – and now our new understanding of 'epigenetics', as outlined in the *Nature* article, actually lends credence to a Lamarckian form of inheritance too. At least I was right about something, though it is a poor consolation.

Outside, we part with a brief smile and a polite peck on each cheek. Then I pretend to be fastening my overcoat as I watch Erin walk away from me, her slender figure consumed by a teeming, faceless crowd.

On Chiswick Common bars of sunlight probe cracks in the cloud to form small pockets of warmth I pass in and out of as I amble homewards. A few hardy dog owners battle with their obstinate pets and with eternal crosswinds that seem to be gathering force as the day advances. All part of a rather grim start to the year that will, no doubt, flicker briefly into spring before another dry and unsatisfying summer ensues.

All that coffee has dried me out too, and I devour a large glass of water the moment I arrive home. I am also, paradoxically, drowsy, and in my room I curl up on the duvet – still clothed – and stare out through the misting sash window. Inclined on the bedside table next to a miniature skyline of medicine bottles is the one photograph from my mother's collection I have chosen to keep, a picture of our family when I was less than five years old: my father, his brother, my mother and I. Not yet the people who will disturb the fine equilibrium of each other's lives. Not yet the people I will come to know at all. But what I owe now to those other selves, and to all the other selves we pass through being, is for greater minds than mine to grasp. I can only haul myself, once again, into sleep where the past continues to unburden itself onto the future in fractured dreams in which, amidst their silent swells, images foam close to the surface and then are lost again to the deep. Sheila and the waving heads of corn, a figure towering above her, the face always turned away or in shadow. Constant motion. Nothing is ever still in those dreams, the detail always blurred and smeared like a blot on a northern.

Printed by Amazon Italia Logistica S.r.l.
Torrazza Piemonte (TO), Italy

16256015R00151